THE FAKE WEDDING PROJECT

T0182726

OTHER TITLES BY PIPPA GRANT

For the most up-to-date booklist,
visit Pippa's website at www.pippagrant.com.

The Last Eligible Billionaire

Not My Kind of Hero

The One Who Loves You (Tickled Pink #1)

Rich in Your Love (Tickled Pink #2)

The Three BFFs and a Wedding Trilogy

The Worst Wedding Date

The Gossip and the Grump

The Bride's Runaway Billionaire

Copper Valley Fireballs Series

Jock Blocked

Real Fake Love

The Grumpy Player Next Door

Irresistible Trouble

THE FAKE WEDDING PROJECT

a novel

PIPPA GRANT

This is a work of fiction. Names, characters, organizations, places, events, and incidents are either products of the author's imagination or are used fictitiously. Otherwise, any resemblance to actual persons, living or dead, is purely coincidental.

Text copyright © 2024 by Pippa Grant
All rights reserved.

Pippa Grant® is a registered trademark of Bang Laugh Love LLC

No part of this book may be reproduced, or stored in a retrieval system, or transmitted in any form or by any means, electronic, mechanical, photocopying, recording, or otherwise, without express written permission of the publisher.

Published by Montlake, Seattle

www.apub.com

Amazon, the Amazon logo, and Montlake are trademarks of Amazon.com, Inc., or its affiliates.

ISBN-13: 9781662513343 (paperback)
ISBN-13: 9781662513350 (digital)

Cover design by Caroline Teagle Johnson
Cover image: © Olga Andreevna Shevchenko / Getty

Printed in the United States of America

THE FAKE WEDDING PROJECT

Chapter 1

Dane Silver, a.k.a. a man very unaware of his own romantic situation

Someone is breaking into the house.

It's broad daylight. My dog is beside me. There are neighbors nosy enough to notice—if any of them are home.

And someone is definitely jiggling the living room window on the side that overlooks the backyard.

Not that I can talk. This isn't my house. I technically broke in too.

But my sister told me where to find the spare key for her little cottage, and the person now banging the lowered blinds of the window wouldn't do that if they knew where the spare key was.

Mine was a legitimate break-in.

This break-in is more likely criminal.

But is there crime in the little town of Tinsel?

Not likely.

I look down at Chili, who's sitting beside me on the overstuffed yellow-checkered couch that faces a brick fireplace with a television above the mantel.

My fluffy tan mutt stares back. He's about fifty pounds of some golden retriever, some Labrador, and some something else. I could get him a doggy DNA test, but he's a good dog, if a bit lazy, and that's what matters most.

"You gonna do something about that?" I ask him.

He yawns. Then looks back at the window to the left of the television and fireplace. Been a while since I took stock of Lorelei's house, but I'm reasonably certain the window is at least five feet off the ground.

Whoever's breaking in is going to a lot of work considering the front and back doors are both unlocked.

And there's an arm flinging itself up over the sill, making the lowered blinds bang more. It's a slender arm attached to a slender hand with slender fingers tipped in pink.

Definitely not Lorelei's arm.

She's not the pink-nail-polish type.

I look at Chili again.

He grunts at me and lays his head back down on the couch, where he's in the direct path of most of the rotating fan's track.

As a puppy, he would've been racing to make a new friend. But since he hit two years old, he's happiest when someone else does the sniffing and investigating. I've had dogs all my life, and I've never had one this lazy.

Until you're talking about food. Then, don't get between the beast and his breakfast.

Trust me on this one.

From outside the window, there's a grunt far more feminine than Chili's grunt.

I set aside my laptop—work can wait—and pull myself to my feet. Debate tossing on a shirt.

You wouldn't think it could get above ninety in this part of Michigan, but August has been brutal. Glad my grandparents have air-conditioning.

Wish Lorelei did, too, but that's a future project for her fixer-upper. And the heat wave should break in a few days.

We hope.

I walk through the breeze coming off one of the two fans circulating air in the little cottage, earning another disgruntled noise from my dog, as the intruder's second arm hooks itself over the windowsill and bangs the blinds more.

There's one more grunt, and then a woman's curly, brown-haired crown pokes under the blinds. She huffs and heaves, propelling the rest of her head through the window.

And then she lifts her face.

Recognition clicks instantly, and I'm so caught off guard, I stumble backward.

Her gaze lands on me, and she goes slack jawed and wide eyed, then *ack*s and tumbles off the windowsill, banging the blinds around.

"Are you friggin' kidding me?" I hear Amanda Anderson mutter as I catch myself and leap toward the window.

And yes.

That is definitely Amanda Anderson. Thick, curly brown hair. Brilliant brown eyes. Natural olive skin. Pouty lips that were always more prone to smiling back in high school.

She's in a black tank top and short jean shorts, sitting on the ground amid the holly bushes with her arms braced behind her, staring at me like I'm a ghost.

"You're not friggin' kidding me," she says.

"What are you doing?"

"I need to see Lorelei." She winces. "Actually . . . that's not right. I . . . need to see you. But I didn't know you'd be here. I knew you were in town, but I didn't know you were *here* here."

Amanda Anderson needs to see *me*?

It's been years since the last time we spoke to each other.

Not because there's any animosity between us.

Not exactly.

Our families have hated each other for generations, though no one in my family has been able to explain why in any manner that's made sense.

Their feud is the soot mark on the otherwise happy, peaceful town of Tinsel, Michigan, where it's Christmas all year round.

Even on days like today when you could fry an egg on the sidewalk.

I've lived in San Francisco since I graduated from college. Last I heard through Lorelei, Amanda had moved to New York to pursue a career as an actress.

Not surprising.

Especially to anyone who watched any of her performances with the high school theater.

She lit up the entire stage.

Which is an opinion I've kept to myself, even knowing that Lorelei and Amanda often had lunch together at school despite our families' feud.

They make me was what Lorelei always told our parents. *They want our families to get along, so they make me.*

The teachers made me wouldn't have been an excuse I could've used if I'd gotten up the balls to ask her on a date.

"This is better." Amanda's face doesn't match her words. Her face says *this is terrible and I want to go live in a hole.* Which isn't the kind of nice that I remember her being. "This way, we can keep Lorelei out of it. She'll never have to know, and she won't have to take sides, and it'll all be over before you laugh about it with her later, when I'll be long gone to stew in my own mortification for the next forever. Can I come in? I really don't want to talk about this with witnesses."

I glance at the houses in view from the backyard.

Doesn't look like there are any nosy neighbors snooping, but you never know.

"They're all downtown for . . . erm . . . a meeting," Amanda says. "But I don't know for how much longer."

"What kind of meeting?"

"Can I *please* come in?"

"Back door," I tell her. "It's unlocked."

"Oh. Well. That would've been easier, wouldn't it?"

My guard is up. I'm already testy for having been guilted into spending an entire week in Tinsel before my grandparents' anniversary party. I'm hot and sweating and need to put on a shirt.

And despite all that, I smile at Amanda's self-deprecation. "Have you and *easy* ever gotten along?"

"You laugh now . . . ," she mutters while she leaps to her feet and strides quickly past the window up the stairs to the deck just off the living room.

I grab my T-shirt and pull it on—*fuck*, it's hot—and then look at Chili again. "Still not moving?"

He pops one eye and gives me a silent no.

Lazier than usual today, but then, we haven't been in heat like this in forever.

The screen door clatters as Amanda lets herself in. "Yep. That was easier." She looks me up and down and winces again. "Can we sit down? Preferably on opposite sides of the room with me closest to the door when you decide you want to murder me? Which you don't have to do. I'll fix this. Cross my heart and triple pinkie promise, I will."

She hasn't changed at all. Still unpredictable. Still prone to the dramatic side. Still always able to make me smile no matter what's coming out of her mouth.

My heart gives a painful thump.

I had such a crush on her in high school.

Not that I ever had the courage to tell her that. Family feud aside, she preferred dating the football players and the class president. Not the guys who were in band and on the mathlete team.

No shade to Amanda.

She was always kind to everyone, but the popular crowd was where she belonged. Where she fit.

I scratch my chest where it's starting to drip sweat and gesture her to the blue La-Z-Boy nearest the screen door, then seat myself once again on the couch, but this time on the other side of my dog.

Farther from her.

At her request.

She sits at the edge of the chair, crosses her legs, and weaves her hands around one bare knee. "There's no easy way to say this, so I'm just gonna go for it. And before I tell you what I have to tell you, I want you to know that I'm very, very, very sorry. I will fix this. I will set this right. I will tell them the truth. I just . . . haven't yet."

I lean back and hook an ankle over my own knee.

College and then city life have helped me get over feeling like the geeky band guy who blushes at the slightest look from an attractive woman, but there's something different about facing your original high school crush fifteen years later.

Especially after coming to realize just how off you felt growing up because of always having to be on guard to never let your family know you'd had any kind thoughts about *the enemy*. Or that you didn't understand why you had enemies, and why everyone couldn't just get along.

Tinsel might be magic for everyone else, but for me, it's nothing but stress and unease. I was not built to be a participating member of a long-standing family feud of indeterminate origins.

Not when it overshadowed every shining moment of my childhood.

"The truth about what?" I ask her.

I honestly can't guess what she's about to say. I never could. And that was half my fascination with her.

For as much as I like predictability in my own life, I still envied the whirlwind of unpredictability that she thrived in.

She sucks in a breath that has her chest lifting, highlighting the curve of her breasts, and she squeezes her eyes shut before she answers. "That we're engaged."

Chili lifts his head and gawks at her.

My jaw meets my chest.

She peeks at us out of one squinty eye, then sighs and opens both eyes again. "I'm sorry. I truly am. I don't know why I said it. My grandma told me that when she announces her retirement this weekend at the party for her fiftieth anniversary of working at the bakery, she's leaving me the gingerbread bakery, and I can't bake, and I love Tinsel, I do, but I belong in the city. New York City. It just—it feeds my soul, and I like to think that I give it something back too. And Lorelei and I were talking about dinner right before I went to see my grandma and she said you were coming to town and might join us even though you and I haven't seen each other in years and I was thinking about how we'd have to be so sneaky to have dinner without my family finding out—"

"Breathe," I interject.

Can't help myself.

I don't think she's drawn a full breath since she walked in the door.

Also, I need to breathe.

I need to breathe, and I need to think.

My fingers curl into fists and then stretch out on their own as I hunch forward. If it wasn't so hot, I'd leap up and start pacing.

Engaged.

Engaged to Amanda Anderson.

While I'm not getting engaged to *anyone* at this point in my life, the news doesn't have me as shocked as I would've thought it should.

Or as horrified.

She takes a massive breath that makes her chest rise and fall again, drawing my attention to the hint of cleavage at the neck of her tank top, and then she dives right back in. "So you and Lorelei and our families' stupid fights were already near the top of my brain, and I looked out the window of the Gingerbread House and I saw your family's Fruitcake Emporium, and then Grandma said I'm the only person who can take the gingerbread bakery now, and the next thing I knew, I was blurting out that I was engaged to you. I panic-engaged us because being engaged to a Silver is basically the only thing worthy of instant disinheriting and it seemed kinder to tell her that being in love with the enemy was the reason I can't take over the bakery."

"Breathe," I say again.

"I'm breathing. Also, I don't personally think you're the enemy. I promise. I know you're a nice guy. Lorelei says so."

"Breathe more."

"I'm so sorry—"

I hold up a hand, cutting her off. Chili grunts—that's his annoyed *someone's interrupting my sleep* grunt—and puts his head back down on the couch.

"Ohh, is that your dog?" Amanda says.

I don't answer.

My brain is spinning too fast, putting a puzzle together and taking me on a path that is far, far, *far* from my preferred predictability as I give in to the desperate need to move right now. The fan hits me as I pace, then the other fan, but neither offers relief.

I don't think like this.

I don't jump to conclusions or solutions like this.

I say and do the predictable thing, always—*You need to tell them we're not engaged, or I will*—except my entire being is revolting over that idea.

And instead, there's an unexpected whisper in the back of my mind telling me to *stop, drop, and think.*

Think about how I didn't want to take this entire week in Tinsel for my grandparents' anniversary party, but my dad guilted me into it. *Might need an extra set of hands for last-minute plans. You don't come home enough. Already told us you won't be home for Christmas.*

Think about how I've been cutting our conversations short every time he starts complaining about anything around Tinsel.

About how his favorite thing to complain about is Amanda's family.

About how I said *I got a promotion at work*, and the first thing I heard was my uncle cackling in the background. *Bet none of them Anderson kids get promotions as fast as our Dane does.* Like I'm not a person, but a prop in their war. Just like always.

Dane's valedictorian. Those Andersons have never done that. Dane aced his SATs. Those Andersons have never done that. Dane's first clarinet. Those Andersons have never done that.

About how the fruitcake shop isn't doing well, and everyone's denying it, and if they'd all pull their collective heads out of their collective asses and address the problem instead of blaming the Andersons for god only knows what reason, maybe they could find a solution that isn't trying to destroy *that gingerdead family.*

Yes, *gingerdead family.*

It's fucking stupid.

My heart's doing its own thing that it needs to get over, and get over immediately.

If I do this—if I propose—*suggest* this idea that's growing louder and more persistent in my mind—it's purely for the reason she already said.

I don't think you're the enemy.

Lorelei has to sneak around to have dinner with one of her oldest friends.

No one knows why our families started fighting in the first place.

Who cares what they did?

What I care about is that I have to hear *alllll* about it. Every week. Like clockwork.

"You told them we're engaged," I say slowly.

"That we've been secretly dating long distance for the past year and we've decided to elope to Vegas next month," she whispers.

"They believe you?"

She visibly swallows and looks away. "My mom had to take my grandma to the hospital to be checked for a heart attack."

I stop pacing and spin to stare at her. *"Holy shit."*

She flaps both hands. "She's fine. My grandma, I mean. She does this all the time. She's had *heart attacks* over my uncle getting a fishing cabin, over her supplier raising prices for the first time in fifteen years, and once over the fact that she went all the way into the city to get a specific bedding set from Macy's and they didn't have it in stock."

She bites her lip. "I mean, I *think* this is just like those times. My mom promised to text with updates. And she said I definitely could *not* ride along for the trip to the hospital. But that's why I know the neighbors aren't home. Not the ones who would've seen me coming in the back, I mean. They're having a meeting to discuss who'll take over Grandma's role for the Jingle Bell Festival if this heart attack is real. Which I'm nearly certain it isn't. I think. I hope."

I slowly close my own jaw again.

Amanda's phone dings.

She pulls it out, looks down, and blows out the heaviest breath I've ever heard another human being blow out.

Her eyes water. Her chin trembles. And then she forces the fakest smile I've ever seen in my life as she flashes the screen at me. "See? She's fine. It was just indigestion."

Her voice wobbles, and I have to rub my own chest. "She had her heart checked lately?"

"Every time she supposedly has a heart attack. She has the arteries of a twenty-year-old. Good genes. Can't be all the gingerbread she's eaten over the years." She's forcing a cheerfulness about this like she wasn't honestly terrified she'd given her grandmother a heart attack.

You can tell that the nonchalance about the idea of her grandmother having a heart attack is fake.

Considering some of the performances I saw her do in high school, this has to be hitting her hard.

Or she's playing you, the ever-present voice of *people like Amanda Anderson don't fit into lives like ours* whispers in my ear. With a side of *she's one of them gingerdead people.*

I tell it to shut up.

Lorelei has always insisted that Amanda's never been one of *those Andersons* who likes to torment us, and I trust my sister's judgment.

"At the risk of sounding like an asshole," I say slowly, still weighing how much chaos I want to bring into my life for this trip home, "it's fucking ridiculous for your grandmother to fake a heart attack over not liking someone you claim to love enough to want to marry. Especially someone she's never met."

Her eyes flare wide again, and her lips part before she slowly clamps them together.

"It's fucking ridiculous that if we tell my family we're engaged, they won't give you the time of day either," I add.

"If we . . . what?"

"We've been dating for a year," I say slowly.

This could work.

I broke up with Vanessa a year and a half ago. I've taken a few solo trips while I worked through it all.

Amanda eyes me the same way I should be eyeing myself right now. "I'll set the record straight as soon as Grandma's home tonight. But I wanted to tell Lorelei—you—before you heard it from someone else. Because the whole Jingle Bell Fest committee might've heard. And then kicked me out while they tended to Grandma's heart—indigestion."

"When was your last serious boyfriend?" I ask.

"*Psh.* My roommate is the best friend a girl could ask for, and I get to spend my days with dogs and my nights exploring the city. Who needs a boyfriend?"

"Your family knows that?"

"They don't always believe me, but I also haven't dated anyone in—why are you smiling? What's going on? What's with the questions?"

"Days with dogs . . . Are you a veterinarian? What happened with acting?"

Her mouth works like she doesn't know what to answer first, and then she sighs. "I'm a dog walker," she grumbles out. "And I love it. I do. I just—my family doesn't understand why I love it so much. As for being an actress, it wasn't—let's just say the stage and I are soulmates, but the rest of the gig wasn't in line with my personality."

A protective streak sparks to life inside of me. "Did someone—"

"No. No. No one hurt me. It just—the constant rejection, the uncertainty, and sometimes the personalities of the cast and crew. I have the world's best roommate now, and I made enough connections when I was trying to break into the theater that I was able to get hired by a company that only services high-end clients. But I'm still *just a dog walker*. Not a *real job*. Of course I can *give that up for my family*."

Protective is rapidly morphing into *fury*. "That's what they said to you?"

"More or less. But for real—one of my cousins is a cancer researcher. The other is doing amazing things as mayor of his wife's hometown in Oregon. My brother just got a job at a high-end bakery in Italy after eloping himself. Being a dog walker . . . it sounds lame in comparison."

"Does it make you happy?"

"*Yes.* I love my job. I'm outside all day, every day. My dogs are hilarious and fun, and they've introduced me to so many amazing people. I can pay my bills and have time to be involved in my neighborhood and there's a never-ending supply of new things to see and do in the city, and—I know it sounds silly, but when I'm in New York, I'm just—I'm where I was meant to be. And I *am* acting. We just restarted a community theater, and we're about to have auditions for our first show."

My mind is made up.

We're doing this. "We should stay engaged."

Her eyes go comically round.

Relatable. I'm goggling at myself internally too. This isn't like me.

It's not like me at all.

But then, it *is* like me to dislike coming home more every time I do it. And that's not a recipe for happiness.

"Dane, I'm so sorry, I didn't mean to—" she starts, but I interrupt her.

"How stupid is it that our families are holding on to a generations-long fight when no one knows what it's about anymore?"

She doesn't immediately answer.

"Do you know what it's about?" I press.

She shakes her head, and there's something firm enough in it that I believe her.

"I don't either. And it's fucking ridiculous. You like Lorelei. She likes you. You should be able to visit her when you're in town without climbing through a back window while you hope the neighbors don't notice. So we stay engaged. We make our families work together if they don't want to lose both of us. We end the damn feud. Are you in? Or do I have to tell Lorelei you broke my heart because your family didn't approve? You know she's likely heard by now. It's how Tinsel works."

It's low.

I know it's low.

All the way around.

But I fucking *hate* the way our families fight. The idea of coming home puts me on edge every time.

It makes me feel like a pawn instead of a human being, and it's overshadowed every major accomplishment I've had in my life.

Early last year, when I thought I would marry Vanessa, that we'd have kids—I didn't want to bring them home.

They didn't even exist, and I was already thinking about how I didn't want to put them in the position that I grew up in. I didn't want them to have to hide it if they became friends with an Anderson. I didn't want them to feel like half of their identity was hating someone else and every good thing they ever did was a chip to be used in a poker game of animosity.

I'll have kids one day, and I'll feel the same then as I do now. They don't need a cloud of anger and hatred hanging over their lives.

So what if we end it?

What if we take advantage of this moment, of Amanda's spontaneity, and we make a real plan, and we *end this*?

"That's . . ." She licks her lips while she stares at me, apparently at a loss for words.

"A big risk," I acknowledge. "It could backfire. But you don't want to inherit a bakery. I don't want to spend the rest of my life hearing more about what's wrong with your family than what's right with mine. So what are we out if it doesn't work?"

I know what I'm risking.

I'm risking conflict inside my family instead of them having a united front against the Andersons. I'm risking being cut out of my family completely if they can't look past their old prejudices to see that Amanda's a nice person.

I don't know what her relationship is with her grandma. I don't know what she wants it to be.

But if she was willing to blurt out that she's engaged to the enemy to get out of inheriting a bakery, can it be that fantastic?

She's staring at me with ever-darkening eyes, and she licks her lips once more.

Fuck it.

If I'm doing this, I'm *doing this.*

I drop to one knee in front of her. "Amanda, will you do me the honor of being my fake fiancée so that we can bring some peace to this town?"

She searches my eyes with hers, her pupils dilating just enough to be noticeable as her breath comes in shallower and shallower bursts.

After what feels like an eternity, she gives me a solid nod. "Okay. Okay. I'm in. Let's do this."

My heart leaps. Not the only part of me leaping, if I'm being honest.

I'm engaged to Amanda Anderson.

This week will be interesting.

An alarm beeps on my phone.

Shit.

Family cookout tonight.

I'm due there in an hour. Which, I suppose, means *we're* due there in an hour now.

I lift a brow at Amanda. "Good. Because we're starting right now."

Chapter 2

Amanda Anderson, a.k.a. a big-city dog walker who is currently very confused

Dane Silver is hot.

Which should not be the thought at the top of my mind, *ever*, especially now as he's driving us through town to meet his family and also tell them the lie that we're engaged.

But *break the family feud*?

And by pretending to be madly in love?

That. Is. So. Hot.

I shiver like I haven't sweated through my bra twice over already today.

And like I haven't shivered six times already at the memory of him not only offering to go along with my charade, but also giving me a solid reason to believe there's greater good in it.

Don't ask what happened to my belly when he dropped to one knee.

That was stress. Had to be stress.

"You're sure you're okay with this plan?" he asks as he pulls his rental car out of Lorelei's driveway to take us to his grandparents' house for a cookout.

"Kinda my own fault." There's no *kinda*. This is 100 percent my fault.

I thought I was walking into the Gingerbread for hugs and welcome-homes and excitement over Grandma's fiftieth anniversary of running the bakery, and instead, I walked into a massive guilt trip.

Amanda. You're a dog walker. If you were headlining Broadway shows or walking red carpets like you thought you'd be when you left for New York . . . but there's no one else. Surely you can give up walking dogs for your family? For your hometown?

Like New York isn't where I belong. Like the job that I love doesn't matter. Like my friends and neighbors in New York don't make me feel warm and welcome and free to be myself. Like the kids who keep showing up asking when they can audition for our first show at the community theater don't matter.

Like just because *someone else could do it*, it's not important enough for it to be *my* dream. Like because I don't have blood relatives there, it can't actually be home.

The biggest problem making me realize just how much bigger this problem is, though?

I haven't told my family that *I wrote the play*.

They don't know my community theater is doing *my play*.

I'm afraid to tell them because I was so vocal about being an actress and then . . . it just didn't work.

What if my play is just as terrible?

I don't want to hear the *oh, Amanda*s that would come.

Didn't you learn that theater isn't really for you as an adult all those years ago?

So I haven't told them.

I haven't told them why I care so much, and I don't know how.

"Doesn't matter whose fault it is," Dane says. "What matters is that we can still back out."

"After the cookout," I reply.

The cookout is our trial run. If we can win over even one member of Dane's family tonight—Lorelei excluded—then we agree that we'll continue this and see if we can knock down the walls one by one before our "elopement" next month.

If we can't—well.

We haven't agreed yet on what comes next after the cookout if we can't. I think we should still try my mom and Grandma tomorrow. He's been less committed.

"You look like you're about to throw up," he says.

"It's how I prep for all of my roles."

He slides me another look. One side of his mouth hitches up. "Uh-huh."

I shouldn't trust him this much, but Lorelei has always said he's the best man she knows, and I adore Lorelei, so we're doing this.

If I have other options, I can't think of what they might be.

We're both putting a lot on the line here. We could both completely lose our families over this. There was something in the set of his jaw and the faraway, haunted look in his eyes while he was pacing Lorelei's living room that made me suspect this is about something bigger to him.

But I still put him in this position, so I feel like I owe it to him to be honest. "Do you ever feel like your family loves you, but not enough to trust you to do what's best for yourself, even when you're nearly thirty years old, and you start to resent it, but then you do something immensely stupid and realize that you might completely lose them over it, but also, you're mad that they've put you in this position in the first place and you're trying not to be mad because you know they're doing what they think is best, but it's just . . . complicated?"

His entire body lifts with the size of the breath that he inhales, and his cheeks puff as he blows it out. "I'm here, aren't I?"

My heart squeezes. "That part makes me a little sick to my stomach," I whisper.

I love my grandma. I love my mom. I want both of them to be able to retire and enjoy their time outside of the bakery, even if Mom's retirement is still several years away.

But that's the point of Grandma announcing me as her successor. To have someone in the wings for whenever Mom's ready to step aside, too, which will likely be sooner rather than later.

And me belonging in New York aside, I'm not the right person to run it.

I would rather that they think I've betrayed them by loving the wrong person than tell them the truth that living here and running the gingerbread bakery would make me miserable, and I'd ultimately destroy it.

Not because I'd want to destroy it. I love the Gingerbread House. I have so many good memories from the kitchen. Helping little kids put together their own gingerbread houses that actually taste good. Helping Mom and Grandma swap out the nutcracker decorations with the seasons. Riding the float in the Christmas parade and tossing out miniature gingerbread cookies to all the kids along the route.

But I can love the Gingerbread House and also know that running it is not what I'm supposed to do with my life. It's like loving the tree at Rockefeller Center and knowing you're not supposed to have one of your own in your dinky apartment. Or like adoring a Monet at the Met and knowing that it, too, doesn't belong in your apartment.

There are things you embrace in your everyday life, and things that are better left for short visits.

Tinsel is for short visits.

New York is where my heart and my life and my creativity are.

"At least you know how to act," Dane says. "I'll be the weak link here."

"Do you believe that us faking this engagement to end a feud is a good thing to do?"

"Yes."

"Just feel that, and you'll do great."

I hope.

I don't know his story or what his family expects of him. Actually, I don't know much about him at all. We quickly covered that he moved to San Francisco after college to work at an engineering firm that manages automated assembly lines for various manufacturing companies around the world. He has an adorable if lazy dog who's chilling in the back seat. And he wants to end our families' feud badly enough that he's willing to pretend to be engaged to me to do it.

"How can a guy go wrong when his fiancée believes in him?" he deadpans.

For the first time in what feels like centuries, I actually laugh.

He slides me another look. "I won the school spelling bee when I was in fourth grade."

I would've been in third. Was I there? "You're very smart."

"My dad had everyone over to celebrate, and the first thing both my uncle and my grandpa said was *Those Andersons have never had a kid win a spelling bee. Take that, idiots.*"

I wince.

"That's what makes me sick to my stomach," he adds. "As a kid, I didn't understand why it made me feel gross inside, but I can tell you now exactly what the problem is. They make every win about beating your family instead of about celebrating that one of us grandkids did something pretty cool. I'm done with this feud. If our families can't fucking get over this . . . I don't know the next time I'll voluntarily come back to Tinsel."

Oh.

I swallow, then have to swallow again.

No big deal. All that's riding on this fake engagement now is my best friend's brother not walking away from his hometown entirely.

No pressure.

None at all.

"I'm sorry the feud hurt you," I say. "For what it's worth—I hated it when we were growing up too. I just wanted to be Lorelei's friend, and I couldn't, and I still don't entirely understand why. I just know it's easier to sneak around to see her than it is to deal with my family being mad at me."

He frowns as we approach downtown Tinsel. I don't think the frown means he's unhappy, though. Any *more* unhappy, I mean.

It's more that I'm realizing he has resting grumpy face when he's thinking.

Every time he's frowned that specific frown in the hour or so since we agreed to keep up this fake engagement, at least for tonight, within moments, he's spouted off some brilliance about why it's a good plan. "If tonight goes well, I need to move into your cabin with you for the week."

I choke on air.

We've agreed that we're not telling Lorelei that our engagement is fake. She doesn't need to carry this secret, and we need *no one* else to know if it's going to work.

We've agreed that I'd come to the cookout his family had planned tonight because if this were real, we'd be racing to tell his family the minute mine found out. They won't forgive him if the rumor mill reaches them first, and we're already in the danger zone.

We've agreed on a story for how we reconnected, when we started talking, and when we knew it was love.

And we agreed that if we need to break up after tonight, we'll work out the details later, even if I'm a little on edge that us breaking up tonight could make my life way more complicated.

Especially since it drove my grandmother to one of her "heart attacks."

But this is the first time he's caught me truly off guard. "What? No. There's only one bedroom in the cabin."

"You told your family we're eloping next month. We're telling mine the same thing. If we want them to believe we're madly in love, we have to stay together. Overnight. We can't stay at Lorelei's. She'll figure out we're faking. I'll sleep on the couch, but I need to stay at your family's cabin with you."

I stare at his profile. He has thick dark hair falling over his forehead, a prominent nose, and lips that aren't too thin or too thick, and he's sporting a five o'clock shadow on his cheeks and square jaw. His cheekbones are chiseled of stone, much like they were in high school, but he's bulkier now than he was then. He's still on the slender side—tall and wide but slender—but there's definition to his legs and arms that wasn't there before.

I didn't pay a lot of attention to him then. Then, he was Lorelei's academic older brother who was headed to Stanford to study to be an engineer.

We don't get a lot of kids leaving Tinsel and heading to Stanford. It was a big deal.

Big enough that there was a lot of eye-rolling at every family function of mine. *Ooh, they think they're so special, having someone who's smart. Or dumb enough to take on the loans that'll come with that. Just wait until Amanda's lighting up the Hollywood screen. They'll see who's the better product of Tinsel then.*

Dane's right.

The fighting between our families serves absolutely no purpose.

It's a stain on the town, causing the mayor and other community leaders to intervene basically every month to get things done if our families have conflicting opinions.

And they do.

Mostly out of spite. Grandma's said so herself. *Those new streetlamps would've been a good idea if I'd thought of them.* Or *Those Silvers know we need to update the welcome sign, but they're arguing just for the fun of it.*

While I'm sure eventually our generation would drop the bickering, it should end *now.*

Why am I a grown adult who still has to sneak around to have dinner with her hometown BFF?

"I'll tell her we didn't want to ruin the surprise," he adds. "Chili and I have always stayed with her when we're in town. She would've been suspicious if I'd told her I was staying anywhere else."

I glance over my shoulder at his dog in the back seat.

Chili doesn't even crack an eyelid.

He is easily the laziest dog I've ever met. Or possibly the most tired. "Have you had his bloodwork checked recently?"

Dane grins, which is adorable.

Have I ever seen him smile before?

I don't think I have. Or if I have, it didn't register the way it does now.

"Yeah, his bloodwork is fine," he says. "He's decided his purpose on this earth is to see how little energy he can expend and still survive. His favorite treats are hot dogs, and he'll pick them over chicken or steak, but that's pretty much the only thing he jumps at these days. Not that he gets treats often. I lean vegetarian."

Another smile creeps onto my face despite all the reasons I've felt like I'd never smile again today. "You *lean* vegetarian?"

"Some days you can't beat a hamburger."

He turns onto Kringle Lane, the main street through downtown Tinsel, where our families each have their own shops right across from each other.

Even during a ninety-degree heat wave, you can count on Tinsel to be a winter wonderland. Fake snow covers the easement between the sidewalks and street. The flower boxes are full of decorative candy canes mixed with poinsettias that won't bloom for a few more months. The hot chocolate stand at the end of the street is open and running a solid business with the tourists despite the heat.

Likely it's iced hot chocolate.

When the sun goes down, holiday lights will twinkle on around all the old-fashioned streetlamps.

I crack my window, and *yes*.

There it is.

I smelled it earlier, when I stopped in to see Grandma and Mom at the gingerbread bakery, but I still love the ever-present cinnamon, pine, and woodsmoke scents lingering together.

Tinsel wasn't always a holiday town. But sometime in the 1960s, with my family's gingerbread bakery well established and the Silvers' fruitcake shop doing good business, the dairy just outside of town started offering eggnog year-round. The corner market added a section of ornaments that you could get anytime. The businesses in downtown started leaving their holiday lights up well into the New Year, and then the fashion boutique on Main Street changed its name to Mrs. Claus's Attic.

The rest of the town followed suit, and soon, we were *the* destination for people who wanted to celebrate Christmas in July . . . and August, and February, and why not May, and so on. Streets were renamed with holiday themes. The parks in town too. Within a few short years, everything was Christmas all year round.

Grandma says our family started it.

I'm sure Dane's family says the same.

I know the mayor stops by and asks Grandma and Mom to *please* not chase customers away from the Fruitcake Emporium on a regular basis. I can only imagine what she has to ask the Silvers to do.

My grandma does enough volunteer work on the various holiday committees around town that people won't outright tell her to get over herself, but I've sat in on enough meetings to feel the tension that creeps in when someone says something nice about Dane's relatives.

Shame.

That's what I'm feeling.

Shame.

Shame that our families make the entire community walk on eggshells.

This isn't how the behind-the-scenes of a Christmas town should feel.

We pass the Gingerbread House on the left and the Fruitcake Emporium on the right. Zero doubt the Gingerbread House is playing a Dolly Parton Christmas album. I can almost taste the frosting that we use for gluing houses together, and out of habit, I wave to the two four-foot nutcracker statuettes guarding the door.

The one on the left is holding a surfboard. The one on the right is wearing a swimsuit.

It's how Grandma does Christmas in August.

Next month, she'll replace them with schoolteacher nutcrackers. October, they'll be ghosts. November, turkey farmers.

Every year, she ponders if she can change up the nutcrackers to aim a middle finger at the Fruitcake Emporium, and every year, my mom reminds her that we're the classy family in the feud.

I will carry the secret to my grave that I actually like their fruitcake.

Lorelei used to sneak it to me in her lunch box at school.

"Do you like gingerbread?" I ask Dane. It seems like something his fiancée should know.

"I like building gingerbread houses."

"Tell me you don't mean with the store-bought kits."

"I do not use store-bought kits."

"Store-bought kits are the reason people hate gingerbread."

"I promise, I only use gingerbread that Lorelei bakes."

"She's so good in the kitchen. I can't bake anything, but even I know store-bought kits are a travesty. They give gingerbread a bad name. Do you know how many kids have to be told every year that they can eat the gingerbread houses that they make at Grandma's place? And then how many kids *like* it, even when they think they won't?"

He slides a raised-brow look at me.

I lean back in my seat and sigh. "I can love Tinsel and care about my family's business and still not be the right person to live here and take over."

"I had the same conversation with my grandpa two years ago. About living here. Not about taking over the Emporium. Similar enough, though, I suppose." He squeezes my knee, and it takes every ounce of willpower that I possess to not jump at his touch.

Not because it's bad.

More because it's *good.*

Which is, I suppose, bad in its own way.

We need to be comfortable touching each other if we're going to pull this off. Just another role. That's all this is. One more role.

I've played parts opposite plenty of guys that I didn't want to touch me in any other circumstances.

But between thinking Dane's hot because he wants to end our family feud, the way he's answered every single objection I could think to raise before I raised it, and the relatability of knowing he, too, prefers city living to Tinsel—I could be wrong, but I think I accidentally signed myself up for a very good fake fiancé.

Provided us carrying through with the charade for a week doesn't give my grandma a real heart attack.

I would *not* be doing this if I thought it was putting her at risk of anything more than swallowing her pride.

He's right. The animosity needs to end.

We pass downtown, which means we're about three minutes from his grandparents' house.

"Tell me again who I'm meeting tonight and what I have to say to each of them to convince them that I'm not out to steal the Fruitcake Emporium," I say.

I'm in. I'm in all the way.

And I'll be the best fake fiancée Dane could ask for in the process, and I'll win over his family.

I have to.

If I don't, if we can't pull this off—I don't want to think about what it'll mean for either of our futures.

Nothing will be the same after this.

I just hope we can make it better instead of worse.

Chapter 3

Dane

The scent of smoked turkey greets Amanda and me as we circle around back at my grandparents' house, making my stomach turn.

Roasted meat is not my favorite scent. Turkey might be the worst.

But it's not a Tinsel cookout if you're not smoking a turkey.

Probably mashed potatoes and gravy inside. Green bean casserole. Hawaiian rolls.

Definitely fruitcake.

If you can't do a Tinsel cookout without a smoked turkey, you can't have more than three Silvers in the same location without also having fruitcake.

"You're serious about liking fruitcake?" I ask Amanda as my uncle Rob comes into view at the smoker. He's wiping his forehead with his apron and doesn't spot us right away. There's a red-and-green-striped pop-up shelter between the smoker and the back door, set up with folding chairs and two big fans, but it's empty.

"I am." She smiles at me, and it's like staring into the sun. I know I should look away, but I can't help it.

You're not seventeen anymore. Get it together. This isn't about high school fantasies. It's about leaving Tinsel better than how we found it.

"About time to prove it."

"Seriously?"

"It's not a—"

"Amanda?" Lorelei's shrill whisper from the window to our left cuts me off. "What are you doing here?"

It's still over ninety degrees, which makes the turkey smell extra nauseating. My shirt is clinging to my chest. Pretty sure my deodorant has failed. The one thing I want most right now is a dip in the lap pool back at my condo building in San Francisco and to not have to do this.

Instead, I wrap my arm around Amanda and tug her close, bringing all her body heat and the scent of cinnamon sugar and the feel of the smooth skin of her upper arm into my personal bubble. "She's with me."

Lorelei's eyeballs go wide, but not evenly.

One goes wider than the other, and then the second goes wider than the first.

They cross momentarily as she gasps, and then—

I stifle a sigh.

My sister doubled over laughing at this announcement was not how I saw this going.

Yelling from my uncle? Yes.

Outrage from my grandpa? Also yes.

Guilt from my grandma? Undoubtedly.

Disappointment from my dad? Inevitable.

"If you wanted coal in your stocking this year—" Lorelei starts.

"We're engaged," Amanda says stiffly, clearly offended—or at least faking being offended very well.

She wraps her arm around my waist, crowding even more heat into my bubble.

I wince, catch myself, and make myself gaze adoringly down at her instead.

Too much?

Not enough?

Shit. I'm bad at this.

Also, she can likely feel how wet my shirt is.

"You are *not*," Lorelei whispers.

Chili harrumphs in her direction.

Pup needs a pool too.

"We *are*," Amanda insists so strongly that I believe her.

Even though I know better.

"We kept it a secret because we knew our families wouldn't approve—and *you* know it too—but it's just—it's just right." She beams up at me again.

My heart gives another painful thump.

You did this to yourself, dummy.

Pretend to be engaged to Amanda Anderson to end the family feud. Not so I can live out a high school fantasy of being her boyfriend.

Uh-huh.

So much for *older, wiser, more confident* me.

This was the stupidest idea in the history of stupid ideas.

"If the family doesn't like it," I say, sweating more now that I'm actually telling the lie and realizing the very likely consequences, "then that's their problem."

Lorelei's smile drops.

She looks between Amanda and me, studying each of us in turn, before looking down at my dog. "Are they serious?" she whispers.

Chili rolls his eyes and flops to the ground, lying in as much of the shade of the house as he can get his body into.

"Dane wanted to tell you when we started dating, but I begged him not to," Amanda says. "That's such a heavy secret to carry, and we didn't know if it would work out, especially since it was long distance for most of it. The last thing we wanted was the judgment we knew would come, you know? We're so sorry we didn't tell you sooner, but—"

"Amanda was right," I cut in. "We know you can keep a secret, but that doesn't mean you should've had to."

Ninety-degree sweats have nothing on the *blatant lying to my sister* sweats.

"Is that one of them gingerdead kids?" Uncle Rob suddenly bellows. "What is *she* doing here?"

If I never hear the word *gingerdead* again in my lifetime, it will be too soon.

The animosity runs deep. Sometimes petty and childish too.

"Meeting the family, because we're getting married," I reply evenly, looking over Amanda's head and straight at my uncle.

Pretending to be engaged and lying sucks.

But this feud is stupid. It doesn't serve the community. It doesn't serve my family. It doesn't serve Amanda's family. And I truly am sick and tired of half of the updates I get from my family about life back home being nothing more than them bitching about something the Andersons did.

There's a reason I don't live in Tinsel anymore, and it's not about turkey or fruitcake or wanting to live someplace where Christmas is only a small part of the year.

Not that I see the end of the feud making me want to move home, but at least I'll quit making excuses to get off the phone with my family faster and faster every time we talk and planning shorter and shorter obligatory visits every time.

I don't even read half their emails anymore.

Uncle Rob's face does nearly the same thing Lorelei's just did.

The back door bangs open, and Aunt Teeny charges out, followed by my cousin Esme, who's a few years older than me.

Uncle Rob's been the fruitcake master of the family for about twenty years now. Esme's been his shadow since she moved back home after getting a business degree. Grandpa asked me a few years ago to move home and help us expand into adding an ornament shop—fruitcake doesn't make the profit gingerbread appears to make, which is also a sore spot for my family—and when I declined, he roped Lorelei into it instead.

"I didn't just hear someone say that our Dane is engaged to one of those *Andersons*, did I?" Aunt Teeny says.

Esme catches her six-year-old daughter, Jojo, by the arm as the kiddo darts out of the house too.

She doesn't look nearly as horrified as her parents.

I glance at Amanda and try to silently telegraph *Let's start with her*, but I think she's quicker on picking these things up than I am.

"No running outside until the smoker's off," Esme says to Jojo, but she's staring at me the whole time.

Lorelei tumbles out the door, too, followed by my grandpa, my grandma, and my dad.

Whole family's here.

And why am I here?

For my grandparents' sixty-fifth-anniversary party.

Which is happening this coming weekend.

The day before Vicki Anderson, Amanda's grandmother, is having her own anniversary party to celebrate half a century of working at the Gingerbread House. Where apparently she's announcing her retirement.

She planned her party on purpose to steal our thunder, Grandma told me when I arrived in town yesterday. *It's not even her real work anniversary. She started at the bakery right after her honeymoon, and she would've been married to that Anderson man for fifty-eight years this year. You know she's making up that this is her fiftieth anniversary. It's all a scam to get more attention on her and steal any attention on us.*

Don't care if it's intentional or not. I care that the animosity stops and my family recognizes me—and Lorelei, and probably Esme too—as more than trophies and pawns.

I don't know how they can live here. I truly don't.

I drop my arm from around Amanda's shoulders and link my fingers through hers instead, tugging her along and ignoring the blip in my chest at the way her tiny hand fits inside of mine.

An hour into this, I've decided the next time I get a fake fiancée, she won't be someone I've ever had a crush on.

"Yes," I say to Aunt Teeny. "You heard right. Everyone, this is Amanda. Amanda Anderson. One of *those* gingerbread Andersons. And we're getting married."

"Next month," Amanda adds. "In Vegas." She gives them all a finger wave like it's totally normal to tell your family's enemy that you're eloping with one of them soon. "Nice to meet you all. I can't wait to get to know you better."

Objections erupt around the backyard.

"Vegas?"

"Next month?"

"How long has this been going on?"

"I thought you hadn't dated anyone since Vanessa."

"Does she know about Vanessa?"

"Can I be a flower girl?"

Jojo's little voice is what makes the adults finally stop.

They all look at her.

Then at me.

"We're keeping the wedding small," I say.

That might be the exact wrong thing to say.

Or it might be the exact *right* thing to say.

Lorelei and Esme share a look.

And I know.

Zero doubt. No question.

The feud is causing more headaches for my sister and my cousin than they've let on.

Let's see if we can win just one of them over. One of them besides Lorelei.

That was our plan.

Looks like all it took to win Esme over was Amanda setting foot on my grandparents' property.

But I don't think the rest of them will be nearly as easy.

"We thought it was best to elope since we didn't want a massive cake fight breaking out between all of you at the reception. Or . . . before the wedding even starts," Amanda tells my family.

"We would *never* start a food fight at a wedding," Esme says quickly. "That's *so* unsophisticated."

"Absolutely," Lorelei agrees. "You don't have to elope to hide from *our* side of the family doing terrible things to ruin your big day. We can be the bigger people. You have to get married here. A Silver can't marry an Anderson and *not* get married here."

"I'd love to help you plan your wedding. It'll be so much fun." Esme swings her daughter up into her arms. "And of course Jojo will be your flower girl. This could be her only chance. I wouldn't want to ruin that for her. Ever. Especially when your wedding would be the wedding of the century in Tinsel."

Shiiiiiiiiit.

The good news? We have allies who know all the right things to say.

The bad news? They're both about to steamroll us into something.

Amanda looks at me.

I stare back.

I don't know her anywhere near well enough to read her mind, but I've watched enough holiday movies in my lifetime to know exactly what my line is supposed to be here.

"What would make you happy, my darling?" I say.

"Oh my god, *swoon*," Lorelei whispers.

Amanda's eyes narrow the smallest fraction of an inch.

I think she's silently telling me off for making her make this decision right here, right now.

Tough.

She's the one who got us into this pickle.

Even if I'm the one who insisted this was a good idea. And I still stand by it.

"It *was* always my dream to get married at the gazebo in Reindeer Square," she says. "With the whole town there. And a cake from

Reindeer Bakes and in a Mrs. Claus dress like the one your grandma used to wear."

Fuck.

She's good.

She invoked *my grandma.*

My entire family draws a loud, collective breath and looks at Grandma, who's eyeing both of us like she's considering the best curse to put on our children.

Someone dialed the summer up to eleven. Sweat's dripping down my ass now too.

"Who does she think she is—" Uncle Rob starts, but Lorelei elbows him in the gut.

"He's a man in love despite all the reasons he knows you won't like it," she says. "And how are you all going to feel when he comes home for Christmas and the Andersons accept him as one of their own when you have this amazing chance to accept Amanda as one of *our* own but you're being dicks purely for the joy of being dicks?"

"I love your sister," Amanda whispers.

"Mostly same," I whisper back.

"Her grandmother plays that god-awful country Christmas album—"

Amanda interrupts him. "I love Dolly."

"Dad. Go check the turkey," Esme says. She beckons us closer. "Amanda. Dane. Chili. Get in here out of the heat so we can all talk about your wedding without our brains frying. Pia over at the bakery is one of my best friends. I'll make a call and get a cake arranged. You just tell me the date."

"Why wait until next month?" Lorelei says as she, too, hustles us into the miraculously cool house. The kitchen is dimly lit, and I smack my hip on the sideboard that's always been too close to the back door, but we're in air-conditioning. Beautiful, cool air-conditioning. "This is Tinsel. We can whip up a wedding in a week."

"And then you can get married on Grandma and Grandpa's actual anniversary," Esme adds as she pushes us toward the kitchen table, where all the sides are already set out, including three different fruit-cakes beside a plate of sugar cookies that I know will have come from Lorelei. She bakes the best cookies. Which is not what I should be concentrating on considering what my cousin is saying. "Next Monday. You can stay a couple extra days instead of taking time off for Vegas next month, and then it's an even bigger celebration this weekend."

Lorelei claps her hands. "Oh, that's such a poetic date for such a poetic romance."

"We can't ask all of you to drop everything to help us plan a wedding in a single week," Amanda says.

"It's our absolute pleasure," Esme says.

Lorelei's eyes go shiny like she's about to cry. "We get to be *sisters*."

I can't remember the last time I've had this many *fuck*s in my head in a one-hour time period.

"My family—" Amanda starts, but Lorelei blinks at her as her eyes get shinier and her chin trembles.

Shit.

Shit.

My sister will hate us if she ever finds out this was all fake.

"—will be so excited that I'm not eloping like my brother just did," Amanda finishes weakly as she casts a glance at the fruitcake.

I swallow.

Hard. "I didn't want to wait a whole month to get married anyway."

Uncle Rob appears at the back door. "Do you like turkey?" he barks at Amanda.

She turns on an instant smile that I'm absolutely positive is fake.

It has to be.

How can she not be feeling guilty to the core of her soul at how upset Lorelei will be when we "break up"?

Which is now happening in no more than a *week*.

"I love turkey," Amanda says. "But not as much as I love fruitcake."

Lorelei stifles a smile.

Uncle Rob stares at Amanda. "Someone get her a piece of fruitcake."

"Am I being selfish if I ask for the whole loaf?" Amanda replies.

Uncle Rob stares harder.

Dad pushes one of the fruitcake plates with an entire fruitcake to Amanda.

Aunt Teeny provides a fork.

Grandma stares in silent disapproval.

And Amanda dives in.

No gagging. No funny faces. No flinching.

Instead, her eyes slide shut, and a smile teases her lips as she chews her first bite.

A soft mewl escapes her lips. "Oh, god, I've missed this."

"When have you ever had it?" Uncle Rob asks.

"I snuck it to her at school all the time." Lorelei's wiping her eyes and beaming at us.

"And I sometimes order it under my roommate's name," Amanda says as she digs in for another bite.

She doesn't say *I know it's wrong to love fruitcake.*

She doesn't say *This is so embarrassing.*

She just dives in like my family's fruitcake is her oxygen.

Have I been had?

Is this really about her not wanting to inherit her family's gingerbread bakery, or is this about her wanting easy, free fruitcake.

I mentally shake myself.

It's not about fucking fruitcake.

But I still think she likes the fruitcake more than she'll ever honestly like me.

Liking me isn't the point.

Ending the family feud is the point.

And our timeline to solve this just got cut down to seven days.

Play stupid games, win stupid prizes.

I think we're fucked.

Chapter 4

Amanda

"One week," I say faintly as I unlock the door to the cabin at the edge of Tinsel that I use every time I visit my family. After the cookout, Dane drove us back to Lorelei's house so I could get my rental car, and then he followed me out here. We won over his cousin, so we've agreed that the fake engagement is still on. "*One week.* And they're planning an actual wedding. *An actual wedding.*"

"If they don't think it's real, this won't work. And they're right. If this were real, it *would* be the wedding of the century in Tinsel."

He doesn't seem aggravated. Just patient with a side of pensive as he follows me inside. We're both pulling suitcases, and he has a backpack too. Chili trudges along like it's an insult to his doghood that he's not sleeping in front of a fan right now.

"My grandma called while we were on our way out here. I lied to her. I mean, it's the truth that your cousin is setting up a cake, but it's a lie that we're getting married." I will not hyperventilate. I will not hyperventilate. I will not hyperventilate.

I did this to myself.

Now I get to face the consequences.

"Her heart okay this time?" Dane asks.

I sigh. "Now she says she's getting the flowers. Not because she approves, but because your family would screw them up."

He sighs too.

"Can we honestly pull this off in a week?" I ask him.

"Are we willing to live with what happens if we don't try?"

And there's the kicker.

If our families weren't feuding, would I still be expected to move home and work in the bakery?

Probably.

But if there wasn't that pride that went along with running a better business than the Silvers do, would it be easier for Grandma to swallow the idea that the Gingerbread House might not stay in our family forever?

I don't know.

I don't want to think about it.

So instead, I think about something possibly worse. "Lorelei's never going to talk to me again when we break up."

Dane shakes his head. "Yes, she will."

I'm not panicking. I'm—okay, yes. I'm panicking.

All the things that could go wrong—"The next step is that we *actually get married* because I can't—I can't—"

Because I can't tell my family the truth that I don't want to give up the life I love in New York to help my mom run the bakery, and I'll be letting Dane down if I bail on this fake engagement before seeing if we can carry it through to a point that our families attempt to get along.

I feel like I'm seven years old again, pulling a fire alarm at school because I wanted to see what would happen, and then lying to everyone about it being me. Knowing how disappointed my parents would be if they ever found out.

Doing stupid, rash, impulsive things without considering the consequences.

And now look where we are.

"Hey." Dane's hands settle on my shoulders, and it's like I'm connected to the earth again.

Not floating in a bubble of panic.

"We can call it quits anytime," he says. "You want out, we'll end it now. This isn't about torturing ourselves."

I drop my head to his chest like we've done this a thousand times. Who knew being fake engaged to someone for a few hours could make them feel like your best friend? "No. This is bigger than us. If I can't—if I can't be what my family needs, then maybe I can be what Tinsel itself needs. I'm okay. I am. I'm just being a little melodramatic. That's all."

"You've had a lot thrown at you today."

"Says the man who woke up this morning with no clue that he'd be going to bed fake engaged to a complete mess."

"Eh. I could use more fun in my life."

I suck in a deep breath. "So we're doing this."

"I'm in as long as you are. We have Esme *and* Lorelei on our side, and I think I can sway my dad with a few more days. That's practically half of the family with just one horrifically awkward cookout."

So many objections swirl in my head.

But what if I lose my mom and grandma over this?

How will I pay everyone back for the wedding when it doesn't happen?

What if Lorelei truly does hate us when we break up or she finds out this is fake?

What if I'm never welcome in Tinsel again?

I shake my head and pull away, grabbing my suitcase as a shield from all my fears. "I can take the couch."

"Take the bed. I was sleeping on the couch at Lorelei's anyway."

"No, really, I—"

"Do we have to arm wrestle for the couch?"

He's teasing, but there's a stubbornness in his eyes that tells me he'll fight to be a gentleman about it.

"I'll take the bed tonight, but if you don't sleep well, you take it tomorrow. Deal?"

He makes a noncommittal noise as he sets his backpack on the couch. "Spare pillow anywhere?"

"Hallway closet. I'll grab you one after I put my bag away."

I duck down the short hallway to the bedroom, looking for breathing room and knowing that between the heat and this fake engagement, I might not find it for a while.

This is good for everyone, I tell myself. *It's good for Tinsel. It's good for Dane and Lorelei. Clearing the negativity is good for Mom and Grandma.*

Why are good things so hard sometimes?

I wash my face to scrub off the remnants of sweat from the day, then head back out to the living room, completely forgetting to stop at the linen closet.

But Dane has helped himself. He's laying out a Christmas quilt on the couch in the living room.

"Little hot for that, isn't it?" I say.

"Protecting your couch from my sweat." He pulls his shirt over his head, leaving him standing bare chested in the middle of the cozy little hideaway. "Your grandma say anything about how she's feeling? Think she'll be up to meeting me tomorrow?"

My mouth is suddenly too dry to answer, courtesy entirely of being this close to a buff, half-naked man who's been my unexpected savior today, but I make myself talk anyway. "She—she's good. Not happy that the doctor told her to lay off sampling the gingerbread. Upset that your family got to meet me before she gets to meet you. But yes. She says she wants to meet you to make sure you're worthy of marrying me. And to decide how much she wants to spend on our wedding flowers."

He stares at me for a long moment.

"I'll pay her back for the flowers. And I'll pay Esme back for the cake." How, I don't know. Somehow. I will. I have to. No matter how many extra dog walks I have to sign up for. I couldn't live with myself if

I knew this was a farce and let them pay for it anyway. "Also, we should probably talk about how we're going to break up since it's going to have to happen in the next week."

"As friends," he says without hesitation, "who realized the spark isn't there for a romantic relationship the way it should be, but who have no regrets about trying to make it work."

The fact that he doesn't have to pause to think about it hurts my heart.

Just a little.

Like the barest amount.

I can hardly feel it anymore.

Chili lifts his head from his spot on another folded quilt on the floor beside the couch, and he snorts at me.

Did the dog just call me a liar?

I shake my head and look back at Dane. "That's brilliant. So long as we're friends, they'll have to stay friends too."

"Or at least something closer."

"We need to tell everyone we want a simple wedding. I don't want everyone going to extreme lengths and spending a lot of money, but they need to believe we're getting married."

"Amanda . . ."

"What?"

"When someone from my family is engaged to someone from your family, there will be no stopping our families from trying to one-up each other in planning this wedding, and I don't think anyone in town will discourage it." He holds his phone up to show me a text from Esme.

> Pia is so excited that you two are uniting our families that she wants to make the biggest, best wedding cake that Tinsel has ever seen. She's expecting you Friday morning to pick flavors. This is the best news ever.

Wow. Guilt grows faster than my favorite hot dog vendor can serve up a half dozen sauerkraut-and-mustard dogs. And he's working on breaking a world record.

"But it'll be worth it if our families call a truce," he adds. "Even better if they actually start to realize they might like and appreciate each other the way they like and appreciate everyone else in town."

Chili grunts. I'm guessing that's agreement.

I sink into the chair next to the couch, remember belatedly that it has a broken spring that likes to poke people in the butt—I should definitely warn him about that spot—and slide to the floor by the dog instead. "Do you honestly think this will work?"

Dane's gaze settles on mine. "What are we out if it doesn't?"

I stroke his dog's soft fur and contemplate the question. "My place in my family," I whisper.

Chili whimpers and shuffles so he can lay his head on my thigh.

Sweet dog. I like him.

Dane shifts onto the couch. "If your family can't accept the life you want to live for yourself, then they don't deserve you. And I'd say that no matter how you want to live your life and no matter who your family is."

"They're *family*."

"Being family doesn't give anyone a free pass to dismiss your goals or to treat you like you're not capable of deciding how to live your own life, or like they own you. Being family means respecting each other and the choices you each make. Would you ask your grandma to quit being a gingerbread baker to go live in New York with you?"

"Of course not."

"Then they can fuck off." He clears his throat. "And please consider that said far more politely than it came out."

There is so much more to unpack here. "Does your family not support you living the life you want for yourself too? They sounded so proud of you tonight."

They did.

When they weren't muttering about his choice in women.

"They just wanted you to know I'm the better one of the two of us. Their opinion. Not mine. All based on the dumb feud." He clears his throat and looks away. "I emailed you a get-to-know-you questionnaire I found online. Things we need to be able to answer about each other if we're going to pull this off."

I can't concentrate on a questionnaire right now.

Not when my heart is aching so hard for him.

How is it possible to have this much compassion and worry over a man I barely know?

"My grandma will likely accuse you of using me just so that a Silver can get their hands on the Gingerbread House," I tell him. I don't want to. It feels like kicking him when he's already down. But he needs to know.

Instead of seeming offended or defensive, though, he rolls his eyes. "She's on to me. I'm an evil family-feud-loving mastermind who lives to destroy the lives of my family's enemies. Mwaha. Ha. Ha ha."

I don't even try to suppress a smile. "You need to work on your evil villain laugh. That wouldn't scare a toddler."

"I thought fiancées were supposed to support a guy's dreams."

Was he always this funny? Why didn't I know he was funny? "I'll do better tomorrow when I'm more used to being someone's fiancée."

He shakes his head, clearly amused this time, then gets up. "C'mon, Chili. Outside one last time before bed. And clearly, we all need sleep."

"I'll take him."

Dane lifts a brow at me.

"I'm a professional dog walker. I think I can handle Mr. Cutie-Patootie Lazybones here. Plus, I promised my mom I'd check the mail-box." And I need to breathe a little more.

And think more.

And process more.

It's been quite a day.

"You good with Amanda taking you out, Chili?" Dane asks the dog.

Chili grumbles, but he pulls himself to his feet and nudges my hand.

"Who's the sweetest boy?" I say while I scratch behind his ears.

He harrumphs, but he also licks my face.

Just once.

But he does it.

Victory.

I love winning dogs over. They're my favorite kind of people.

"How long have you had Chili?" I ask while I get up to grab the dog's leash.

"Seven years."

"Did you have dogs before that?"

"Always."

I smile.

I like dog people almost as much as I like dogs. "We'll be back. Make yourself comfortable. And I'm serious that you can have the bedroom if you want it."

"Good here. Thanks."

He grabs his laptop again while we head for the door. He mentioned that he's working remotely this week rather than taking the whole week off for vacation, so I expect he'll be grabbing his computer a lot when we're here.

Not spending his time getting to know his fake fiancée.

Which is probably how it should be.

Outside, crickets are chirping. Frogs out on the lake behind the cabin are singing too. There's no moon, so the stars are bright overhead, and I even see a shooting star.

The temperatures have dipped enough that it's easy to take a full breath of the night air while Chili does his business, even if it's still warm. We make a very slow walk to the mailbox, but I don't mind.

I walk a couple of older dogs who can't be rushed either. They make me slow down and take in the world differently than when I'm clipping along with a half dozen energetic friends on leashes.

And tonight, I get to enjoy the night and mull over everything that's happened since I arrived in Tinsel this afternoon. I want to call Yazmin, my roommate and New York bestie, but with the windows to the cabin open, I don't dare.

I don't want Dane to think I'm spilling the beans of our secret to anyone who'd blabber here.

But I do text her on the way back to the house after I grab the single envelope from the mailbox.

> FYI—I kinda did a thing and got accidentally engaged to my home BFF's brother. We're trying to fix our families' long-standing hatred of each other. If my mom or grandma call, can you please tell them that you adored Dane the few times you've met him, that you like that he's vegetarian like you, and that you're thrilled for us getting married in Vegas next month?

She calls instantly.

I don't answer, but text her again.

> Can't talk. I'll call tomorrow when I'm alone. Tell my mom I'm madly in love, and then tell me everything you tell her if she messages. Promise?

Girl, you owe me a story and dinner for this. I. Am. Dying. WHAT IS GOING ON? she texts back.

My big mouth and a very kind man who can see the good in things that I can't. Promise I'll call ASAP with more deets, I tell her.

Waiting impatiently, she texts back.

Chili and I reach the house, and that's when I realize something's weird about the envelope I grabbed from the mailbox.

It doesn't have a name or address on it.

Someone dropped it off.

And when we open it up and see what's inside, all three of us—even Chili—gasp.

Today's been full of surprises.

And it seems there are even more on the way.

Chapter 5

Dane

Amanda's up early, moving through the kitchen fixing coffee not much later than the sun.

Guessing she slept about as well as I did last night.

Wonder if she's having second thoughts about continuing our fake engagement.

I'm not—while I might not have slept great, I don't have regrets about our plan. A small amount of guilt that Lorelei will be disappointed when I don't marry Amanda, yes. But any regrets about putting myself in a position to make my family choose between me and the feud?

Nope.

Especially since *someone* clearly knows something more about our family histories than we do, and decided it was time we were let in on some old, old secrets.

I pull myself off the couch, stretch, and head into the small kitchen with Amanda. Chili stays behind, moving only to yawn and put his head back down on his quilt bed.

Coffeepot's making noises while she stares, again, at the letter that someone dropped off here sometime since she arrived. We left it on the scarred oak kitchen table when we went to bed last night after both of us read it a dozen or more times.

"Do you think it's a warning?" she asks.

I shake my head. "I don't know what it is."

Technically speaking, I know *what* it is.

It's a letter, written by my great-great-great-grandmother in the late 1800s to my great-great-great-great-aunt Lucy, who hadn't yet come to America from Germany.

And it spells out very clearly that a man named George Anderson had left my great-great-grandmother Maud brokenhearted after leaving her days before their wedding to marry a *trollop*—my great-great-great-grandmother's word—named Minnie.

There's no question that Maud is my great-great-grandmother and that Lucy is my great-great-great-great-aunt.

Uncle Rob and Dad got Grandpa and Grandma a printed family tree going back ten generations for Christmas when I was in high school. I was fascinated with it. Used to go to their house to stare at it hanging over their mantel. Been a few years, but I know where I come from.

I know the names.

But I don't know what it means that someone delivered a copy of this letter to the mailbox where Amanda's staying. Beyond that I'm in this fake engagement until we get answers to this too.

"I tossed and turned all night wondering if this is why our families don't get along," Amanda says. "I don't know all of my relatives back that far the way you do, but George *Anderson*? That can't be a coincidence, can it? And then I started wondering why George and Maud broke up. Was Minnie pregnant with George's baby? Was there some kind of arranged-marriage situation somewhere? Was Maud really brokenhearted? Or was that the family's story, and Maud actually broke George's heart? No, please, don't get offended, this isn't about *your* family specifically. Or even mine. It's just a thing I wonder after the number of plays and musicals I've read and seen. I'd ask the same thing about any family letter like this."

"There might be more."

"Right? The number of possibilities of what actually happened could be endless."

"More letters."

She stares at me.

I tap the letter. It's not original—it's a photocopy. "We need to figure out where this came from."

"Your family. Has to be. Mine doesn't know where the feud started."

I suck in a deep breath and pinch my eyes closed.

"I didn't mean that in the offensive way," she adds quickly. "I'm not implying your family does and they're lying. I promise, I'm not."

"I'm not offended."

"You look offended."

"I'd like a cup of coffee before I remind you that any of our relatives could be guilty. They could've started fighting for any reason from George and Maud to someone breaking someone else's window a hundred years ago. Which isn't about you or me."

She stares at me again.

Clearly, we both need coffee.

Or possibly something stronger, considering that her eyes are getting shiny and her chin's starting to wobble.

Fuck.

I hold my hands up in supplication. "I don't care who's at fault. It doesn't matter. What matters is that they all pull their heads out of their asses and quit making it so that if *our* kids want to get married someday, they don't have to go through *this*."

So Tinsel's mayor doesn't have to continuously intervene to keep one of our families from sabotaging the other during parades and cookie bake-offs and snowman-building contests. So I can have one conversation with my family that doesn't remind me of how mean and petty they can be. So that Lorelei can have dinner with Amanda when she's in town without the two of them having to sneak around to make it happen.

Hell, they could even publicly be friends on social media.

Wouldn't that be something?

Amanda swipes her eyes and turns away, staring at the coffee maker instead of me. "I know. *I know.* I just—you're so logical and smart and you know exactly what we need to do, and why, and how, and I'm just—I'm *not.* I got you into this and you're doing all of the planning and the *why*s and I'm just daydreaming about a romance gone wrong well over a century ago."

You're so smart, Dane. Look at those grades. Look at what a good job you have. Those Andersons can't touch what we've got in you. Ignorant assholes. We made sure they saw the write-up of you and your volunteer work at the dog shelter too. They acted like they didn't see it, but we know they did.

Sometimes, I want to daydream about a romance gone wrong, too, but hell if I've ever been able to admit it out loud.

"You ate half a fruitcake last night," I say instead. "You're definitely pulling your weight."

"*I like fruitcake.* Especially your family's fruitcake. I've tried fruitcake all over New York City, and nothing else comes close. I meant it when I said I order it under my roommate's name. You can check the receipts. There are probably two a year from Yazmin, which is really me ordering as her."

If she weren't an Anderson, my family would be thrilled that we're engaged. Even Lorelei doesn't like the family fruitcake, which is the biggest reason she's not working at the Fruitcake Emporium.

"So you're still in? We're still engaged for the next six days or until our families come around on their own?" I ask her.

She looks at the letter, then back at me. "I don't know if this will solve my problems at the bakery, but I know the town deserves to have our families' feuding end. Even if it all goes to hell, we'll know one day our own great-grandchildren will read the social media posts about how we tried to fix it, and that'll have to be enough."

"No boyfriends for you, but you want kids?" I ask, then instantly regret it.

Yes, Amanda, I paid very close attention to how you feel about dating. That's the most important part.

But she just smiles. "I never wanted a fiancé either, but look at us now."

The coffee maker stutters the end of its cycle, and she leaps to grab two mugs. "Sugar? Cream? Milk? Iced to brace ourselves for another day of this awful heat? I should know how you like your coffee."

"With good company."

"So somewhere else."

"Hey. Nobody's their best before coffee. And you're very good company." I step behind her and settle my hands on her shoulders.

She stiffens but almost immediately relaxes and leans back into me, and for one more split second, I wonder what it would be like if this was real.

If I was in a real relationship with Amanda.

"Thank you for lying to me," she says.

"Who do you keep in your life who makes you feel like you're not good company? They need to go."

"Just me."

"How do you take your coffee?"

"Intravenously, preferably."

"Second choice? I need to know since we're engaged."

"Eggnog lattes are my favorite. Heavy on the eggnog."

"Seriously?"

"They're delicious."

"I know. They're my favorite too."

She looks up at me, blinks twice, and then grins. "No way."

"Favorite part of coming home is that you can get eggnog year-round here."

"*Mine too.* But I can't say that in front of my mom or grandma. They'll think it's code for *I want to move home.*"

"I tell Lorelei sometimes. She doesn't believe me."

Amanda slides out of my hands and skips to the fridge. "Have you ever had it on ice? I think today calls for iced eggnog lattes."

"Agreed."

She turns with the eggnog, then slides a look at the wide doorway from the kitchen into the living room. "Well, good morning, lazybones. Finally decided to join us, did you?"

Chili saunters into the room and snorts at both of us.

I take him out while Amanda finishes our eggnog lattes.

It's still early, but you can already feel the heat starting to rise. Steam lingers on a lake beyond the pine trees. The morning birds seem muted, like they, too, would rather go hang in a pool than hunt for food when it's this hot.

Amanda steps out onto the back porch with both of our coffees before Chili's found the perfect spot to do his business. He's not prone to wandering—that would take effort—so I've let him off his leash to find whatever he wants to find out here.

She hands me an oversize snowman mug with ice floating in the tan liquid. "Do you have your phone on you? We should go over your questionnaire now and worry about that letter later. Grandma and Mom will start calling soon about me bringing you to the bakery to meet them, so I should know more things about you and vice versa."

"Pretty good logic there," I murmur while I pull my phone out of my pocket.

"I'm trying."

"Of the two of us, you're far more likely to pull this off without a slip."

She wrinkles her nose, but then she sips her coffee.

It's like watching her eat fruitcake all over again with the way her eyes close and her head lifts, highlighting the curly tendrils of hair not tucked into her bun wrapping the base of her long neck. She sighs in satisfaction, sips again, and sighs deeper with a soft *mmm*.

Whatever Amanda thinks she's lacking in strategic planning for a fake engagement, she makes up for in spades with the emotions that radiate out of her pores.

Ecstasy over coffee. Joy over my dog. Worries over her family. Eagerness to prove her worth.

I sip my coffee too.

Damn good latte.

"Okay. Let's do this," she says. "First question."

I clear my throat and look down at my phone as I realize I've been staring at her. "Favorite food."

"Breakfast, lunch, dinner, dessert, or snack food?"

I blink at her.

She starts to smile. "I like to eat. Don't you have favorites for every meal?"

"That's a question I've never been asked before."

"Lucky day. I'll bet I can come up with a few more. What's your favorite meal? Not like, *I like steak and eggs*, but like, *I never skip breakfast*."

"No steak."

"Right. Mostly vegetarian. Will it bother you if I have a steak?"

I shake my head.

"Not that I eat a lot of steak," she continues. "I'd rather buy a ticket to a Broadway show than blow my grocery budget on a steak."

The way this doesn't surprise me in the least has me smiling again. "What would you eat instead of going to a Broadway show?"

"Fruitcake."

We stare at each other for a split second before we both crack up.

"I'm mostly serious and only a little kidding," she says through giggles.

"I'll get you a hookup so you never have to pick again."

"My hero."

Her eyes sparkle brighter than the holiday lights hung all over town year-round, and her laugh rings out more merrily than any Christmas bells.

Any doubts I had about lying to my family last night evaporate.

Ending our family's fight will be worth it, and somehow, I'll find a solution to her bakery problem at the same time.

It'll set her free.

It'll set all of us free.

Chili suddenly bolts to his feet.

My dog unexpectedly leaping up is concerning enough that I set my coffee down. "Chili? What's up?"

A massive *arooooooof!* explodes out of his mouth, and then he's gone, racing through the trees.

"Chili!" Amanda exclaims. "It's just a squirrel!"

I dash off the porch, chasing after him.

My dog doesn't run away.

My dog doesn't *run*.

Unless he's going to dinner.

Who knew Michigan squirrels counted as dinner?

And now that he's running, I don't know where he'll end up.

Or how he'll have the energy to get back.

Chapter 6

Amanda

Taking a dip in the lake wasn't what I expected this morning, but chasing Chili with Dane all the way out here made it an easy decision.

"Go dry off," Dane says to Chili as he helps the dog to the shoreline.

Chili grins at him.

I stifle a laugh while I tread water. I'm not far out—just far enough that it's too deep for me to stand up. "You should come back and swim," I call to Dane after he's made sure Chili's settled in the shade again. "We can finish talking out here. It feels *so good*."

Especially after yesterday's heat.

How did I forget how much I love a dip in the lake?

Dane gets Chili leashed to a park bench, and then he strips off his wet T-shirt and his shorts, going down to black boxer briefs.

It's not the chill of the lake making my nipples tighten.

That's the effect of looking at my hometown best friend's brother practically naked.

When I say I don't date, it's not that I'm opposed to the idea.

I just rarely find a man who's interesting enough to take along with me while I sightsee and enjoy the city. Or who's worth giving up the time I'd otherwise spend seeing shows and exploring museums and discovering new restaurants.

Especially when there's always that lingering question in the back of my head: *Will my family approve? What if they find something wrong with him?*

Grow up hiding your best friend from your parents because of a generations-long feud, and you get paranoid about how your family will react to the people you want to bring into your life.

Yazmin says my preference for not dating is a defense mechanism.

She's probably not wrong.

But here in Tinsel, Dane Silver is fascinating. I already know my family *doesn't* like him and we're pretending to be engaged anyway, so why not enjoy the fact that he's legitimately sexy as hell?

Plus, he got me fruitcake.

You don't want to know the number of people who've mocked me for liking it. Actually, you can probably guess.

It's not a small number.

So people who feed it to me without mocking me get extra bonus points.

Dane wades out. His dark hair is standing up at all angles after the dog chase into the lake, and he runs his fingers through it, pushing it back one last time before he does a shallow dive and slips under the surface.

He appears beside me a few seconds later. "Little colder than my pool back home."

"You have a pool?"

"Condo complex does."

"You swim?"

"Most days."

I can see it. He has that long, angular swimmer's body, and he's far more solid than I would've given him credit for in high school.

Actually, I wouldn't have thought about him like this in high school.

But my brain and my libido are on overdrive this morning.

"You?" he says.

My face goes hot. "Hm?"

"Do you swim?"

Right.

Swimming.

He's not asking about my libido.

"I'm more of a splasher-arounder," I tell him.

He smiles, and *damn.*

I haven't had enough coffee yet today, but that blue-eyed smile that brings out two matching dimples is waking me up more than the cool water in the lake.

Especially in various parts of me that I usually handle all on my own.

Am I having a reaction to this fake fiancé thing?

Or is this some kind of Tinsel woo-woo magic?

Or maybe just gratitude that he's a nice guy? It's so weird to me that Lorelei and Dane are both fabulous people, but my mom and Grandma insist on hating on the Silvers.

"Am I in danger of being splashed?" he asks.

Is he flirting with me? Or am I hearing things? "Only if you want to be."

His smile deepens, making his eyes crinkle at the edges.

Wow.

He has long eyelashes.

Incredibly long eyelashes.

How did I not notice that yesterday? Or ever?

"How about you stay here and do your splashing-arounding while I go for a swim. Then we can go grab some breakfast and continue with all of those questions."

"Deal. But I might head back to the house to finish my coffee. And I'll take Chili if I do."

He chuckles. "Good luck with that."

"With Chili?"

"Yep."

"He's a good boy. He'll come with me."

"He just used a week's worth of energy chasing a squirrel and then fairies in the lake. He's gonna have to be carried inside."

I suppress a shiver at the idea of a soaking-wet Dane in nothing but his underwear carrying a fluffy fifty-pound dog.

And then I shake my head.

This is fake.

Yes, we could be real friends, but sleeping with Lorelei's brother while we're pretending to be more than we are will make things complicated quickly.

And who's to say he's feeling the same thing?

He's already told me he's in this to make our families quit fighting both for himself and for Lorelei.

Not for me. At least, no more for me than for me being able to hang out with Lorelei openly when I'm home.

"I can carry your dog," I tell him.

He studies me, smile still lingering. "I believe you."

"But I'll talk him into walking on his own before I'd have to."

"You deal with difficult dogs a lot?"

There's something about being home that puts me on edge whenever someone wants to talk about my job. It's not *normal.* It's not a job that's needed in Tinsel because people walk their own dogs here, and dogs have yards to play in that are just one door opening away. But Dane seems genuinely curious, not judgmental or mocking, so I shake my head. "Not often. But occasionally. Usually when we cross paths with another dog that one of mine doesn't like."

His gaze dips to my lips—*hello*, belly on a roller coaster—and then shifts like he's studying my shoulders.

Like he's curious how strong I've gotten from walking dogs.

I suppress a shiver again, but not well enough.

"Cold?" he asks, lifting his gaze to meet my eyes again.

"I like it," I reply. "It'll be a good balance before the day gets really hot. Do you have a dog walker for Chili?"

He nods and starts to answer, but a voice interrupts us from shore.

A familiar, guilt-inducing voice.

"Yoo-hoo! Amanda! We need you at the bakery, sweetheart!"

Grandma Vicki.

She's here.

At the edge of the lake in her bakery pants and a reindeer T-shirt.

"Is that—" Dane starts.

"My grandma," I whisper.

He and I stare at each other for a moment.

"Time to get out?" he says at the same time I blurt, "We should kiss."

We stare at each other again, but this time, his face is telegraphing about a million conflicting thoughts going through his head while I'm sure mine is telegraphing horror that I just said that out loud.

"I mean, she'd expect it," I whisper. I'm not wrong. But I'm suddenly feeling awkward as hell.

"No, yeah, you're right. Kissing is normal for an engaged couple."

"So, yes to the kiss? We don't have to if you don't want to."

"We'll kiss. Once. You go to shore and tell her I'm doing my morning swim and I'll be in later."

Oh my god.

He's in his underwear.

He can't get out now.

He'd flash my grandmother.

And I forgot that, and once again, he's used that quick brain of his to save the day.

"Amanda?" Grandma calls again.

"Okay," I say. "One kiss, then you go swim, I'll get her to town. Do you want to get Chili, or do you want me to see if I can convince him to head back to the house?"

"I'll get him."

"Okay. Okay. So now we kiss." I am *never* this awkward onstage.

It's different when it's real life.

"Amanda!" Grandma hollers.

"Just a minute!" I call back.

When I look back at Dane, he's smiling again. "Grandparents, man."

And just like that, all my tension leaves me, and it's the most natural thing in the world to propel myself closer to him and press a quick kiss to his lips.

But he wraps an arm around me and tugs me closer, clearly tall enough to be anchored on the lake bed, and the next thing I know, I'm having a *real* kiss.

One that has our bodies flush and him gripping me under one leg and parted lips and mingled breath and chilly noses and a flush breaking out over my entire body.

I don't live for physical touch. For kisses. For sex.

Other people are not the adventure that I crave.

Yazmin is right. I have too many hang-ups around relationships, all rooted in having to grow up hiding my best friend.

But I don't want to break this kiss.

It feels *safe*.

And at the same time, it's an absolute thrill.

For one fleeting moment, I let myself pretend that it's real.

That Dane *wants* to kiss me. That it's not just for show.

That I can trust him.

"Amanda!" Grandma hollers again, breaking into the moment and making me break the kiss.

"Sorry," I gasp.

One of his eyebrows twitches. His smile is gone. "For what?"

"For—I don't know." For my grandma? For me liking the kiss? For me getting us into this situation? For me forgetting why we're doing it?

He quirks a half grin. "Then don't be sorry. I need to check in with work, and then I'll join you in town. Don't make up too much about me without texting me what I'm supposed to know, okay?"

"I'll do my best."

"Amanda?"

"Yeah?"

"We have to plan this wedding, or the town will plan it for us."

"Right. Crap. *Crap.* Okay. Okay." I'm babbling, and I need to stop. "You'll come to the bakery, and then we'll say we have to go get lunch to plan the wedding. That's good. Really good. Cut them out and make them want to be involved. Or maybe they'll come with us. Or maybe—you go swim. You go swim, and then *you* text *me* how we're going to solve this, okay?"

He nods, his grin growing. "I'll text you."

And then he's gone, pushing off for a swim.

I linger in the lake for just a moment, watching the powerful way his body cuts through the water, his long arms making it look easy in a way that I very much know it's not.

I have a failed semester of swim team in high school to prove it.

After watching Dane for long enough to sell the ruse—probably longer than necessary, but I'm enjoying the view—I turn and head back toward shore.

It's time for me to face the music.

Chapter 7

Dane

Amanda tastes like eggnog frosting on a gingerbread cookie.

It's the only thing on my brain for the entirety of my swim. Through a shower accompanied by a boner that I rub out while trying *not* to think about her. While I handle a few emails from work and spend half an hour on a project that will be overdue at the rate I'm going. As I convince Chili to get in the car to go hang with Aunt Lorelei.

While I'm facing my sister at the rear of the small ornament shop next door to the Fruitcake Emporium.

"You should've told me," she whispers.

"If it didn't work, you would've had to pick sides, and neither one of us wanted you to feel like you had to."

She rolls her eyes and tugs on Chili's leash. "C'mon, you big old fluffy rug. I have a fan with your name on it."

"Amanda wanted to tell you." The fib slides off my tongue like I'm a natural-born liar. But I believe it's likely true, so it's close enough to satisfy the guilt weighing down my iced eggnog latte. "I'm the problem."

Lorelei eyes me.

I stare back without blinking. "Also, she wants to keep things small with the wedding."

"Oh, no freaking way."

"What the bride wants . . ."

My sister pulls me into the doorway of the ornament shop and lowers her voice to barely above a whisper. "Zero chance, Dane. *Zero.* If you want a small wedding, elope tonight and never come back."

I wince. If I leave town . . . I might not ever come back. Which means I'd see Lorelei even less.

She doesn't notice. "Everyone in town wants to see this wedding. There's not a single person here who doesn't have a story about how they've broken up fights between our families at some point. The people who aren't rooting for full reconciliation between all of us are showing up with popcorn to see whose grandparents throw fists first."

I wince again, and this time, she sees it.

"They're not throwing fists." She pulls a face. "Esme and I are on it on our side, anyway."

"Appreciate the help."

"We're doing what we can." She blows out a breath. "Regardless of whether or not you told me when you should've, I'm thrilled for you. There's nothing I love more than two people I adore finding happiness together. Don't let our families get you down. Concentrate on the happiness."

Yep.

She's going to throttle us when we break up.

Both of us.

Especially if she ever finds out this is fake.

"Thanks for keeping Chili for a while," I say. "I don't think he'd eat everything in the bakery if I took him there, but I also didn't think he'd chase a squirrel. Ever. So I'm not taking any chances."

"Have you met Amanda's family yet?"

"Nope. You all got the honor of both of us first."

Huh.

That lovely eggnog-iced-gingerbread flavor doesn't taste so good when I'm lying to my sister. Not that I'm lying about Amanda meeting our family first.

More that I'm lying about us being in a relationship at all.

Lorelei gives me one last long eyebrow-arched look. "Don't fuck this up."

"She wouldn't have said yes if she didn't mean it."

That part, at least, is true.

I give Lorelei a quick hug. Not too long—the morning's already steamy hot—but hard enough that she should know I don't want to fuck anything up.

That I don't want to cause her any pain.

"Grandma and Grandpa are convinced that Vicki Anderson's timing her anniversary party with their anniversary party to steal their thunder," Lorelei murmurs to me.

"I'm aware."

"Just saying. I have no idea what you're walking into on the other side."

"Have you ever heard the real reason our families hate each other?" I ask her.

"They sometimes talk about the fit the Andersons threw the year Grandpa made a fruitcake house and won the gingerbread house contest, but just like you, I have no idea why they'd been fighting for the decades before that."

The fruitcake house happened before Lorelei and I were born.

I've seen faded pictures, though.

It was epic. A glorious monstrosity. No idea how the whole thing held together, but it will be family legend for generations to come still.

Pretty sure it won for the mere fact that it was outlandish and shouldn't have made it to the contest at all.

And we can't talk about how epic it was without also talking about how glad we are that it made the Andersons furious.

Is it possible to have been born the wrong species? I'd rather be a dog.

I rub Chili's fur once more, then head around the building and across the street.

The Gingerbread House looks exactly as you'd expect. The plastered exterior walls are painted to look like a gingerbread house with candy canes "growing" among the poinsettias in the flower boxes beneath the picture windows flanking the door. Surfer nutcrackers stand guard too. The angled roof has bright-white globs of frosting dripping over the edges. Painted fiberglass, I'm sure. Large, multicolored holiday bulbs line the roofline, real lights intermixed with painted fiberglass bulbs so that it looks lit up, even in the daytime.

The building itself is a work of art.

Grandpa tried to make the Fruitcake Emporium just as quaintly themed for a few years there. One year he painted cherries on the windows that looked like giant bloody butts. Another year, he tried raisins.

Don't ask what people said about that. Just don't.

He finally conceded that there's not a lot you can do to compete with a real-life gingerbread house, so instead, he replaces the red-and-green awnings as soon as there's a hint of fading, he keeps the windows spotless, and he and Grandma go overboard with even more poinsettias and shaped rosemary bushes and Christmas cacti in their flower boxes.

Plus the red bench with a fiberglass Santa for anyone to sit next to and take pictures with all year round.

Get that free advertising with the store name right behind them, he says.

I push into the gingerbread bakery, expecting bells to jingle, and instead, a hearty *Ho ho ho* interrupts the country Christmas music.

Dolly Parton.

Just like Uncle Rob likes to complain about.

Cinnamon and ginger linger in the air. It's cool inside, but nearly as bright under the lights as it is outside under the sun. One wall is covered in pictures of kids holding their gingerbread creations. Another has shelves with knickknacks for sale. There's a train running around the shop close to the ceiling, and the floor, which is likely painted stamped concrete, looks like a flat layer of gingerbread. Gumdrops of all colors—the fake, foot-high kind—are positioned around the perimeter of the dining room. The back wall menu, behind the register and the display cases, looks like it was written by an elf, with curlicue letters and snowflakes.

The woman behind the counter gawks at me. Another woman in an apron pauses and makes a *you shouldn't be here* face at me too. She's helping a table full of kids assemble gingerbread houses on one side of the bakery while the adults that I assume are their parents sip out of mugs on the other side of the café.

I nod to both of them and stroll toward the hallway along the side wall.

Sign says **Restrooms and a Peek at the Magic**. Cute sign too. Just as ornate as you'd expect inside a gingerbread house.

Logic says this is the only way to get to the kitchen.

And sure enough, there's a large window next to the door where anyone can watch what's happening in the back.

I pause to take in the hallway and the kitchen itself.

Even the kitchen door looks like it belongs in a gingerbread house.

You are Amanda's fiancé and you are allowed to go in there, I remind myself.

I wonder if I need to put on disposable booties over my shoes. Do I need a hairnet? Where's the nearest sink for washing my hands?

Overthinking time.

Awesome.

I spot Amanda as she walks by the window. She's grimacing with a fresh trash bag in one hand, but she freezes, looks fully at me, and makes a face so comical that I smile despite myself.

And then it's all whirlwind action.

She charges the door. "Dane! You're here. *I told them you were coming*, but they think since I don't have a ring, that somehow means you don't care." Her eyes roll so hard I'm temporarily worried she'll pull something in her eye sockets, but they seem fine when she meets my gaze again. "And I still can't freaking bake," she adds in a whisper. "I never could."

Oh.

Huh.

That's . . . a new smell coming out of the kitchen.

Little smoky.

Not oven smoky, though.

More like burned-out-appliance smoky.

She grabs me by the hand and pulls me into the kitchen.

No orders to wash my hands. No disposable booties to cover my shoes. No hairnets.

Definitely overthinking.

"Mom? Grandma? Meet Dane. And be nice or I'll tell Santa to bring you coal in your stockings. Dane, my mom, Kimberly, and my grandma Vicki."

Two women turn and look at me.

They're related by marriage, not blood, but they could pass for mom and daughter.

They're both white, pleasantly plump, and average height. They're both wearing candy cane earrings. They're both in jeans and T-shirts covered with aprons decorated with snowmen.

They even both have red and green stripes in their hair, which you can see through their hairnets.

Kimberly has maybe two inches on Grandma Vicki. Her hair is in a bun under her hairnet, though, whereas Grandma Vicki's hair seems short and curly. Kimberly has Amanda's brown eyes. Grandma Vicki's are ice blue.

And they're both watching me like they'll destroy me if I make one wrong move.

"Morning, ladies. It's a pleasure to—"

Grandma Vicki snorts.

Kimberly nudges her.

"*Grandma.* Be nice." Amanda slips her hand into mine and leans into me. "Until you can tell me what Dane's done to you that's so horrible, you can keep your opinions to yourself."

"He's trying to steal my bakery," Grandma Vicki says.

"The Silvers aren't stealing the bakery," Kimberly says. "We won't let them."

Amanda sighs a sigh so deep and heavy that I feel it in my own gut. I squeeze her hand, and she leans more heavily onto me.

We were never friends, exactly, in high school, but we weren't enemies.

I'd definitely say we're friends now.

No matter what happens next.

"I don't want your bakery," I tell her family. "It's a very nice bakery. But gingerbread isn't in my life plan."

They narrow their eyes as one.

Shit.

Amanda hasn't told them *she* doesn't want the bakery.

She made up being engaged to me to get out of it.

And now I'm the guy taking away their retirement plan.

"There won't be a bakery if we don't get the mixer fixed," Amanda says. Under her breath, she adds, "Or if I touch it again."

The mixer.

That's what's smoking.

Or was.

"Anything I can do to help?" I ask.

I'm playing with fire.

They think I want to steal their bakery.

I don't, even if my wheels are spinning trying to find a solution for them that doesn't involve Amanda moving back to Tinsel.

Or me. I am definitely never moving back to Tinsel.

But I'm the fall guy now if Amanda doesn't want it. That's why we're faking this engagement.

So is it better for me to be helpful and feed their suspicions to win them over, or is it better for me to stay out of it?

If we want everyone to get along, I have to prove I'm a nice person.

Best way to do that is to be helpful.

"You can stay out of my kitchen," Grandma Vicki mutters.

"Did I tell you the Silvers are getting us a wedding cake from Reindeer Bakes? Oh, I did, didn't I?" Amanda says. "That's why you're doing the flowers. Right. But I don't think I mentioned that I saw Dane's sister this morning on my way in. She offered to shop for a wedding dress with me. I'm thinking tomorrow or Thursday would be good for that. Can't put it off much longer, can I?"

Kimberly and Grandma Vicki both suck in a breath.

It's uncanny.

There are clear differences in their facial structures and their builds now that I'm looking closer, but their mannerisms are so similar. Amanda said at some point in the past day or so that Grandma Vicki won the daughter-in-law lottery when Kimberly married her dad.

I can see it.

"I'm taking you shopping for your wedding dress," Kimberly says.

"And I'm making the wedding favors for the guests in addition to handling the flowers." Grandma Vicki snorts softly. "Can't have his family giving everyone fruitcake at my granddaughter's wedding."

"I like fruitcake," Amanda says.

Kimberly gasps.

Grandma Vicki puts a hand to her heart.

"Oh, no, ma'am." Amanda shakes her finger at her grandmother like she's scolding a dog, and I have to suppress a smile. "You're not pulling that baloney two days in a row. Go take your antacids and do whatever you have to do to come to terms with the fact that I love this man, I don't care who his family is. And considering you can't even tell me what they did that was so horrible, it's high time you got over it."

Both older women gawk at her.

I clear my throat and cross past a prep table covered in trays of raw gingerbread men and approach the mixer like I'm not having a reaction in my heart and my stomach to Amanda casually dropping an *I love this man*. "This happen often?"

"Only when—" Kimberly starts, but Vicki silences her with a look.

"Only when I'm around," Amanda finishes. She's almost cheerful about it. "Last time it smoked like this, it needed a new motor."

"How quickly does your repair person usually get here?" I ask Kimberly.

She winces. "A couple days."

"We've got this," Grandma Vicki says.

I would not want to see her and my own grandma in a stare-down.

But instead of worrying about how the world could end if those two ever ended up in the same room, I angle for a look at the serial number on the mixer and do a little googling.

"We've got this," Grandma Vicki says again.

I ignore her and look at Amanda. "Motor's in stock at a place up in Grand Rapids. We can have it back here in two hours. Three or four, if we stop for lunch and ring shopping."

Kimberly makes a noise.

But Amanda—

Amanda smiles so brightly at me that the sun itself pales in comparison.

And then she flings herself at me for a full-body hug and a hard kiss on the lips.

It's pretend, I remind myself while I hug and kiss her back.

Just pretend.

But I've lied enough in the past twenty-four hours. I can't lie to myself too.

I can't pretend it's not my teenage dreams come true to be holding and kissing this woman, even knowing we have an expiration date.

That everything about her body molding to mine feels even more perfect than I dreamed it would.

That I don't want to let go.

She's beaming at me as she pulls out of the kiss. "See?" she says to her grandma. "He's the absolute best."

"Any fool can get a motor," Grandma Vicki says.

I look her square in the eye. "I can replace it too."

She stares at me like she's trying to read the lies littering my soul.

But fuck it.

I'm pissed now.

I didn't do a single damn thing to this woman. I can have her shop back up and running by midafternoon. And she's being a butthead.

"I'll call Wade," Kimberly says. "If he—if Dane can't fix it today, we'll have a backup plan."

Grandma Vicki hasn't stopped staring at me.

I don't stop staring back.

I don't care how old she is. She's being rude, and she's putting Amanda in an awful position.

Just like my family's done to me for my entire life.

Starting to see why it was preferable to pretend to be engaged to the enemy to telling her grandma that she doesn't want the bakery.

Grandma Vicki apparently likes getting her way.

"Do you need a credit card for the motor?" Amanda asks.

"This one's on me."

"If you break my kitchen—" Grandma Vicki starts.

Kimberly leaps between us. "Thank you, Dane. Whether you can do it or not, we appreciate you trying."

I nod to her. "Anything to help Amanda."

I would. I'm still the sucker who'd do anything to help Amanda.

No regrets, though.

Not when she beams at me again.

I can practically hear her voice in my head. *We're making progress on my mom!*

Amanda's a whirlwind in the kitchen, tossing off her apron and grabbing her small wallet and phone from one of the drawers in the desk in a small office.

"No time to waste," she says as she darts back into the kitchen. She pecks her grandma on the cheek, then her mom. "We'll be back."

She grabs my hand again and hauls me out of the kitchen, down the rest of the hallway, and out the back door.

"What happened to the mixer?" I ask as I unlock the car and open her door for her.

She does one of those comical eye rolls again where her eyes roll unevenly. "Me. I happened to it. Me and that stupid recipe."

"What's wrong with the recipe?"

"It's in code, and I can never remember if *snowflake* means pound or tablespoon, if *candy cane* means cup or quart, and if *salt* actually means salt or if it means ginger."

I open my mouth.

Close it.

And then gesture her into the car.

"The code is so no one who's not family can steal the recipe."

"I guessed that part."

"Right. Naturally."

"But unless you put frozen butter and yarn and screws and bolts in that bowl . . . I think odds are good the mixer was on its way out anyway, and you had bad timing."

Her eyes meet mine, and then she sighs.

"Hey." I grab her hand again before she can sit. She looks so damn sad. "Doing the big things isn't always easy, but this'll be worth it in the end."

She glances back at the bakery, which is just as ornate on the backside, complete with fake gingerbread windows and a fake gingerbread chimney coming off the top of the house.

And then she sighs again. "If we can pull off planning a full wedding that neither one of us intends to follow through on and break up in a way that doesn't make everyone who's thrilled for us hate us and everyone who's not thrilled about us hate us too."

When she puts it like that, I get another knot in my stomach. But I still squeeze her hand again. "We will."

I hope.

Otherwise—nope. Don't even want to think about who'd be hurt by *otherwise*.

Chapter 8

Amanda

Dane Silver is a lot funnier than I ever would've suspected.

And I don't say that only because he's parking the car in front of a ring shop after we picked up the motor for the mixer.

He's cracked me up at least a dozen times since we left Tinsel, pulling me out of my head and all the worries that we're doing the wrong thing. And now he's parking in front of a jewelry store.

This one is only funny because it's outrageous.

"You are *not* spending the money to buy me a ring," I tell him.

"I'm sure they have a return policy."

I gawk at him. "Are you serious right now?"

He cracks a grin.

And now I'm doubled over in the front seat, laughing until I have tears in my eyes. "Jewelry stores—do *not*—have—return policies," I gasp out.

"They don't *advertise* return policies," he counters. "Who'd do that? *Fellas, get her some bling for her birthday. If she says no, we'll double your money back.* Not happening. Doesn't mean they don't have return policies. We should go ask."

"Dane—"

"My grandmother was staring at your hand last night too."

"I'm splitting the cost with you." My credit card is groaning at the debt this charade will cost me. But if our ruse makes our families call a truce, it'll be worth it.

"Not necessary."

"I got you into this—"

"—and I insisted on playing along. Until we find a solution to your Gingerbread House problem, I have more to gain than you do. I'm buying you a ring."

We have a stare-down in the front seat even if my heart blips at the reminder that we have no plan for the Gingerbread House.

Only a plan for ending a feud.

Which won't solve the bakery problem.

He kills the motor on the car.

Which means the air-conditioning peters off.

I have exactly forty-two seconds before this car gets too hot to continue this stare-down. "You play dirty."

"When we break up, we'll auction the ring off as the ring that brought peace to Tinsel, and they can donate all of the proceeds to charity. Maybe to fighting family charities. That's money well spent."

"I repeat, you play dirty."

He grins again. "Shall we go find you the ring of your fake dreams?"

I grab his hand. "Promise me we'll stay friends after this is over."

He studies me, his smile slowly going more serious. "Are you a friend who keeps in touch every month or a friend who runs into someone after three years and picks back up right where you left off?"

"Is there a wrong answer if I want to stay your friend?"

He shakes his head. "I just like knowing what to expect."

"I'll send you memes that make me think of you and you can call me if you ever want to talk, and then whenever we're in Tinsel at the same time, we'll have eggnog lattes and you'll bring the fruitcake and I'll bring vegetables, and we'll have a picnic at the lake."

His eyes crinkle at the edges as he smiles at me. "Your optimism is inspiring."

"I *will* send you memes."

"I believe you. Let's go get a ring."

The heat's already rising in the car, and he's getting out, so it looks like my options are sweating it out solo in the car or agreeing to walk into the jewelry store.

I don't have to let him buy me anything.

We can look and say there was nothing that inspired either of us or fit right.

He opens my door for me and takes my hand as I step out, then holds it all the way into the store. "Do *not* give them any suspicion that this is fake," he murmurs as we walk in.

Not that I would—if we're not telling Lorelei, we're certainly not telling a stranger. But it becomes apparent immediately why he's concerned.

The jeweler looks up from whatever he's doing at a desk behind the counter, and his face breaks into a broad smile, flashing bright-white teeth. He has brown skin and short, dark hair, with a well-trimmed beard, and he's in a suit. "Dane Anderson! It's about time you—ah, oh. Hello, there."

Dane's lips twitch. "Raoul. Meet Amanda. My fiancée."

Raoul's face says *These words do not compute*—I feel you, Raoul, I do—but he quickly recovers and flashes that brilliant smile again at me instead, extending a hand as he reaches us. "Amanda. So lovely to meet anyone who can capture this young man's heart."

Up close, I realize he has a few silver strands woven into his dark hair, and there are more crinkles at the edges of his eyes than I expected.

"She's a granddaughter of the gingerbread family," Dane says.

Raoul sucks in a breath. "No wonder I hadn't heard. Or possibly I should be saying, How have I not heard?"

"We broke the news to our families yesterday."

"How'd they take it?"

"About like you'd expect." Dane turns to me. "Raoul's family has been doing wedding jewelry for my family for about four generations now. He might know more family secrets than I do."

And we're lying to him too.

Fantastic.

But I smile brightly. "So you're practically family."

"Practically," Raoul agrees. "Though I take no sides in disputes. You need a ring?"

"We do," Dane says.

I pinch my thumb and index finger together. "Just something little."

"Definitely something big," Dane corrects.

Raoul nods. "Can't go *Romeo and Juliet* without something big."

"We need a statement piece."

"A bold statement piece."

"At least two carats."

"Hello?" I wave my hands at both of them. "Does the wearer get a say in this?"

They both study me for a minute.

Then they shake their heads in unison.

"No," Dane says.

"You can pick the cut and the setting," Raoul assures me, "but I can't in good conscience let this young man walk out of here with a ring his family can argue with. Not for you, my dear. Not with the curse you're breaking. Come, come."

I trail after him, casting a sideways glance at the necklaces and earrings and watches in cases closer to the door as we move deeper into the store. "Curse? Is that why our families fight?"

"You don't know the story?" Raoul asks me.

My pulse bumps. "No. Neither does Dane. Do you?"

Is it my imagination, or is Raoul looking at me like he's still on Team Silver and isn't sure if he can trust me?

"We think it'll be easier for both families to come to peace with us if we can address why they don't get along," Dane says, making me wonder if he feels it too. "And we won't breathe a word about how we heard anything, if you can help."

But after one more moment of studying us both, Raoul shakes his head. "Your guess is as good as mine. If my father knew, he didn't tell me. I don't know if anyone knows anymore."

Dane and I share a look.

Someone knows something, or we wouldn't have gotten a copy of that letter last night.

"Ah, here we are." Raoul slips behind the farthest counter, any suspicions or hesitations he might've had either masked well or slipping away. He bends and fiddles with his keys, and a moment later, I'm staring at a tray of diamond rings.

Unlike my occasional window-shopping trips in the diamond district in New York, though, this time, I'm up close and personal with these gems.

Teenage Amanda used to dream about having a billionaire boyfriend who would buy the whole jewelry store for me. There would be the starter rings that were upgraded every year to bigger diamonds and fancier settings.

Not long into my dog-walking journey, I met a billionaire.

My dreams changed.

I started saying I'd rather build snowmen in Central Park or spend a day at the Met than have all the jewelry in the world. And I meant it.

But staring at a row of sparkly diamonds, even knowing this is for an act and not real?

That Dane is committed enough to the ruse to buy one of these?

That the world will see me wearing his ring on my finger?

I suppress a shiver.

There's something about buying a ring that makes it feel almost real.

"One of them catch your eye?" Dane asks me.

I point without conscious thought and despite my best intentions to insist something smaller is better. There's a round-cut diamond inset among diamond, emerald, and ruby chips, making it look like a brilliantly sparkling snowflake on a poinsettia.

It's so Tinsel.

"Ah, wonderful choice," Raoul murmurs. He's put on gloves.

I briefly wonder if I should, too, but Dane takes the ring from Raoul without gloves, lifts my left hand, and slips the ring onto my finger.

His touch sends a warm thrill through my arm, and he doesn't let go after he has the ring on my hand.

Instead, he turns my hand in the light, making the diamond flash and sparkle and sending little rainbows dancing off the floor and walls. "It fits."

"Lucky finger size," I stutter.

"Want to try others?"

I shake my head.

Raoul's saying something. I think about the diamond's color and clarity.

But that's not what I care about.

What I care about is Dane holding my hand, both of us staring at the massive engagement ring currently sitting on my finger.

This is pretend. This is pretend. This is pretend.

And even if it wasn't, I made up my mind years ago that I can't be bought with jewelry.

It's not the jewelry. It's the guy.

Nope. Nope nope nope.

It's the weight of having my grandma wanting me to take over the bakery and me faking an engagement to get out of it while realizing I've accidentally picked the exact right guy because he wants to use our engagement to break a generations-long family feud.

Who could be immune to having big feelings over that?

"Amanda?" Dane says quietly.

Right.

We're an engaged couple in love, and we have an audience. "It's so beautiful. I don't think I deserve it."

He loops an arm around my shoulders, pulls me in for a hug, and kisses my head. "Goofball. Yes, you do."

I don't need a boyfriend.

I like being bound to no one. Exploring where and when I want. Not worrying if someone else isn't in the mood for noodles or pizza or girl dinner. No guilt or shame when I change my mind at the last minute. Just pure freedom.

With a side of knowing that my family can't disapprove of *no one*. There's nothing to disapprove of. There's no tests for *no one*. No insistence that *no one* pledge their loyalty to the Andersons over the Silvers.

But I'm starting to wonder what Dane would think of the Met. If he's ever been to a Broadway show on Broadway. Would he go to a baseball or hockey game just to experience the vibes in the crowd? Or people-watch in Central Park?

Would he come see the inaugural play that we're doing at our revived community theater?

The play that I wrote after being so inspired by the city itself? But that I'm not telling anyone about, in case it actually sucks?

I could tell him.

He wouldn't mock me.

But I don't.

Instead, I sigh heavily and hug him back as tightly as I can. "Thank you."

For everything.

For absolutely everything.

Chapter 9

Dane

I've never truly believed hell exists, but I'm reconsidering tonight.

Because I think I'm there.

My phone is exploding with texts from my family and some local friends. It's eighty-nine degrees, and I'm in an ugly Christmas sweater. Half the town is staring at me.

At us.

At Amanda and me in the middle of Reindeer Square for the annual Tinsel holiday photo shoot.

It's not her family or my family.

Not *only* them.

It's the whole town.

We're gathered around the gazebo that has Santa and four of his reindeer on top. The townsfolk are all dressed up in some variety of reindeer antlers and jingle bells and ugly sweaters, and the town hired a drone operator to get the best shots. Shop owners use the photo in annual mailings and on their websites, and every year, Tinsel outdoes itself.

My sweater smells like cedar and mothballs courtesy of the fact that it's lived in a cedar chest for the past fifteen years. Amanda's mom's cedar chest, to be precise.

She saved it since Amanda's dad passed away.

I'm wearing my dead fake father-in-law-to-be's ugliest Christmas sweater.

Correction: I'm sweating through his sweater.

And everyone wants to see Amanda's ring.

And talk about how I saved Christmas at the Gingerbread House.

One, Christmas is still four months away. I didn't *save Christmas*. I fixed their industrial mixer. And two—

Getting Amanda a ring was the worst thing I could've done.

"There's the man of the hour," my old English teacher says. Mr. Briggs claps me on the shoulder. He's in an ugly Hanukkah sweater and shorts. "Never thought I'd live to see the day that a Silver would save the Andersons. And marrying one too. Don't end this in tragedy. That's an order."

"No tragedies here."

"Good. Amanda's performance in *Taming of the Shrew* will always be my favorite, but that doesn't mean I need you two going real-life Shakespeare in this town."

"No real-life Shakespeare."

"I mean it."

"Mr. Briggs, my fiancé has already assured you there will be no tragedies happening here." Amanda slips to my side and squeezes my left hand, leaving her free to lift the engagement ring for the teacher's inspection.

It's all anyone wants to see.

We knew it would be when we decided that we had to come to the photo shoot.

That we had to be out in public, letting our families see the town's excitement over our impending wedding as one more solid example of why they need to pull their heads out of their asses and let this stupid feud go.

"How did you two meet? I haven't heard the whole story," a woman dressed like a Christmas tree says.

"Dane was on a trip to New York for work, and I was walking dogs past his hotel when he was waiting on a ride, and one of my dogs humped his leg," Amanda says.

I slide her a look. This is a new version. Or at least new details of the version we've agreed on and told other people.

She throws her hands in the air. "I'm tired of not telling the truth about what Mr. Fluffles did to you that day."

Mr. Fluffles humped my leg.

I file that one away for the questions Lorelei will have when that reaches her in approximately forty-two seconds.

"Anyway, after I got Mr. Fluffles off of Dane's leg, I asked if I could buy him coffee to apologize. And *then* I realized who he was, and I couldn't take it back without being rude, and honestly, I've always adored Lorelei, and she always spoke so highly of Dane that it wasn't truly hard to want to have coffee with someone from back home. One thing led to another, and here we are."

Amanda smiles.

Her ugly Christmas sweater is one of the gingerbread scenes from the movie *Shrek*.

She has an entire series of them stored at her mom's house. It's unexpectedly charming that she can tell a whole story with her Christmas sweaters.

Also, I was incredibly glad that her mother wasn't home when we were going through the Christmas sweaters.

But now—"Amanda!" Kimberly calls. She's in a blow-up gingerbread costume. "Grandma and I are over here, and they're about to start."

"Dane," my dad calls at the same time from the other side of the gazebo. Like the rest of my family, he's wearing the fruitcake version of a Green Bay Packers cheese hat. "Over here. With us. We have an extra hat for you."

Amanda looks up at me, and she doesn't have to say a word. The question is obvious. *We're in this together, so whose family do we both stand by?*

Something shifted the minute I slipped it on her finger at Raoul's shop.

I don't believe in soulmates. I think love is hard work and some people are better at it than others. I think you have to be good at communicating and forgiveness if you're going to make it work. I think we all change over time, and you can never know what life will throw at you.

But when I took Amanda's hand and slid that ring onto her finger, it was like something off-kilter in my life fixed itself.

It makes zero sense. There's no logic to it.

This isn't real.

She wants to be my friend. Nothing more. And I'll never tell her how much of a crush I had on her in high school.

Not if I want to maintain any of my dignity.

But without any discussion, we link hands again, then both turn to our respective families.

"Dane and I are staying in the middle," she calls to her mom as I report to my dad, "We're good here, thanks."

Silence settles over the square.

Some people look at Amanda and me. Some subtly shift farther from us. Some angle closer. Some look at our families.

Even the fake snowmen seem to be gaping at us, waiting for whatever will come next.

"Whoopsies," Amanda says. "We forgot to ask how much popcorn we'd need for this. Can we get this picture show on the road? My makeup is melting off, and I have a hot date tonight."

The tension breaks as other families—not our own—crowd around us and echo the calls for the photographer to get started.

It's hot. It's sticky. My hand is sweating, but Amanda doesn't let go.

If anything, she holds on tighter.

We're both taking a massive risk of being disowned, and I don't think I realized the full implications until just now.

There's a rustling in the crowd around us, and it takes me a minute to realize why.

Lorelei and Esme are pushing through.

"We're with you," Lorelei says as they reach us.

Amanda sucks in a loud breath, then launches herself at my sister and hugs her tight.

Esme punches me lightly on the shoulder. "Doing Santa's work here. I'm proud of you."

"Squish in closer," the photographer says over his megaphone. "Quit changing spots, but squish closer."

Esme hands me a fruitcake hat.

Amanda lunges for it and puts it on her own head before I can take it, and then she smiles at me. "I love fruitcake."

"You can keep it."

She links her hand in mine once more and squeezes.

It's hot. It's humid. There are too many bodies crowded around. I want to go take another dip in the lake.

We don't have a solution to her Gingerbread House problem yet.

And I might be on a path to tearing my family apart.

But so long as Amanda's gripping my hand, I can survive this.

So long as she's gripping my hand, I think I can survive anything.

And that's exactly the kind of thinking I need to *not* believe in.

Now, or ever.

Chapter 10

Amanda

Me and my big mouth.

I have a hot date tonight.

Now the whole town is wondering what we're up to. Which means we have to get caught on a hot date. Which means I have to figure out the best hot date to have with a fiancé that they all believe I've mostly dated long distance.

So that they can all see that this is real and we're choosing each other over our families.

And once again, Dane comes to the rescue and answers the question for me.

Beach picnics are hot in this weather.

And romantic. And semiprivate, but also public enough that someone will see us.

"Do you think it'll actually work?" I whisper to Dane while we set out toward the beach behind the cabin. Chili ambles along slowly behind us, lured by the promise of food. He had a good day with his aunt Lorelei.

Or so we assume. Lorelei reported he snoozed in front of a fan all day.

"Making people think this is real, or tricking our families into getting along?" Dane asks.

"Yes."

"If anyone can pull off a miracle, it's you."

I peer up at him.

He's in board shorts and a plain white T-shirt, carrying a box of candles that we found in storage and canvas grocery bags filled with our impromptu feast. I'm in a two-piece swimsuit made of boy shorts and a crop top tank, carrying beach towels and a beach blanket.

I'm half convinced I'm going to drop my new engagement ring on the shoreline before tonight's over.

"You realize I'm the same person who randomly decided today to tell people we met while a dog was humping your leg?" I say to him.

He smiles. "That's the part that makes miracles fun."

My heart flutters.

It's not supposed to do that, but it does. "Did you ask your family about the letter?"

"Not directly. I asked my dad if he knew how many generations of Silvers were haunting him to make him want to keep disliking your family, but he didn't think it was a serious question. You?"

I shake my head. "I don't think Grandma was ready to hear it. She's pretty mad. There was a lot of muttering about *fruitcake-house-building shitheads* and some *even if you say the vows, it won't last* going on too. Sorry."

"They'll come around," he says.

"Will they?"

"It's barely been a full day. Let's see how it looks this weekend."

If he has faith, then I will too. "I hoped it would be magic. Super simple. That they'd look at us and believe we were happy and decide to just do the right thing."

He squeezes my arm briefly. "We still would've had to keep it up for a few days so they wouldn't get suspicious that we're playing them."

"I know. You're right. But that sounds more fun than stressing that we're committed to this through the weekend without any clue if it'll work."

"I'm having fun with you anyway."

I glance up at him, but he's moving on toward shore.

Leaving me with something to contemplate.

Why *can't* this be fun? I want to stay friends. I like him. We're in this together. And it's not like we're scheming for bad reasons. We're not trying to steal inheritances or sabotage anyone's business. We're doing this to make things better.

So again, *why can't this be fun?*

We get our picnic set up on the beach, complete with the candles around the picnic blanket. Close enough for ambience, not close enough to catch the blanket on fire.

Been there, done that.

And when I tell Dane the story, he laughs until he nearly snorts chickpea salad out his nose.

He pays me back by telling me about a time in college that he almost got arrested for public indecency, which is so not what I ever would've expected of Lorelei's straitlaced older brother.

And yes, he times the best parts just right so I come close to snorting fried chicken out my nose.

Payback.

It's hilarious.

We get halfway through his emailed list of things we should know about each other before I get a tingling between my shoulder blades. "Someone's watching us," I whisper as I lean in, smiling at him, and peck his cheek.

"Nice job letting us know, Chili," he says.

The dog grunts in his sleep, and I crack up.

The sun is dipping low, but not so low that what I propose next is a bad idea. "We should go for a canoe ride."

Dane sweeps a glance around the lake.

My family's cabin isn't the only one on the lake, but there are only a handful of other homes out here. A half dozen or so.

Most are owned by locals who live here year-round, but there are one or two that are vacation rental homes.

You can generally tell who's home by the Christmas lights sparkling on the houses when the sun goes down. And there's zero doubt that the locals would be spying and taking pictures and sharing them all around town tonight, so that tingling between my shoulder blades that says that someone is spying is pretty much expected.

"This one your canoe?" Dane asks, pointing to an upside-down canoe halfway between my uncle's cabin and the neighbor's house.

"I think so."

He eyes me.

I grin.

"Exactly how sure are you?"

"This much?" I hold my hands about a foot apart.

"On a scale of one to ten, ten being most sure, how sure are you?"

"Six . . . and three-quarters?"

I love how easily he smiles. Back in high school, I thought he was on the uptight side. But he seems mildly amused by nearly everything now.

Except our family's feud.

I wonder if the feud is the entire reason he seemed uptight in high school.

And how much of a shame would that be?

"Six and three-quarters," he repeats, shaking his head with his smile growing. "Good enough. Chili, want to go for a canoe ride?"

The dog doesn't answer. Dane still rises and dusts his hands on his board shorts, then heads over to the canoe while I gather up most of what's left of our feast.

Dessert is going with us out onto the water.

He brought me fruitcake.

After consulting with Lorelei in a completely not-suspicious way—I hope—I grabbed two oatmeal cranberry cookies from Reindeer Bakes for him.

And also talked to Pia about the wedding cake.

That wasn't awkward at all . . .

Chili volunteers to guard the fruitcake and cookies for me while I run back up to the cabin to put the leftover food away and toss the trash.

Okay, the dog doesn't really volunteer.

He's sleeping on a beach towel. Quite soundly, in fact.

Pretty sure he won't eat dessert.

While I'm at the cabin, I run out to the mailbox.

Just in case.

But it's empty. No junk mail. No catalogs or bills.

No letters.

Dane's right. If we want to know where it came from, we need to ask questions. We can't just sit here and wait for more to magically show up.

So I need to get up the courage to ask my mom and grandma tomorrow what they know about how the feud started. No matter what they might tell me.

I dash back to the shore as he's turning the canoe over, and *holy hell.*

Dane's lean, but he's solid. His back muscles flex. His biceps flex. His thighs are tight as he squats, and I suddenly need seventy-six more drinks.

I see fit guys around the city all the time. This isn't something new.

But Dane's so kind.

He's funny.

He's thoughtful.

He's quick on his feet.

And when you put the whole package together, you get a guy who'll likely make a very lucky woman very happy one day.

I'm trying to be happy for her—provided she deserves him, which she better, whoever she is—but my dinner is suddenly sitting sideways in my belly and my ring finger feels like the rock on it is dragging it down to the bottom of the lake while I'm still on the shore.

"How old is this thing?" Dane asks me as he pulls it toward the water.

"At least a few years, I think." Has it always been here? I can't remember. I didn't pay attention the last few times I was here.

"Have you ever seen anyone use it?"

I shake my head.

He grins again. "Guess we'll find out if she floats."

"Are there paddle thingies?"

"Oars? Yeah."

He kicks off his shoes as he gets the canoe into the water, wading out as he guides it deeper, rocking it a little side to side.

I place my shoes near Dane's and head out with the small bag of dessert.

"Hold on." He waves me back. "Testing it for leaks. Can't have you sinking in the middle of the lake."

"I can swim."

"Chili can't."

I crack up. "Yes, he can."

"Not twice in one day."

Chili lifts his head enough to grunt in Dane's direction.

"Is he picking on you, you poor thing?" I say while I rub the pup's head.

He blows out a long-suffering breath and puts his head on my foot.

And once again, I'm cracking up.

While on a beach picnic with my pretend fiancé and his dog, getting ready for a dessert canoe ride at sunset.

It's a role that hasn't been in my dreams for a long time, but it's a role that's giving me the squishy-glowy kind of warmth in my chest.

Which is *not real.*

But what can be real?

Being a good friend to Dane.

He's a good guy. He deserves to be treated well.

And some of that means having fun with him.

"I think she's good," he calls. "You ready for your sunset dessert cruise?"

Aw, we're even on the same wavelength with what to call the canoe ride. "Absolutely. Chili? You coming?"

The dog sighs, then lumbers to his feet like he's put out, but he knows we need supervision.

This dog.

He's the best.

Almost as much as his owner.

Chapter 11

Dane

Amanda brought me my favorite cookies.

I'm so startled when she pulls them out as we're floating in the middle of the lake that I almost drop an oar.

"Lorelei said you like them," she says quickly.

Ah.

Right.

She asked. This isn't Tinsel magic. "I do. They've always been my favorite. Next to Lorelei's snickerdoodles, anyway. Thank you."

"You got me a ring. Cookies seemed like the least I could do."

That ring has been taunting me all day.

While we were driving back to Tinsel, she kept looking at it. While I was fixing the mixer, she kept looking at it. While we were lining up for the town picture, when she wasn't talking to the people around us, I caught her looking at the ring.

Always with the softest of smiles.

I wanted to know what she was thinking, but I didn't dare ask.

In case I didn't actually want to know what she was thinking.

Chili's happily settled in the center of the canoe between us. He opens one eye and squints at me.

Calling me out on starting to like Amanda as an adult person who's sometimes impulsive, sometimes insecure, always entertaining, and rarely rude?

Or is he asking if he can have a bite of my cookie?

Could be either.

I bite into the cookie and a sigh of *this is bliss* slips from my lips.

There's a lot I don't miss about Tinsel.

But this cookie?

"I talked to Pia a little about the wedding cake, but it looks like I should call her back and tell her we want a cake of cookies," Amanda says.

Like this is real.

Like we're actually having a wedding.

Of course we're talking about it like it's real. She's going dress shopping with her mom in two days. We have an appointment with Pia on Friday to talk about flavors. It feels real because we *are* planning a wedding.

We're just not following through with it.

Probably.

Shit.

What if we have to actually *get married* to convince our families to get along?

It's like a game of chicken, but instead of racing two bikes at each other at full speed, we're seeing who blinks first over our threat to have death do us part.

She's happily nibbling on fruitcake again. Her hair is tucked up in a messy bun on top of her head, and I can't stop glancing at her belly button ring peeking out between her tank and the bottom of her swimsuit.

It's no surprise at all that her swimsuit is bright with splashes of color making an optical illusion of a design. Is it flowers? Or is it a bunch of stars between geometric shapes?

Either way, it's Amanda.

"So Raoul . . . ," she says, giving me a look I can't quite interpret.

I lift my brows and wait.

"He thought you were going to show up to get a ring for someone else. Or was I reading that wrong?"

Nope.

Didn't expect that.

"You read that correctly."

"He knew your last girlfriend?"

"Knew of her."

"But didn't meet-meet her?"

"Correct."

"You went ring shopping?"

Not my favorite topic, but I'm the one who suggested we keep up this engagement-and-wedding-planning ruse. I'm the one who took her to meet Raoul. I owe this one to her. "I did."

"What happened?"

"She was bored and I didn't know it."

"Bored by what?"

I blow out a sigh. "I sometimes work long hours. I didn't always like her favorite restaurants. Swimming as exercise was cliché. I'd rather go sailing than golf. And on, and on, and on." To include that she got invested in my family's feud and didn't understand why I didn't want to talk about it too.

Amanda wrinkles her nose. "And you were still going to propose to her?"

"Did propose."

"You *proposed* to a woman who thought you were *boring*?"

"Didn't know she thought I was boring until I proposed."

"Oh, Dane. That's—that's a special level of hell. I'm sorry."

She's not wrong.

It was hell. Actually, it's the only time I can remember that my family didn't find a way to blame the Andersons or suggest that my engagement breakup was better than anything the *gingerdead family* could've done.

It will not be the same next week when Amanda and I have called it quits. We're going to have to absolutely sell that we're better off as friends and want to remain friends.

Otherwise, this will be my second broken engagement, but *all those damn Andersons' fault.*

Shit. We really are going to have to get married.

I lift a shoulder. "Better before an actual wedding. And at least I was boring enough to propose on a private boat cruise instead of a sports event where she could've told me how much she didn't want to marry me while we were being broadcast on the jumbotron."

She stares at me for a beat, and then she cracks up. "Sorry. Sorry. Not funny."

But she's still giggling. Waving her arms like she's trying to stop. Rocking the boat just enough that Chili lifts his head and snorts at her like he's saying *dump me in this lake and I'll dump something on you in the middle of the night.*

"It's just—here you are, again, about to not have a wedding, and it's so unfair." Her cheeks are flushed. So is her chest above her swimsuit.

I shake my head, but I cannot help smiling when she's laughing like this. "You laugh now. Wait until I make you go through with it because we haven't fully ended the feud by Monday and I don't want to have two failed engagements on my hand."

"I'm sorry," she says again. "It's not funny."

"So long as you don't dump me because I'm boring, I think I'll live."

"You are *not* boring." She fans herself. "Not in the least."

"I can be."

"Did you work late every night?"

"Few times a month. Not every night. Not even close. I travel about a week a month, but it was less when I was with her."

"And could she take herself to her favorite restaurant?"

I blink.

Then blink again.

She finishes off the last bit of her fruitcake. "Honestly, just because people are a couple doesn't mean they can't have their own likes and interests. Or maybe I'm the weirdo for believing that. But if you love someone but want to do something they don't like, why not do it on your own? Or with a friend?"

"I . . . don't know."

Chili makes a noise like he, too, wants to know why I hadn't considered that it wasn't my job to like everything my girlfriend liked.

I look down at him, and *oh shit.*

That's not the noise he's making.

He's making the *my fur is wet and I don't like it* noise.

There's a layer of water in the bottom of the canoe.

And we're in the middle of the lake.

It's not a huge lake, but we're not exactly a stone's throw from shore either.

"Why's there water in the bottom of the canoe?" Amanda whispers.

"Leak." Only answer.

Chili rises all the way to his feet and shakes, making the canoe tip back and forth, which makes Amanda shriek and grab the edges.

And then she throws her head back and laughs again. "In case you were wondering, I'll never be upset that you like to swim for exercise."

I grab the oars and start paddling, and as I do, I realize I'm smiling.

We might very well sink this canoe before we get back to shore.

And I'm with Amanda on this one.

It's freaking hilarious. "Start bailing water," I tell her.

"With what?"

"Your hands?"

We lock eyes, and we both crack up again.

With her hands?

There's zero chance she's bailing this canoe out *with her hands.*

"Paddle faster!" she shrieks between gales of laughter. "Why aren't there two sets of those paddling thingies?"

"Oars?"

"*Oars!* Those! Yes. Why aren't there two sets?"

Chili snorts at me.

I paddle faster.

Amanda starts scooping water out of the bottom of the canoe with her hands.

Our gazes meet again as she's making zero progress. She laughs so hard she snorts. I'm laughing so hard I almost can't breathe.

It's coming in fast now. We've sprung a leak, and the canoe is done for this world.

But we're still a good ways from shore.

"Your extra cookie!" Amanda lunges for the brown paper bag resting near her seat, and the canoe rocks sideways again.

Chili grunts.

I paddle even harder.

Amanda puts the bag with my cookie in her teeth and goes back to scooping water out of the canoe with her hands, her engagement ring sparkling and catching my attention with every handful of water that she dumps out of the canoe.

We make it to about ten yards from shore before the canoe gives up on life.

Chili stares at me like I've betrayed him, like he wasn't out here in the lake himself just this morning of his own free will, then pushes off and swims for land.

"You good?" I ask Amanda as we make a swim for it too.

Her eyes are dancing. Hair soaked. Dog-paddling while she holds her head far back, the bag with my cookie still clenched between her teeth.

It's funny, but it's also making something warm swell in my chest.

She's going out of her way to save a cookie for me when I can get another one tomorrow.

But when getting another one tomorrow would mean talking to the woman making our wedding cake.

For our fake wedding.

I rescue the cookie bag as we reach ground I can stand on, then wrap an arm around her and pull her closer to shore, to where she can stand too.

We're smiling at each other like absolute fools.

And that's the only explanation for what happens next.

Which is me kissing her.

I can't help myself.

Who could when this close to a ray of sunshine?

Especially a ray of sunshine who's looping her arm around my shoulders and kissing me back.

Our bodies line up with her breasts pressing into my chest, both of us dripping wet. Her swimsuit is cold but the skin just above it hot as I grip her waist.

Lips hot.

Nose cold.

I catch myself parting my lips to taste her, and that's when I remember I shouldn't be doing this.

I break the kiss, panting. "Sorry," I mutter at the same time as she says, "You're right, that'll convince them."

We stare at each other for a beat before Chili saves the day.

By shaking all the water out of his fur, directly onto us.

Amanda shrieks, then laughs and bends over to rub his fur.

I subtly adjust my cock, which needs to get the message that we're not doing this.

But she's right.

Every bit of this is selling the ruse for anyone who's spying on us tonight.

Pretending to be engaged to Amanda is a good idea.

This will work.

It'll make our families at least lighten up on their fighting and feuding.

But I hadn't considered one very important thing.

And that's how many moments I'd forget this isn't real.

Chapter 12

Amanda

The very worst part of being fake engaged to Dane is how much I'm starting to like him.

I can't remember the last time I laughed so hard on a date.

The last time I lost myself in the moment with a man to the point that I forgot where I was with the desperate need to kiss him.

How much I didn't want it to be so awkward when the kiss ended.

Sorry.

He apologized for kissing me.

What does that mean? That he wanted to kiss me but he didn't want me to know he wanted to kiss me?

Or does it mean that he was only kissing me because I kissed him first and he was apologizing for not being into it?

And now we're back at the cabin and we're pretending everything is normal and that we didn't just have an impulsive kiss on the lakeshore when I'm pretty sure the sun had dipped too low for anyone to actually see us kissing, despite my own insistence that the kiss was a good show for anyone watching?

"Shower's all yours," I tell him as I step into the living room after a quick shower that didn't do anything to calm the rapid-fire questions in my head about our kiss. My hair is damp, and I'm in a light tank top and pajama shorts.

And my engagement ring.

I'm wearing my engagement ring too.

He's turned on all the fans and opened all the windows to let in the rapidly cooling night air. Chili's chilling on a blanket next to the couch. Dane's shirtless, which is truly unfair of him, working on his laptop. He sets it aside and rises as I take a seat in the armchair next to the couch.

"Thanks," he says.

Just *thanks.*

No *I'm still thinking about that kiss too.*

No *we should have more fun while we're pretending to be engaged.*

No *sorry I got carried away.*

No *this was a stupid idea, give me the ring back, I'm out,* either, though.

Just *thanks*, and then he's off to shower.

Without inviting me to join him.

Just like I didn't invite him to join me when I went first in the shower.

He slips down the hallway, and I move to the floor to rub Chili's fur. "You're the best part about this situation," I whisper to him.

He squints at me through one eye like he knows I'm lying.

Today was fun.

Not all of it. Definitely not all of it. Like Grandma being so mad about me being engaged to Dane.

Mom seems like she might come around first.

Especially after Dane fixed the mixer.

The town photo wasn't the best.

Really could've done with that happening a week that I wasn't home.

But starting the day with eggnog lattes with him? The swim in the lake? The trip to Grand Rapids? The date on the beach and the canoe ride?

Fun.

Yes. Definitely fun. Far more fun than having a fake fiancé should be.

Headlights flash through the window, and I leap to my feet.

Is someone dropping another letter?

Chili hardly moves.

I dash through the kitchen and out the back door, circling back against the house to see if I can catch a glimpse of—

Lorelei.

It's not someone dropping off another letter. I'm not solving that mystery tonight by hiding on the side of the house and watching to see who's either for or against us based on what another letter might say.

It's Dane's sister.

And she's climbing out of her car on the small side gravel parking area, which means she's likely headed to the front door.

Which opens into the living room.

Where Dane's stuff is scattered about, making it clear we're not sharing a bedroom.

Crap crap crap.

I retrace my steps, dashing through the kitchen door and back into the house.

Chili lifts his head, but he doesn't bark at me.

Two options right now.

One, I let Lorelei in the house, and she sees that Dane's stuff is all over the living room while he showers solo.

Or two—the option I take—is to race back to the bedroom.

Lorelei knocks at the door as I scurry down the hallway and into the bedroom.

Is the front door unlocked?

Would she let herself in?

Surely not.

If we don't answer, she'll assume we're doing what fiancés do, and she'll go away.

I think.

I hope.

I fling myself into the bedroom and instantly wish I hadn't.

Dane left the bathroom door open.

He left the bathroom door open into the bedroom, and I can clearly see his outline against the fogged-up glass of the shower, and *oh my holy big apple.*

Walk away, Amanda.

Turn around.

Do not keep standing here.

I totally keep standing here.

Staring at the lean, dark-haired, broad-shouldered man who put an engagement ring on my finger, while he strokes his cock in the shower, his head thrust back, eyes closed, hair wet, hand jerking up and down over his impressive erection.

Turn around, I order myself again.

Problem is, I've never been the best of rule followers.

And *oh my god.*

My mouth is going dry. My nipples are buzzing. There's a pull between my legs that hasn't been prompted by a man in probably three years. At least.

Another loud knock pulls me out of my stupor.

I dash to the edge of the bathroom door, just out of sight, then angle in with my back to the door. "Dane," I hiss, trying to send my voice his way without being too loud and also without getting caught watching him.

There's a *clunk*, then a *"Fuck!"* from inside the bathroom.

"Your sister's here," I whisper.

The shower door audibly clicks open. At least, I think that's what that noise was. "Amanda?" he says hoarsely.

Oh, god.

Was he thinking about *me* while he was stroking himself?

I hope so, and then I immediately tell myself to stop hoping so.

This is pretend.

He apologized for kissing me.

We're not doing this for real. We're not.

"Hi! Hey. Yes. Yes, it's me," I ramble, still hovering half-in, half-out of the doorway, facing the bedroom rather than him.

"What are you doing?"

"Your sister's here."

Silence.

More silence.

The loud kind of silence, I mean, where the water is pounding down in the shower and night bugs are chirping outside and where Dane isn't saying anything.

It's the ultimate white noise silence.

"I haven't let her in," I whisper. "I thought it would be better if she thought we were . . . you know."

If she thought we were doing together what I accidentally just saw you doing solo.

Is the window open?

Can she hear us?

Crap crap crap.

"Hello?" Lorelei calls from somewhere distant but still close enough that I spin and stare at the open bathroom window. She's still outside. Likely still on the porch.

Would she circle the cabin looking for us?

Or would she leave if we don't answer?

"Kill the lights," Dane hisses.

The lights.

The lights.

What are the—*the lights.* Right.

I fumble for the switch and flick it, but not all the way, so the lights get caught in a blinking pattern that probably means my uncle should have the wiring checked in the cabin.

But then I hit it again, and this time, I plunge the room into total darkness.

Except for the lights coming in from the bedroom and the shaft of porch light streaming through the bathroom window, which are illuminating Dane in all his glory.

"Get in here and shut the door," he says.

He's still hoarse.

He's still sporting a very impressive hard-on, which I try just as hard to not look at, but it's kind of unmissable.

Even without full bathroom lights on.

Just *holy hell.*

Have I ever been this affected by a penis?

Likely.

Just not for a long time.

"Should we make . . . noises?" I ask.

"Shut the window."

It's the first time in the past two days that he's been abrupt with me.

Hey, Dane, people think we're engaged. Okay, cool.

My mom wants to know where my ring is. I'll get you one.

I just watched you rubbing one out in the shower and we probably both know it. This has gone too far.

I leap to the window and wriggle it closed. It groans and creaks, which Lorelei can likely hear, but maybe she'll think one of us makes really weird noises when we're having sex.

And now I'm thinking about having sex.

With Dane.

My hometown BFF's brother.

My pretend fiancé.

And it's not just the shower steam heating up the bathroom.

Can't be, actually. There's not a lot of it, and if Dane's anything like me, his shower tonight is on the cooler side to compensate for the heat of the day.

The dunk in the lake helped, but not enough once we dragged the canoe out of it and helped Chili back up to the cabin.

Much better.

Much, much better.

Think about a wet dog.

Not about Dane naked.

I slide a glance at him.

He's turned his back on me and ducked back into the shower.

"I didn't see anything," I lie.

"Not like I have anything you haven't seen before," he replies.

I think.

He's talking into the showerhead, and I'm trying to not stare at his perfect ass cheeks.

"I didn't want to let Lorelei in while it's clear someone's sleeping on the couch."

"Good call."

He doesn't invite me into the shower with him.

I don't ask to join him.

And as I'm thinking this can't get any worse, my phone dings loudly with an incoming text message. The sound echoes around the room.

Dane doesn't turn back to look at me. Instead, he keeps scrubbing his head under the flow of water.

I glance at my phone.

The preview tells me Lorelei stopped by to ask if we wanted to participate in the . . . and then I can't see any more of the message.

But if I check the message and she sees I checked the message, she'll know I wasn't having sex with her brother.

And now I'm thinking about Dane naked again.

It's going to be a long, long, *long* night.

Chapter 13

Dane

It's official.

I have taken self-torture to new heights.

Pretending to be engaged to my high school crush, when she has no idea how I've ever felt about her, is messing with my head.

So is the fact that she's every bit as fun as I thought she'd be.

Every bit as bright.

And completely not interested.

While I was jerking off in the shower to fantasies of making love to her after staring at her in her bathing suit wearing my engagement ring all night, she was going out of her way to not look at any part of me while warning me that my sister had shown up.

I give it a 65 percent chance she saw what I was doing.

Thank fuck she couldn't possibly know what was going on in my mind.

I'm almost feeling normal again early the next morning as we drive into town.

Almost.

But not quite.

There's an ever-present clock ticking in my head, reminding me that we only have five days to fix our families before we're supposed to get married.

"Lorelei *and* Esme emailed me to make sure you and I would do a snow globe together!" she's saying as she looks at her phone. I'm driving to give myself something to do that's not staring at her and wondering if she rubbed one out in the shower before me. Though if she did, she probably wasn't thinking about me.

"Apparently our generation hasn't pissed each other off yet," I say, which feels like the wrong thing to say, but I don't know what the right thing could be.

"I don't think we will either," she says. "I heard somewhere that tradition is just peer pressure from dead people. I feel like that's what this feud is. Peer pressure from dead people to keep hating each other. But screw that. Esme says there's a prize for the best snow globe, and she also says she knows where the best leftover holiday decorations are stashed for us to use."

Don't be fooled by the word *snow globe.*

It's not what you think.

It's much, much larger.

The town of Tinsel picks a theme for holiday decorations every year. This year's is *snow globes.*

Which means we're having life-size snow globes put all over town, much like some cities do temporary installations of themed statues like cows or ducks or giant gnomes.

A few years back, an artist donated two dozen fiberglass elves for Tinsel businesses to paint with themes. I heard all about that *gingerdead elf* that Amanda's family painted that looked like a gingerbread elf. And about how using fruitcake colors on my family's elf made people think we were repping Wisconsin or Ohio football instead of Michigan football, which—again—was a rumor blamed on *the gingerdead family.*

We put blue on our elf too, Uncle Rob kept saying. *Nobody cared that we added blue.*

A year after that, there was a nutcracker theme for the Jingle Bell Fest. Another year, there were reindeer. Snowmen. Snowflakes. Gingerbread men were floated as an option once, but my family shot it down.

I still hear about it anytime Jingle Bell Fest is mentioned. *That gingerdead family better not try to cheat and get more marketing for themselves with the Tinsel Jingle Bell Holiday Businesses on Kringle Lane Statue Contest this year.*

I slide a look at Amanda. "Do they know where the elves went?"

Her mouth goes round, and her eyes light up. "I'll check."

An hour later, we arrive at Reindeer Square with some bonus decorations for our snow globe in tow. At least two dozen massive globes are already littering the grass.

They look like eight-foot-tall clear beach balls.

Have to wonder how they'll hold when covered in two feet of snow. Not that anyone's thinking about snow when it's still pushing ninety today.

Lorelei and Esme meet us at the edge of the parking lot.

"You made it," Lorelei says, throwing her arms around Amanda and hugging her first.

"I told her not to go see you last night," Esme adds with a smirk as she punches me lightly on the arm.

It's too hot to hug, so I appreciate the gesture.

"Oh, did you stop by?" Amanda says.

And then blushes.

Amanda.

Amanda Anderson.

Thespian of the century at our high school.

Blushes at the implication that we didn't hear my sister stop by.

"I did," Lorelei says, "and now I regret it. I will never do it again. Ever."

Amanda blushes harder.

Hell, so do I.

"Esme!" someone hollers. "We need a water bottle! Man down! I repeat, man down!"

We all glance across the square to where Uncle Rob is fanning Esme's husband in the entry to one of the globes.

"I told him to assemble it *outside* the globe before putting it *inside* the globe with the heat the way it is," Esme mutters. She shakes her head, then points to a globe near the gazebo. "Yours is there. If you need help carrying your supplies, grab a shopping cart."

"Dane," Uncle Rob bellows, "get over here. We need your engineering opinion."

"Dane and Amanda are doing the newlywed piece this year," Lorelei bellows back.

And now the entire town is gawking.

Even if they're not here in the town square, even if they don't know why, they're gawking.

"I can't wait to see what you do with yours," Amanda calls to Uncle Rob.

"*Amanda*," someone else hisses from the other side of the square.

She shifts seamlessly and aims a smile at her mother. "And yours too, Mom!"

She grabs me by the hand. "C'mon, Dane. Let's go get a shopping cart and show Tinsel how you decorate a life-size snow globe."

"Do you worry at all that they'll disown you?" Lorelei asks.

I don't know if she's talking to me or Amanda.

But Amanda winces and nods. "A little."

Fuck it being too hot to hug.

I slip an arm around her. "If they don't forgive you, they don't deserve you."

"*Awwww*," Lorelei whispers. "You two make me so happy."

Stab stab stab. All of the guilt over the lie slashes into my gut and makes me want to vomit.

But I remind myself all this is for the greater good.

For our families. For Tinsel. For Amanda. For me.

Who knows? Our kids *could* want to get married someday.

Unlikely, but weirder things have happened.

Like one of the round snow globe covers rolling away with a jar of paint inside so that it's being coated in red stripes while a guy dressed up like Will Ferrell in *Elf* chases it down.

No, wait.

In Tinsel, costumed people chasing holiday decorations isn't that weird.

Amanda swipes her eyes as she smiles at Lorelei, and I don't think that's an act. "You make me happy. I'm so grateful you've always been such a good friend even when it's been hard."

The lying is definitely the worst part.

Lorelei wipes her eyes, too, then flaps her hands at us. "Go, go get started before it gets any hotter. I cannot *wait* to see what you two are planning."

We grab a shopping cart and unload our tools and holiday decor, then head across the square to our spot. I'm frowning as we approach it.

"We brought too much stuff," Amanda says.

"No, these are too big to put on the sidewalks on Kringle Lane."

Not only are they eight feet tall, but they're nearly that wide in diameter too. The bases are maybe a foot high, but easily four feet wide themselves. Each snow globe is on its own trailer for transportation.

The holiday crew must've been up half the night switching over from the photo shoot to putting the snow globes in place.

Amanda looks at me, then purses her lips together and makes a choking noise like she's trying not to laugh.

"You're picturing tourists dodging these all over Kringle Lane, aren't you?"

"Grandma's gonna get run over by a snow globe this year." Her voice is quiet and strangled, and there's no mistaking the utter amusement in her voice.

I stifle my own laughter.

Odds are good no one will get run over by a snow globe.

"Dane," Uncle Rob calls again at the same time Amanda's mother calls her name.

We lock eyes.

There's zero question what's on her mind.

Mine's echoing it.

And it's the right call.

Kiss her.

Ignore both of your families and kiss her.

Kiss her the way you were fantasizing about kissing her in the shower last night.

She's not thinking that last part. That's all my own deal.

I've done this to myself, and now I have to deal with the consequences.

Namely, kissing Amanda and knowing that when she kisses me back, it's not about me.

It's about the show.

But I still kiss her.

I wrap my arms around her waist and pull her tight against my body while I nibble on her lower lip. I stroke my hand up her back while I lick at the seam of her mouth. I tangle my fingers in her hair and touch my tongue to hers when she parts her lips.

And fuck if she doesn't grip me by the ears and take the kiss even deeper herself, pushing her breasts against my ribs and making little noises that say she's loving every moment of this kiss.

She's faking, she's faking, she's faking.

It's not a malicious thought.

I'm supposed to be faking this too.

It's self-preservation.

And it's not working.

How can it when kissing her is setting my soul on fire and sending blood rushing to my cock and making my heart pump like it's found a new reason to live?

"Awww, yeah, look at the man getting his game on," someone crows nearby.

Shit.

We're in public.

And I'm mauling my fake fiancée like a man completely out of control.

Amanda's panting as she pulls back. "Wow," she whispers.

Wow.

One little word that sears itself onto my heart.

Like she means it. Like she's affected too. Like that wasn't fake for her either.

Stop it, I order myself. *Eye on the prize.*

And what's the prize?

Our families getting along. Amanda and Lorelei getting to be friends in public when they're both here. Me not having to listen to constant complaints about home.

Seems like a dumb prize when I'm starting again to want everything I wanted and couldn't have in high school.

"So I'll empty the cart and get back to the car for the rest of the stuff," I say awkwardly.

Like it's not okay for me to kiss my fiancée in public.

I'm gonna fuck this up.

Can't play the part without public affection.

And I can't give her public affection without wanting more.

Yep. Totally gonna fuck this up.

Chapter 14

Amanda

I'm hot.

I'm sweaty.

I'm sticky.

And I want to pull Dane into the coatroom inside Holly & Mistletoe, where we're having lunch with my mom and grandma, and do all kinds of things to him and with him that should not be done in public.

Zero denying it anymore. After that kiss before we put our snow globe display together, coupled with accidentally seeing him stroking himself last night, I can't stop thinking about what it would be like to have sex with him.

Fully naked.

Skin on skin. Tasting him. Touching him. Exploring him.

The heat has fried my brain and ignited my libido.

Except I don't think it's the heat.

I think it's him.

"I program the microcomputers that control automated processes for assembly lines," he's telling my mom.

That sounds like a job I would absolutely not be interested in doing, ever, and also like the sexiest thing in the world.

Just because *he's* the one who said it.

Also? I'm starting to want to eat more vegetables after watching his "mostly vegetarian" diet for the past two days.

Have I ever thought farro looked delicious? I don't think I have. But his farro bowl is so bright and colorful with all the veggies in it, and I keep resisting the urge to try some.

Which I wouldn't be resisting if we were *actually* engaged.

"So you want to automate our secret family recipe?" Grandma says.

Dane covers my hand with his, an easy smile on his face. "I'll do whatever Amanda wants me to do."

Today's swoon factor is dialed up to eleventy bajillion.

I like it.

And I hate it.

"I should probably master making gingerbread by hand first," I joke, then cringe to myself.

I don't want to make gingerbread.

That's the whole point of Dane being here. And I just ruined his attempt at making Grandma reconsider that I'm the best person to take over for her.

"You'll make good gingerbread," Grandma says.

"I really don't think—"

"When—*if* I give you the real recipe, it'll do its magic. You'll see."

The real recipe?

Magic?

I slide a look at Dane.

He rubs his thumb over the back of my hand. "Amanda has her own magic."

"You know, Grandma, when we get married . . . ," I start, but she snorts and waves a hand.

"You're not getting married."

I don't care much about rules and edicts in the general scheme of things. If they work for me, great. If they don't, I push back.

Right now, that rule about respecting your elders is about to fly out the window.

Mom puts her fork down and shoots me a look that silences me, though. "I'm really looking forward to dress shopping," she says.

The look Grandma gives her makes me glad our family doesn't believe in evil eye curses from the head generation.

But Mom doesn't bat an eyelash. "My only daughter having a Tinsel wedding instead of eloping like her brother? I'm taking her dress shopping. She could be marrying a serial killer, and if he made her happy, I'd support her."

"That's love," Dane murmurs.

I grab my mulled wine and take too large of a sip. I don't think she means she'd support me under circumstances *that* extreme.

I don't think. "Maybe if I were dating a serial killer, you should intervene."

She looks at Dane.

So does Grandma.

Oh, for the love of jingle bells. "Being a Silver does not make him a serial killer."

"Are we sure about that?" Grandma asks with the gravity of a woman who's seen stranger things in her time, which is ridiculous.

This is Tinsel.

The most scandalous thing to ever happen here beyond our family's feud with the Silvers was a bad batch of eggnog taking out half of the actors in the annual Christmas village play when I was in high school.

"We haven't had a serial killer in our lineage for at least eight generations," Dane replies, though, equally serious.

I laugh and bump shoulders with him.

He doesn't laugh back.

"We think eight generations is enough to dilute the serial killer genes," he says instead. "Plus, it was a low-key serial killer. Barely ever featured on true crime podcasts."

Lorelei never mentioned *that.*

But I suppose every friendship has its limits when it comes to divulging things like serial killers in your distant lineage. Especially when you know your parents and grandparents don't get along.

Also, he could still be joking.

Couldn't he?

"I love those podcasts," Mom says reverently.

"Not appropriate listening for a gingerbread bakery." Grandma sniffs.

"Which serial killer was it?" Mom asks, ignoring Grandma completely.

"The Egg Beater," Dane replies.

Mom squeaks. "*I just listened to that episode.* The guy who—"

"Oh my gosh, did I tell you how much I loved your snow globe?" I interrupt. "It never ceases to amaze me how many different ways you can incorporate gingerbread into all of the annual Tinsel decorations."

I hate true crime podcasts. I don't want to know how people murdered other people.

But also, did Dane know my mother loves them?

He's winning her over.

And hopefully lying about who he's related to.

But is he? *Is he?* Or is he divulging family secrets to gain my family's trust?

I legit still can't tell.

"Gingerbread is always the answer to all Christmas decorations," Grandma says.

And for her, that's true.

"I want to know how you made yours snow," Mom says.

Mine and Dane's ended up being his family's old snowman holding hands with my family's old elf while snow swirls around inside. Simple, but no one else has blowing snow.

"Engineering secret," Dane says with a wink. "But if you want me to sneak into the warehouse and do it to yours, too, I can."

"Don't touch my snow globe," Grandma says.

Mom sighs.

Then she slides a glance at Grandma before turning back to Dane. "Are you going to make your family's snow globe have snow?"

"If they ask me to. They're not entirely happy with me right now, though, so I don't know that they'd ask much of me."

The truth of that statement hits me in the heart, and I impulsively lean over and kiss his cheek.

And instantly regret it.

His cheeks are rough with stubble and he smells like the best parts of a summer night on the lake.

His gaze flickers to me, warm and kind, and kissing his cheek doesn't seem like nearly enough.

I want more.

I want so much more.

"At least we'll have each other," I say to him.

"And me," Mom says. "I can't imagine abandoning my daughter simply because she fell in love with someone I wouldn't have picked for her. It's your life, honey. I support you. Even when you're marrying into a whole family of serial killers."

Grandma's jaw works back and forth while she watches all of us.

You can *feel* the way she doesn't want to react the same way as *those damn Silvers*, but she also doesn't want to have to be related to one.

"Who's invited to your wedding?" Grandma asks.

"The entire town," I answer without hesitation.

That's the point, right? For the whole town to see a Silver marry an Anderson. Plus, I don't think we could keep them out even if we tried.

Except we're not getting married.

No matter how pretty that ring looks on my finger.

I jerk my hand back under the table as I realize I've been fiddling with it subconsciously for I don't even know how long.

That keeps happening today.

"My dad offered to officiate," Dane tells me. "He's an ordained minister."

"Oh, because he got a certificate off of the internet?" Grandma scoffs.

"Yeah, a few years ago, his best friend was getting married. First time. In his fifties. Pete's bride got really sick, and she was in the hospital, and they didn't think she was going to make it, so Dad got ordained to help them tie the knot ASAP."

"Oh my god," I whisper as I catch myself fiddling with my ring *again*. "My heart."

"She pulled through," he tells me. "Dad did their wedding again when she was back on her feet. Really nice ceremony. He'll do a good job for us too."

The lies should feel awful.

I've never wanted to get married. In my teenage years, I dreamed about lighting up the Broadway stage and having lovers who showered me with lavish gifts.

And then when I started dating—for fun—I met too many men who thought they were the shit and that I'd be lucky to have them, instead of any men who made me feel valued in the same way that I valued and appreciated them.

Add in that I had to hide from my own family who my best friend was for most of my childhood, and the idea of bringing someone home for approval held zero appeal.

But it's been so easy to slip into this lie that we're having a wedding.

"That's so sweet of him, and I know how much it would mean to you." I don't actually know how much it would mean to Dane beyond being an indication that his dad is willing to accept me, if not my entire family.

But I know it'll set my grandma off.

In three . . . two . . . one . . .

"Then *I'm* getting ordained," she says. "We'll *jointly* do your wedding."

"Aw, Grandma, that's so sweet of you too!" She's close enough that I can lean over and peck her on the cheek. "Thank you!"

"Are you having attendants?" Mom asks.

"No," Dane and I answer together.

"We wanted it small," he says at the same time as I add, "It's not about the ceremony, it's about the life we're building together."

"And what she said," he says as I say, "And the small-wedding thing too."

We're vibing.

It's fun. It's unexpected.

And I like it way more than I ever thought I could.

I would date Dane. I would absolutely date Dane if we lived in the same city.

Not that I'd move for him. But if his work ever brought him to New York, and if he wanted to—which is unlikely, considering the mess I keep digging him deeper and deeper into here—then I'd do it.

"Gah, got something in my eyeball," Mom says.

I tear my gaze from Dane's—how often have we been smiling at each other like this?—and catch Mom wiping tears from both of her eyes.

"I wouldn't have picked this for you," she whispers, "but it's so good to see you this happy."

Dammit.

Now my eyes are watering.

But it's not all fluffy rainbows and lovey-dovey heart reasons.

No, that's heavy on the guilt.

Dane squeezes my hand once more.

Pretty sure that's an *I feel it, too, but look. We're making progress. They might all actually get along before we're done.*

I hope so.

I sincerely hope so.

Because if not—I don't want to know the consequences.

Chapter 15

Dane

This is the worst day of my entire life.

Snow globes and lunch with Amanda's family and a few random errands around town that we claim to be *wedding errands* are requiring more touching. More kissing. More accidentally being in sync with her between saying the same things and subconsciously moving closer to each other when we both realize we're being watched.

We're back at Lorelei's house with Chili for dinner. I make excuses about needing to check in with work to give myself a break, but I still hear them talking.

And *this* is half of why we're doing it.

I'm not in Tinsel often. Amanda's apparently not either.

But Lorelei and Amanda are chattering away like they talk all the time. Like it hasn't been months since the last time they saw each other. Like they were even better friends when we were kids than I knew, and that their friendship has only gotten stronger since.

I don't make much progress checking email to minimize the mess that I'll eventually be going back to, and I'm falling farther behind on work this week when I'm supposed to be putting in at least half time to save vacation days.

I'm too busy soaking in the stories they're telling each other about their lives while the scent of fresh-baked chocolate chip cookies fills the air.

Amanda's accidental excursion to a comedy club that ended with her onstage playing right back to the stand-up comic. Lorelei acting as peacekeeper during a committee meeting about changing out the color of the light bulbs on Kringle Lane. Stories about Amanda's dogs acting up all over the city. Lorelei's attempt at a starring role in a low-budget commercial for the Fruitcake Emporium.

Amanda's fear that the play she wrote for her local community theater will bomb.

She wrote a play.

She wrote a play.

And she hasn't said a word to me or her family about it, as far as I can tell.

Because she doesn't think it's a big deal?

Or because it *is* a big deal, and she's afraid no one will support her?

"It's okay if it bombs." There's so much cheek in her voice that I don't believe her. "I failed at being a professional actress, so it would just fit the theme."

"*It's not going to bomb*," Lorelei replies. "When is it? I'm coming. Wait. *Wait.* Does this mean you and Dane are definitely living in New York?"

I freeze, but Amanda has this. "He'll work remotely in New York until after my play, and then we'll head to San Francisco for a few months. Figure out which one suits us best, you know?"

That's when I heave myself up from not working to pop my head into the kitchen and volunteer to grill burgers.

It is absolutely a once-in-a-blue-moon cheeseburger night for me tonight.

It's hot in the kitchen with the oven on, but the fresh cookies are worth it. Even hotter at the grill, and the cheeseburger is even more worth it.

Over dinner, I don't have to say hardly anything.

They keep going.

It's making my chest tight.

Not jealousy. Not envy. I don't feel left out.

I just *want this* for my sister, all the time. To not have to hide how much she enjoys hanging out with Amanda.

I want it for Amanda, too, but I want it even more for Lorelei.

She loves her life here in Tinsel, but I don't believe for a minute that she doesn't dream of going other places and seeing other things too. She's been to San Francisco to visit me a number of times. She took a trip with another friend to Chicago a couple of years ago. I completely believe she'll go see Amanda in New York too.

Plus, while I know she feels like she belongs in Tinsel, I also know working at the family's ornament shop isn't her favorite.

It's just what she does because that's where she's needed here.

Making the torture worse?

All evening, while they're talking, Amanda keeps touching her ring. Glancing at it. Moving her hand to make the diamond catch just right in the light, sending sparkles all over the kitchen.

Reminding all of us that we're planning a wedding.

Which Lorelei keeps exclaiming will make her sisters for real with Amanda.

Absolute. Hell.

We leave earlier than I'd like when Lorelei basically shoos us out the door with a bag full of cookies, plus a wink and a nudge. "I've taken enough of your betrothal time, you crazy lovebirds," she says.

Amanda helps Chili into the car while Lorelei hugs me tighter. "I love seeing you so at peace," she whispers.

At peace.

Not *in love.*

At peace.

She knows this is fake. She has to.

But she's trusting us to do the right thing.

"Feels good," I force out.

"That's how I know it's right. Vanessa never gave you peace. Not like this."

Ah, fuck.

She *did* mean *in love.* She means *You look like you fit in your life now. You've found your missing piece, and hunting for it isn't stressing you out anymore.*

"Go on, go take your fiancée home." She grins at me as she pulls back. "Call me if you need anything else for wedding plans. Might be the only time I ever plan one."

I give her a look, but she shoos me away with a vague comment about a small dating pool.

As we're driving back to the cabin, Amanda twists in her seat to look at me. "I really do love your sister. That's not an act. She was always my best friend in school, even if our families hated it. If she ever needed a kidney, I'd be first in line to sign up to give her one."

I smile. "What if you weren't a match?"

"I'd donate a kidney to someone else in the hopes that my generosity would inspire the right donor for Lorelei. I think the world works like that sometimes."

While I'm not sure I agree, I can appreciate the lengths she'd go to in order to do something good for someone else.

And it makes me like Amanda even more.

I open my mouth to ask her to tell me about her play, but change my mind.

As her fiancé, I should know these things.

But as the man getting too hung up on her, I don't know if I can handle it if she tells me she's embarrassed or afraid everyone will laugh or just doesn't want to share that part of her life with me.

When we get home, she offers to take Chili on a short walk while I unload the leftovers Lorelei insisted we take home.

And moments after I'm done, Amanda comes running into the house, Chili running with her.

Chili.

My dog.

The laziest being on the planet.

Running.

For a second day in a row.

"We got another letter!" Amanda shrieks.

I spin so fast I almost hit my head on an open cabinet door. "What's it say?"

"I don't know. I just saw the envelope and ran up here so we could open it together."

Her cheeks are flushed. Her breath comes in rapid bursts that make her chest rise and fall quickly under her tank top, and her eyes are shimmering with excitement. There's a curl that's come loose from her bun, hanging down and brushing her cheek.

She's so fucking pretty, and her energy is contagious, and she makes me happy.

At peace.

Safe.

I shouldn't feel safe with her. My family has told me since before I could talk that anyone in her family was dangerous to us.

But there's no *why*.

Without a why, I reject the idea that they want to do us harm. And I'm thirty-one years old.

I'm old enough to deserve to know a why if there is one.

But I don't think there is.

I think our families are just assholes who don't know how much their feuding hurts everyone around them and makes me not want to be part of the family.

"Oh, it *is* another letter," she squeals as she slides the envelope open and peeks inside. "Same handwriting. Look."

She pulls it out to show me. I have to grip her hand in mine to slow the vibrations shaking the letter, especially with the old-fashioned script and the fact that my ancestors were still practicing their English after a lifetime of speaking German.

I love how excited she is about this. Like this letter is the magic of Christmas. But better, because it's not about Tinsel. It's not about *Christmas all year round.*

We're in the middle of a heat wave. All the snow here is fake. The music is out of season. The poinsettias aren't blooming.

It's not the magic of Christmas.

It's the inherent magic Amanda carries inside of her.

I wasn't faking when I told her grandma that at lunch today.

"*Oooh*, Lucy was in charge of sending Maud's dowry from Germany," Amanda whispers.

I clear my throat. Being this close to her is making me want to read this letter while I bend her over the table naked. "So there's question about if George stole it."

I'm not interested in the letter. I'm interested in Amanda.

Which I will absolutely not be confessing tonight.

"And they can't tell yet if Minnie is pregnant," Amanda says. "But no one believes George's story about falling for her while they were at church together."

I skim the letter, then skim it again. "It doesn't say what the dowry was."

Amanda spins to me. "*Oooh.* It doesn't."

Her body is lined up with mine and she's tilting her head back to look up at me.

"What do you think it was?" she whispers.

It's a logical question. It should be one with an easy answer.

But my brain is scrambled right now.

I don't want to be logical. I don't want to be analytical. I don't want to pull my phone out and search *popular imports from Germany around 1900.*

What I want is to boost this woman up onto the counter, kiss her until she can't breathe, strip her out of her clothes, and make every inch of her satisfied.

I'm not supposed to fall for my fake fiancée.

This isn't part of the plan.

But she makes it impossible to not like her.

To not *want* her.

I'm staring.

I'm staring into her deep-brown eyes, and I need to stop.

I've heard there's been research saying that if you stare into another person's eyes for a couple of minutes, you start to fall in love.

I like Amanda too much already.

I can't do this.

Falling for someone in San Francisco would be one thing.

Falling for Amanda Anderson is completely different.

"Germans introduced Christmas trees to America," I blurt.

My family had no part in that. It was before our ancestors came here.

But I need something to say that isn't *I want to kiss you.*

Kissing is for outside these walls. When we have an audience.

Not here.

"Do you think Lucy was mailing Christmas trees?"

I shake my head. "Tinsel wasn't a Christmas town until the 1960s. It was probably money."

I can't take Chili out. Amanda already did.

But I have to break away from looking at her. "We need to find out who sent these and see if there are more."

"Would Lorelei know?"

I don't know.

But I know she'd be discreet.

So I nod. "Yeah. We should ask Lorelei. Tomorrow."

Amanda grips my forearm. "I know this is a little inconvenient, and I know it's not fun lying to everyone, but I just want you to know, I've had a really great time with you these past few days."

I swallow. "Same."

Walk. Away. Quit staring into her eyes. Walk. Fucking. Away.

She smiles one of those brilliant smiles, and then she shifts away toward the fridge like she's reading my mind and thinks I'm talking to her. "I'm glad we'll stay friends after this. Want some eggnog? I'm going to have a little bit before bed."

No.

No, I don't want eggnog.

But what I *do* want isn't something I'll be getting.

So I nod.

And then I live with the consequences of my actions.

Chapter 16

Amanda

Dane was going to kiss me.

He was going to kiss me, not for show, and I was going to let him.

Until I got cold feet.

I'm impulsive. I live for fun. Exciting unplanned adventures are my favorite.

But I absolutely cannot lead Dane on and make him an *unplanned adventure*, no matter how much I like him.

So the next morning, when he says he needs to catch up on some work at a coffee shop—*outside* of Tinsel—I take advantage of the empty house and call Yazmin, my roommate back in New York.

And with four days left until Dane and I are supposed to be having a wedding, I finally fill her fully in on *everything*.

Grandma wanting me to join Mom at the Gingerbread House with the intention of taking it over in a few years when Mom retires too.

Me saying I was engaged to Dane to get disinherited.

That not working, exactly, but now we're in this together while we try to get our families to realize the other isn't the enemy while we find an alternative solution for the bakery so Grandma can retire, or at least so Mom can get other help at the bakery that isn't me.

Me liking him.

Thinking that maybe he likes me too.

Yazmin squeals a lot.

"This isn't squealy," I protest. "This relationship can't go anywhere. I don't *do* relationships."

"Amanda. You do relationships. You do relationships when they're worth it. Which isn't often because your standards are so high, which is a good thing. So if this guy is meeting your standards—"

"He lives in San Francisco."

"There are dogs in San Francisco."

"My play—"

"There are community theaters in San Francisco that would love to do an Amanda Anderson original play."

"*You* are not in San Francisco."

"*I* might be your best friend, but I am *not* your soulmate."

Yazmin can occasionally be annoying.

This is one of those times.

"Tell me the heat wave here is frying my brain," I say.

"A guy pretending to be your fiancé so that you can end your family's long-standing stupid feud is *swoon* no matter the outside temperature."

"Maybe I told you the story wrong."

"When's your wedding?"

"We're not getting married."

"Your fake wedding."

I look at my engagement ring and brace myself against the tsunami of guilt that comes with the lies we're telling everyone. "Monday. *Four days.* But *it's not happening.*"

"How are you going to break the news to everyone?"

"We're still discussing exact details, but we'll basically say spending time together made us realize we're better off as friends and not as romantically attracted to each other as we thought."

"You're in over even your own head."

She's not wrong.

"And how's this helping get you out of bakery duty?"

I sigh. "It was supposed to get me disinherited so that they'd find another solution on their own. Instead, Grandma's insisting that I learn everything I need to know for when Dane and I break up."

"Which you're doing by Monday . . ."

"And when I'll be too sad at the idea of watching our families start fighting even worse and have to leave town . . . and get fully cut off for being such a major disappointment."

"Oh, sweetie," Yazmin murmurs. "I hate that they're putting you in this position."

"It'll be okay. It *has* to be okay. We're doing everything we can to leave town better than we found it, you know?"

"None of them deserve you."

A call from my mom beeps in, so on that note, I let Yazmin go and switch over.

Mom's ready for wedding dress shopping.

Time to let more people spend more money on a wedding that will ultimately be canceled. Maybe I can follow Dane's lead and find a way to auction the dress for charity.

I meet Mom at Mrs. Claus's Runway. It's a quaint, holiday-themed boutique formal dress shop, attached to Mrs. Claus's Attic, which is where most locals go for all their ugly and chic holiday sweaters and one-piece fleece holiday pajama needs. Mrs. Briggs, wife of Mr. Briggs, who taught English at the high school, still owns and runs both.

"Oh, my dear, I am *so excited* for you," Mrs. Briggs squeals when we arrive. With the wire-rimmed glasses, curly white hair, and classy red Christmas sweater featuring a quilted reindeer, she looks every bit the part of Mrs. Claus. She often plays it when the community theater has a need. "For *all* of us. An Anderson marrying a Silver! We never thought we'd see the day, but I love that your love is healing old wounds."

"Dane and I have been talking," I say as she leads us past rows of sparkly green, gold, black, and red gowns toward the bridal section in the back. "We realized we have no idea why our families fight. Do either of you know?"

I have homework, and I'm not letting Dane down.

Not this time.

"The fruitcake house was before my time, but I know your grandmother says that was just *one more thing* they'd done," Mom offers.

It's good to have her coming around. "But what other things did they do?" I ask.

"Your grandma has never elaborated. She's always said I don't want to know."

Mrs. Briggs shakes her head. "It's a mystery to the rest of us how it started. All I know is that my mom told me to never get involved in a fight between your families, and my dad was glad I was too young to date either of your grandfathers and too old for either of your fathers too."

That actually cracks me up. "Guess I get to be the one to suffer instead," I joke.

"No, dear, you're going to live your happily ever after forever. Have you and Dane decided where you'll live once you get married?"

"I can walk dogs from anywhere," I answer, not looking at my mom, who quietly sighs like she doesn't want to get caught sighing.

I want to believe that if I told her I'd been writing plays and my local theater was doing one and I wanted to be there for it, that she'd understand, but after the way I walked away from an acting career, I don't want to share until it's been a success.

I want to prove that I can see this through and that it's the right path for me.

Mrs. Briggs lifts a brow. "Not much need in Tinsel."

I've never wanted to squirm more in my life. "I can't decide if I want to go with a white or ivory dress, or if I want to go full Tinsel and do something holiday themed," I say. "What do you think?"

"I think you're gonna be limited to what fits you on the racks because my seamstress is out on maternity leave."

All of us laugh at that. "Fair enough," I say.

The bells jingle, and a familiar voice calls a quick "Hello? Can we join you? We brought homemade tea cookies as a wedding-dress-party-crashing offering."

Lorelei.

And Esme too.

Both of them.

I texted Lorelei that we were dress shopping and asked if she could make it, but she didn't know if she'd be able to leave the ornament shop.

Having her *and* Esme show up?

I think this is good.

I *hope* this is good.

I slide a glance at Mom. One of her eyes twitches, but she quickly turns it into a smile. "If that's what Amanda wants."

Progress.

This is progress.

I beckon them back. "Come join us. We were just talking about how silly it is that no one knows why our families fight."

Esme rolls her eyes. "Whatever the real reason, I doubt it's because of why Grandpa says it is."

"Wait, Grandpa's told you something?" Lorelei asks. "What did he tell you?"

"That when the Andersons were building the Gingerbread House, like the building itself, they knew Great-Grandpa was getting ready to open a fruitcake shop, and so all of the construction lining under the stucco had *fruitcake sucks* written all over it to taunt him."

"Would our great-grandpas have used the word *sucks*?" I ask.

"No," Esme and my mom answer in unison.

They share a look.

And then hesitant smiles.

Lorelei meets my gaze, and I can see the smile she's hiding while my own eyes get hot.

More progress.

"Aww, don't cry." Lorelei smushes me in a hug.

"I'm just so happy," I reply honestly against her shoulder.

I still feel bad about lying. But it's working. And I *am* happy that it's working.

"Well, let's make you happier with a wedding dress," Mrs. Briggs says. "This one's on the house. Seeing a Silver marry an Anderson . . . knowing I might never again have to intervene in a fight about whose car is blocking whose in at a committee meeting . . . that just makes my whole life."

"Mrs. Briggs, I cannot—"

She interrupts me with a dismissive noise and moves to the racks, where she starts pulling dresses out. "Yes, you can. Come, come. I want to see you in this dress. And this one too."

Before I know it, I'm buried under a pile of gowns in my size. Some are pure white. Some are white with green-and-red trim. One's a true red velvet Mrs. Claus dress, which would be brutal in this heat.

Mrs. Briggs ushers me into the changing room in back after setting Mom, Lorelei, and Esme up with champagne and Lorelei's tea cookies in the viewing area.

And I try on dresses.

And more dresses.

And *more dresses.*

This one's too frilly. That one doesn't fit right. This other one is too simple.

I feel like a picky asshole.

But more—it's not *my* opinion. Not mostly. It's Mom agreeing with Lorelei about that dress being *just not you.* Or Mom agreeing with Esme that *this dress will be too much to handle for bathroom breaks during your wedding.*

And then it's Mom discovering that she and Lorelei both have a love of the fried shrimp balls that were taken off the menu at Elf's Landing for being unpopular. Or that she and Esme share a love of punny jokes.

Dane and I didn't explicitly discuss what "let's end the feud" would look like—we both agreed it'll be complex but we'll recognize progress when we see it. Wrangling more people from each of our families to get along is pretty awesome from where I'm standing.

Definitely progress.

Mrs. Briggs is huffing and puffing by the time she gets back to the dressing room with what she's declared to be the final gown in my size in the entire store.

"So I guess this one's it no matter what," I joke.

But once I get it on—no.

No, it's no joke.

I've watched that wedding dress show on occasion with Yazmin. I know what's happening right now.

And what's happening is me staring at myself in the mirror, wearing the wedding dress of my absolute dreams.

It's cream-colored satin with a V-neck and thick lace straps. Pearls are woven into a cascade across the midsection, mixed with red and green gems like I'm wearing a physical representation of a meteor shower in Christmas colors.

Or like I was trying to match my engagement ring.

When I shift, the skirt swishes and sparkles like the real snow in winter in Tinsel. My engagement ring sparkles with it.

My eyes well with tears.

This is it.

And it's all fake.

I suck in a deep breath and blink back my reaction, but Mrs. Briggs is beaming at me.

She knows.

She saw it.

"Let's see if we've finally found you a dress, yes?" she says, opening the dressing room door so that I can step out into the viewing area.

Mom gasps.

Lorelei squeals.

Esme chokes on the champagne she's sipping.

"Oh my god, that's the one," Lorelei says while she pounds Esme on the back.

Esme gives me a thumbs-up while she coughs. Could be agreement. Could be an *I'm okay*.

And Mom dives for the box of tissues. "Oh, Amanda. I wish your father could see you right now."

"Aww, Mrs. A.," Lorelei says, and then she's hugging Mom while all of us start bawling.

Lorelei.

Hugging my mom.

My mom letting her.

This is working.

"I need my phone," I whisper to Mrs. Briggs. "Dane needs to see this."

She hustles into the changing room and comes out with my phone, and I snap a pic of Lorelei hugging Mom and Esme joining them for an even bigger group hug, then send it to Dane quickly before I, too, leap into the hugging fun.

Or try to.

"Don't get tears on the dress!" Esme shrieks.

"Or champagne or cookie crumbs!" my mom agrees.

"My brother is going to flipping *flip* when he sees you like this," Lorelei says, and then we all burst into sobs again.

That's the sign, right?

The crying?

It's a good sign.

Or it would be.

If this were real.

Chapter 17

Dane

The minute Amanda's text message lands, I'm done trying to work for the day.

The accompanying message says she's excited that her mom and my sister and cousin are getting along, but I can barely look at the three women who are supposed to be the subject of the photo for getting stuck staring at the reflection Amanda got of herself in the mirror too.

Wearing a wedding dress.

And not just any wedding dress, but a dress that matches her ring and makes her look like a winter princess.

No, a winter *queen*.

I zoom in on the reflection, studying the way her eyes look misty, the way curls are once again falling out of her bun to frame her face, the way the dress hugs her breasts and caresses her shoulders, how it wraps around her as if it was made for her and her alone.

She'd make a fucking beautiful bride.

But she won't be mine.

So I text back a quick great news, I'll work on my dad, and then I do just that.

He wants help with some last-minute arrangements for my grandparents' anniversary party this weekend.

And I need to bring every ounce of game that I have if I'm going to keep up this ruse solo.

I snort to myself as Chili and I head across town to meet him at the banquet hall.

All I really need to do is picture Amanda in her wedding dress, and I'll look like a lovestruck fool.

Dad's inside the banquet hall talking to the caterer when we arrive. Grandma's with him. I kiss her cheek, then give him a hug, and then they loop me in on the final decisions that have to be made.

Grandma and Dad argue over table layouts—I take Dad's side—and the location of the photo albums—I take Grandma's side—and then about a last-minute substitution for the broccoli salad, since there's apparently a nationwide shortage of broccoli suddenly.

I take the caterer's side on that one, with a very pointed clearing of my throat and accompanying glare, mostly because Grandma starts to say something about *those Andersons probably took the last of it.*

Finally, everything's settled.

But as we're about to leave to visit the florist for final approval on the centerpieces, the caterer grins at me. "And then you're next," he says.

Is it possible to grimace and smile like a lovestruck fool at the same time?

That's what I feel like I'm doing.

"Everything's so last minute that we're asking anyone who wants to come to the wedding to bring their own picnic dinner," I tell him.

"Smart, smart . . . if you want a backup location in case of rain, we're keeping Monday open here. Not that we usually book up on Mondays this time of year, but we're still keeping it open for you."

There's no good answer beyond "Thank you," so that's what I say.

He slides a look at Grandma, who's gone stone faced, then at Dad, who's poker faced, before pulling his shoulders back and looking at me. "And good for you for fighting for who you love. Can't be easy. The town's behind you."

"His family's behind him too," Dad says quickly, angling away from Grandma.

"It would be nice if we knew *why* our families dislike each other so much," I say.

Fuck it.

What do I have to lose here?

Grandma glowers at me. "That Anderson man always passed gas in the grocery store whenever I'd come into the same aisle with him. And no one else ever had that complaint."

That . . . is not what I expected to hear.

"And that Anderson woman was always making comments about how her boobs were better than mine, and wearing skimpy clothes to try to get your grandfather to look at her, the hussy," Grandma continues.

"Mom, I sincerely doubt Vicki Anderson's goal in life is to lure Dad away from you," Dad says.

"The minute she married into those Andersons, she became a different person." She points at me. "If you do the same, you're disinherited."

"Were you related to Vicki Anderson?" I ask her.

"Of course not. Who'd want that bloodline mixed with ours?" She sniffs again, then turns and heads toward the door. "If you boys want me to buy lunch, you better hurry your butts up."

Dad sighs, thanks the caterer, and quickly follows her.

Not for the free meal, I'm certain. More to make sure she doesn't hurt herself while she's mad at the Andersons, or they'd get blamed for that too.

I glance back at the caterer.

He shrugs. "Only thing I ever heard was that some relatives older than your grandparents used to steal clean clothes off the clotheslines the last time they lived next to each other, but I was pretty sure that was made up. And I could never get a straight read on who was the thief and who was the victim."

After a tense lunch with Grandma where I debate leaving at least a half dozen times over the subtle jabs Grandma makes at my taste in women—including calling Amanda *Vanessa* at least once, which I'm pretty sure was on purpose—Dad pulls me to the side. "I'm trying to appreciate your choices here, Dane, but there's just so much bad blood between our families. Are you *sure* you want to do this?"

"*Farting in the grocery store?* If that's the level of crap that has our families fighting, then everyone needs to get over it. Until someone can tell me a real reason I shouldn't marry Amanda, until you can tell me what the hell *she's* done wrong, then she's what I'm choosing."

The image of her in that wedding dress is seared into my brain, and even knowing I'm lying, I believe myself right now.

"This is a big commitment—" Dad starts, but I lift my brows at him, and he sighs and stops. Objecting, anyway. "I suppose if it means you're coming home—"

"We're picking one of our cities and living there."

"I heard a rumor that Amanda's inheriting that gingerdead—*gingerbread* bakery."

"That's an issue she and I will work through together with her family." Mental note: Tell Amanda that's what I told him. "Lorelei's excited. Esme's excited. Kimberly was incredibly gracious and kind when I had lunch with the Andersons yesterday. Is it asking too much that the rest of my family let go of something that doesn't do them or the town any good?"

He sighs. "No. No, it's not asking too much. It's just . . . hard."

"I appreciate you trying." Chili flops down at my feet. He's been trudging along like a champ, but it's time to get him home. "We're gonna have to bow out for the rest of the day. Old man here needs a nap. And possibly a swimming pool."

That earns me a look that I'd say was calling me an asshole if he were anyone other than my father. "I'll tell your grandma."

Ah.

Right.

Breaking bad news to grandma is no one's favorite.

It's too bad she and Vicki Anderson hate each other.

I think they could bond over their disappointment that Amanda and I are engaged.

"We're tasting cake tomorrow morning at Reindeer Bakes," I tell my dad. "You should come. Get to know Amanda yourself. You'll see."

He looks away briefly, then meets my gaze and nods. "I'll clear my schedule. That would be . . . nice."

One more.

One more not quite down, but closer.

Chili and I don't go straight home.

Instead, we stop by the town hall.

I'm operating on a hunch.

The town historian isn't in today—it's a part-time job at best—but the administrative assistant for the mayor tells me she can let me in to look through the archives that they have about the founding of the town.

You tell someone you're trying to understand why your fiancée's family hates yours and vice versa in a town this small, and everyone wants to help.

Annoying as hell that our own families can't see how much the rest of the town wants them to drop it.

Or maybe they *can* see it, and they don't care.

Two hours later, I've combed through every record they have, and I haven't found any letters like the ones that have been delivered to the cabin.

I've found letters from people not related to me or, best I can tell, to Amanda either. About things like horse injuries and bumper crop years and town elections.

Nothing about feuding families.

Nothing with any names I recognize from my own family tree.

No handwriting that looks remotely similar.

But at least it's air conditioned.

When Chili and I head out, I stop by to see the admin one last time. "Probably don't get a lot of people coming in to look through the archives, do you?"

"Oh, I don't know. You'd have to talk to Winona about that. She's in on Mondays." She drops her voice. "She *does* get people coming to see her, but sometimes I think it's just gentlemen who want to impress her, if you know what I mean."

I can imagine what she means. "The wedding's Monday. I'd love to talk to her before then. *We.* Amanda and I both would love to talk to her. If we can."

"You leave me your number, and I'll call and tell her what you're looking for. If she can help, I'm sure she'll give you a ring."

Not much left to do beyond thank her for her time, so that's what I do.

Out in the parking lot, I pull up the picture from Amanda once more.

Fuck, she's stunning.

And as soon as I get home, I need to start dating again.

Whatever it takes to get over this growing attraction to my fake fiancée.

Chapter 18

Amanda

Reindeer Bakes smells like warm chocolate chip cookies. I shouldn't want to swim in anything that evokes feelings of warmth, but the heat is forecast to break this weekend, and it's close enough that I'm letting myself stand in the middle of the pink-and-black bakery and just inhale.

When I open my eyes, Dane's staring at me.

He was quiet once we were both back at the cabin last night. He's trying to save his vacation time for a trip to Thailand—*Thailand!!*—next year, hence why he's working half time while he's in Tinsel. Chili and I went out on the back porch to watch the sunset and mull over the letters.

And for the first time in a long time, I wished that a man was sitting next to me to watch the sunset and talk about how amazing it was to see my mom hugging his sister and cousin and to throw out random theories about the letters too.

He was still working when I went to bed, and when I arrived in the kitchen this morning, he was already up, iced eggnog lattes waiting.

Now, we're having an early cake tasting so Pia knows what flavor we want for our wedding cake.

For our wedding that's in *three days.*

Our wedding that won't happen, but that we can't cancel yet because our families aren't yet getting along and I don't yet have a solution to the question of who will step into the Gingerbread House in Grandma's shoes.

I wrench my gaze away from Dane's and smile at Pia, who's a Black woman just a little older than us. She's wearing a pink apron with dancing reindeer on it and the largest smile I've ever seen on her.

Unlike me, she was happy to join the family baking business.

Also unlike me, she's even better at this than her grandma and mom were, which is impressive.

But the smile suggests she's as thrilled as everyone else in town that Dane and I are tackling this family feud problem.

"Who's ready for some wedding cake?" she asks us.

Chili's paw would be up if he were with us today, but he's hanging with Lorelei again. Apparently cake is his second favorite treat after hot dogs, and he can't be trusted in bakeries.

"Would it be wrong to have a cookie cake?" I ask her. "Dane loves your cranberry oatmeal cookies, and I would die of happiness if my apartment smelled like your fresh chocolate chip cookies every day for the rest of my life."

"Absolutely an option." She gestures to a small table set up near a display case of holiday-themed cupcakes. "But will you try the cake flavors before you decide?"

I grin back while we all take seats. "Oh, the torture."

"Anyone else joining you today?" Pia asks.

"I invited my mom, but she wasn't sure she could leave the bakery again today after dress shopping yesterday," I report.

"No updates from my dad either," Dane says, something in his voice making my heart ache.

Pia looks between us. She apparently noticed too. "You two okay?"

I instantly shift closer to him—natural reaction to the question when all needs to look right between us, plus, it's not awful to be near him—and dial up the smile to an eleven. "Of course!"

"We'd be better if our families had any valid reason at all to object to us being together," Dane says.

"I'm sure they'll come around," I say.

He eyes me like my optimism might be able to move boulders, but it won't budge certain members of our families.

"I hear it's the oldest generation giving you the most trouble," Pia says.

He didn't give me much of an update on his day yesterday, but I heard from Lorelei that their dad was fighting with their grandparents over the wedding and not feeling great about being stuck in the middle between his parents and his kid.

I shouldn't tell you this, but I don't think Dane will because he wants to protect you from it, her message said with the details.

"They're the most set in their ways," Dane says. "You ever hear anything about why they hate each other so much?"

Pia shakes her head. "Whatever happened predates my family moving here. Also, if you tell me you want a gingerbread-flavored cake or fruitcake cookies, you're going to have to find a new wedding cake baker. I'm excited about this wedding and happy to work overtime all weekend on your cake, but I have lines."

Even Dane cracks a smile at that.

I miss his smiles.

Whatever happened yesterday must've been bad.

"Understood," he says.

"I'd never ask you to do that," I agree. "My grandma is already insisting on doing gingerbread men for wedding favors, even though she hates that we're getting married."

Dane sighs again and presses his palms into his eye sockets.

I rub his back. "I'll go charm your uncle and ask about fruitcake favors too."

"And my cake will outshine them all," Pia says. "Here. Let's start with this sample. White chocolate cake with a cherry ganache filling and a pistachio frosting. It's very popular with Christmas brides for its color, and also, it's delicious."

She's not kidding.

I've never been a huge pistachio fan, but she did something magic with the frosting, and the flavors meld together like there's a party of happiness happening in my mouth.

Dane's eyes slide shut as he chews, and he sighs the sigh of a man in utter heaven, the slightest smile curving his lips upward again and peace settling over his expression.

It makes my nipples tight and my heart happy.

He's sexy *and* in a better mood.

"Damn good cake," he says.

Pia grins widely. "And we're just getting started."

The door bells jingle. "We're not open yet—oh. Hello, Mr. Silver. Mrs. Anderson."

Dane and I both spin in our seats to stare at the door.

Our parents are walking in together.

Our parents are walking in together.

We look at each other.

Then at our parents.

Mom showing up or Dane's dad showing up was somewhat expected.

But *together*?

Is this coincidence, or is our plan working even better than we thought on certain members of our family?

"Cake's important," Mom says. "You don't want to pick a flavor that your guests won't like, even if it's your favorite."

"I never turn down cake samples," Mr. Silver says.

They look at each other, then they both hesitantly smile.

"I can't argue with that," Mom says.

"Very good point about the guests," Mr. Silver says.

Dane squeezes my knee, and I gulp hard and blink harder against the heat in my eyeballs.

Pia spins into motion. "Give me five minutes to grab a few more samples. Never hurts to have more opinions, but you two will be in time-out if you make the bride and groom upset, understand?"

The bride and groom.

She's talking about us.

Dane squeezes my knee again. *The lies will be worth it in the end. We're doing community service here.*

I hope he's right.

I'm afraid he's not, but I hope he is.

"Hello," my mom says, extending a hand to Dane's dad. "I'm Kimberly. I'm not sure we've ever been properly introduced."

My eyes bulge, and I stifle a squeak.

They've *never been introduced*?

No way.

But Dane's dad is taking Mom's hand and shaking. "Harry Silver. Nice to meet you."

Are they playing us?

I glance at Dane.

His mouth is slightly ajar like he, too, is questioning what kind of game this is.

My parents were college sweethearts.

Mom grew up somewhere in Pennsylvania and didn't arrive in Tinsel until she and my dad were basically newlyweds.

It's entirely possible my mom and Dane's dad *haven't* ever met. Crossed paths in the grocery store, likely. Probably attended school functions together for us kids. But never actually introduced despite probably knowing exactly who the other was.

Wow.

"Fascinating times," Mr. Silver adds.

"Indeed," Mom agrees.

Pia dashes back in from the kitchen with a bottle of champagne under one arm and an extra set of samples in her other hand. "Beautiful day for a cake tasting, isn't it? Will there be more family coming, or just you two?"

"Just me from Amanda's side," Mom says at the same time Mr. Silver replies, "No one else from my family."

I look at Dane again.

He's closed his mouth, but a muscle is working in his jaw.

I wish Chili was here.

"So, to catch you up, here's our first flavor," Pia says. "White chocolate cake, cherry ganache filling, pistachio frosting."

Mom and Mr. Silver both moan over the cake.

Then they make eye contact and smile a little less hesitantly at each other.

"At least you have good taste," Mom says.

"Not as good as Amanda's," Mr. Silver replies.

I grab Dane's hand and squeeze.

It's happening. They're trying. They're finding common ground. A *Silver* just complimented my taste.

Even if it was a veiled reference to *anyone who picks my son has good taste*, or maybe it's a subtle *I know she likes my family's fruitcake*, but Mom doesn't seem offended.

If anything, she's smiling wider. "She gets it from me."

"You like fruitcake too?" Dane says.

Dane.

Who's supposed to *not inflame the situation*.

Mom's ears go bright red. "I . . . may have enjoyed a piece or two in my time. When I found leftovers in Amanda's lunch box."

I squeak. "Impossible. I always threw it away. Always."

"Not always," Mom says. "Those birthday parties in elementary school would get you every time. You'd forget someone brought cupcakes or doughnuts or cookies, and your afternoon fruitcake snack would end up at our house."

"Lorelei was my best friend," I blurt.

Both Mom and Mr. Silver cringe.

"I know." Mom sighs.

Mr. Silver nods. "I did too."

"And you know what?" I add. "It *sucked.* I never got to hang out with her after school. Whenever one of you would chaperone a field trip, I couldn't be in her group. I couldn't go cheer her on at her softball games, and she never felt like she could get me flowers after a play."

My eyes are getting hot and my chest is getting heavy.

Dane slips an arm around me and squeezes. "I'm good with you being best friends with Lorelei."

Best. Fake. Fiancé. Ever.

I lean into him and squeeze my eyes shut while I stuff down the emotions. "Thank you."

He kisses my hair. "Of course."

This.

This is the kind of relationship I could have.

"I'm sorry, Amanda," Mom says quietly. "I'm so sorry."

"I am too," Mr. Silver says.

"So end it," Dane says. "Quit. Fucking. Fighting. Be better. Do better. For the whole damn town."

Mom's eyes are going shiny too. She blinks quickly. "I will."

Mr. Silver claps a hand to Dane's shoulders. "I'm so proud of you, son."

Dane stiffens, and he barely relaxes when his dad adds, "You're doing what none of the rest of us have ever had the courage to do."

That's odd.

That's *very* odd.

I shoot a look at Pia.

"Cake!" she says like things are getting too emotional in here for her. "More cake. Our next selection is a chocolate fudge cake with a homemade marmalade filling and a cinnamon frosting."

Cake.

Wedding cake.

For the ruse that's coming with entirely too many real emotions.

We're getting close with two generations of our families.

Now if we can just get Dane's uncle and all our grandparents on board, he and I will be able to go back to our normal lives.

But better.

But worse, because I think I might miss Dane more than I can bear to admit.

Chapter 19

Dane

Amanda's on the back porch again while I finish up my work for the day.

She's been quiet since we left Reindeer Bakes with a wedding cake on order for Monday night. I don't know if she's feeling the pressure that comes with knowing we have to tell our families the truth soon, or the same level of guilt I've felt about the lies, but I know a quiet Amanda is not a normal Amanda.

I grab a slice of fruitcake from the log I got from Uncle Rob earlier today and take it out back to her in the still-stifling heat.

"Not out there catching the fireflies?" I ask as I sit down on the back steps next to her.

She doesn't answer right away.

Didn't expect her to. She's too pensive right now.

She's not even nibbling on the fruitcake, though she accepted the plate and has it on her lap.

"I didn't realize how much it hurt that I could never be *real* friends with Lorelei until today," she finally says. "I've always thought that was part of the reason why I'm never interested in relationships, but now I *know* it is. It's the biggest part. Too much judgment from the outside world. *They're wrong* or *you should pick better*, but multiplied because you're getting the judgment from someone else's family too. It's like, I can't look at a man and not subconsciously wonder what his family will find wrong or unworthy about me when I wasn't even worthy of being publicly friends with Lorelei growing up, like it was somehow my fault, so it's easier to just make my own way without anyone else's expectations."

"Family gets in your head in ways you don't even realize."

"They do."

I scoot closer to her and loop an arm around her. "My ex leaving me was the kindest thing she could've done. Even with how she did it. But after I got over being called boring, I started to realize how much she'd complained about everything. *Everything.* Without that noise, the next time I talked to my grandma, when she started ranting about something your grandma had done, I was more or less triggered. Felt like I was back in a dysfunctional relationship with the worst kind of cynic, and that's when it all clicked. Every single time I did something that a normal parent would've just been proud of, my family wanted to talk about how much better it made us look compared to your family instead. I didn't even tell them the last time I got a promotion, because I didn't want to hear that they couldn't wait to rub it in your family's faces. I just wanted to hear a fucking *good job, we're proud of you.*"

"Why did they ever think this was okay?" she whispers, the break in her voice making fissures erupt in my heart.

"It's all they knew."

"I almost had a panic attack when I saw the cost of the wedding cake," she adds. "I can't pay that back."

"Our families pushed it to this. They can pay for it."

For all the guilt I've felt about lying, I don't feel any guilt about leaving it to our families to make things right with the businesses around town who are going out of their way to celebrate our wedding.

Seeing Amanda's pain talking about not being able to be friends with Lorelei sealed it for me.

Someone in town knows why our families are fighting. We wouldn't have gotten the two letters we've received if they didn't.

But not a single person inside either of our families will tell us what happened.

If they know.

Which means they appear to be fighting for the sake of fighting.

Fuck that noise and fuck feeling like I have no worth beyond being a pawn in their fights.

A stiff breeze whips off the lake, rattling the pines and rustling through the oak and maple canopy.

It doesn't bring enough of a respite from the heat, though.

"Thank you," Amanda says quietly while she fiddles with the engagement ring that she hasn't removed once, not even when we've been here alone.

"For what?"

"For doing this with me. You've been—you've been the absolute best. The instant I told my grandma and mom that I was engaged to you, I had so many regrets. I thought you'd be furious. I thought Lorelei would be stuck in the middle, and obviously, she'd pick you, and then I'd be the next reason the mayor had to break up fights between our families. But instead, I feel like I've made another best friend."

"I'm not really the *get angry* type."

"You're the best type."

"It's a phase. It'll pass."

Her eyes soften and her lips tip up as she looks at me. "I don't think so."

"Heat's gone to your brain."

The heat's gone to *my* brain.

When she looks at me like that, I think she wants to kiss me.

I know I want to kiss her. It's why I've avoided her as much as possible since the night she caught me in the shower.

I'm tired of avoiding her.

I'm tired of resisting her.

I'm not tired of wanting her.

"I really am glad I've gotten to know you." She lifts the plate of fruitcake with a smile, then sets it on the porch beside her. "And not for this. You—this you—you're the highlight of this trip home."

Ah, fuck.

She means it.

And she's leaning closer. Tipping her chin up. Eyes dropping to my lips.

Bad idea.

But so was pretending to be engaged to get our families to knock it the fuck off. We still don't have a plan to get her out of inheriting her family's bakery.

I mean, I have ideas.

But none that I think she'll like. *Inherit it and hire whoever the hell you want to stand in there with your mom.*

It's not something I feel like I can say yet.

But what I can do?

I can quit resisting her.

Giving in to kissing her is the easiest thing I've done all week. Angling in to brush my nose against hers, then against her cheek. Our breaths mingling. Her fingers settling on my face. My grip around her tightening.

Until our lips meet.

Soft and hesitant, but only for a moment before we're both all in.

This kiss—it's not because anyone's watching. It's not for show. It's not pretend.

It's real and deep and hot and everything I've wanted not just since she tried to crawl in through Lorelei's window, but since I first watched her onstage in high school.

I'd see her in the hallways, knowing she was an Anderson, that she was off limits, and I wanted her. I saw her in the cafeteria, laughing with friends or arguing with a boyfriend, and I wanted her.

I took a theater class one semester just so I'd be in the same room as her.

This kiss is every dream I had in high school come true.

But better.

Her tongue touches mine, and my skin ignites. She runs her fingers through my hair, and my balls tighten. I let myself explore the soft skin on her shoulders, interrupted only by the thin strap of her tank top, and I'm hard as a rock.

I know this can't go anywhere.

But when she breaks the kiss, I almost whimper.

I want to keep kissing her. I want to pick her up, carry her inside, and take her to the bedroom. I want to strip her. I want to lick every inch of her body, taste her skin, memorize the shape of her body, play with her pussy.

Show her I can make her feel good.

That I'm more than a nice guy playing her fake fiancé.

She stares at me, pupils dilated, lids heavy, breath coming fast, making her chest rise and fall rapidly.

Her nipples strain her tank top.

I want to touch them. I want to caress her breasts and tease her nipples and—

Stop, I order myself.

Myself doesn't listen.

Not when Amanda's moving again.

This time to crawl into my lap, straddling my hips and diving back into kissing me again.

Fuck, yes.

She rocks her pelvis against my hard-on while our tongues clash. I slide my hands under her shirt, stroking the hot, smooth skin of her back, my thumbs caressing her ribs.

And I realize what's missing.

She's not wearing a bra.

Condoms.

I have condoms in my luggage.

Have to get inside.

Get both of us inside.

Strip. Kiss. Touch. Taste. Feel.

She's jerking her hips faster against me, breath coming in desperate short bursts while we kiss. Soft whimpers—the good kind—mix with her puffs of breath.

And I realize she's close.

She's close to getting off.

With me.

The thought makes my cock swell harder and puts me in the danger zone for blowing my load too.

Amanda Anderson.

Wants me.

Not just my cock swelling now.

My heart is too.

Fuck.

"Yoo-hoo, anyone home?" someone calls nearby.

We break apart, my hands shooting straight in the air like *I'm not touching her, I'm not doing anything*, but unfortunately, when Amanda springs back, there's nowhere for her to go.

Except back.

Off the porch.

I jerk forward, reaching for her, while she *ack!*s and tumbles off my legs.

It's only three steps down, and three shallow steps at that, but my heart is racing and adrenaline is making my legs and arms shake as I leap up and dash down the steps to where Amanda's sprawled in the dirt.

"Are you—" I start, but I don't finish.

She's okay.

She's definitely okay.

You can tell by the laughter rolling out of her.

Her cheeks are stained dark red. Her hair has completely come out of the bun she's mostly kept it in this week—my fault—and her hair is spread in a curly mass of glory around her head.

"Hello?" Mrs. Briggs says again.

I check myself—don't want Mr. Happy horrifying my old teacher's wife—and look Amanda over once more. "You okay?"

She grins at me. "Well. *That's* never happened before. Didn't even know it was on my bucket list, and here we are."

I shake my head.

Smile.

Feel the regret and disappointment in my balls that the moment is over, and not likely to repeat itself.

But I still chuckle too. "And this is why I always had a crush on you in high school."

Screw it.

Why not admit it to her?

What's it going to change?

She blinks once. "No."

"Who could spend any time around you and *not*?"

"Oh, dear. Am I interrupting something?" Mrs. Briggs asks.

Amanda stares at me for a hot second before pushing herself up to sitting. "Dane told me not to play the *hop up the stairs with your eyes closed* game, and I didn't listen. Just making sure he can handle me."

Mrs. Briggs smiles at both of us. "I think he's handling you just fine. I forgot to give you a little gift to go with your dress yesterday. Given how fast the wedding's happening, I didn't know if you'd have time to find your something old, something new, something borrowed, and something blue." She pulls a small gift box out of her handbag. "This should cover it all. And I'll let you two get back to . . . your game."

"Mrs. B., you didn't have to do that." Amanda's fully on her feet now, taking the package and hugging the older woman. "I'll return it in pristine form, I promise."

"No, no, this one's yours to keep. Except the borrowed thing, and *only* because it's not borrowed if you keep it. You'll know what's borrowed. You just promise me you'll be happy. The way your love story is bringing some peace to Tinsel . . . bah. Now you've made me tear up. Just be happy. Both of you."

She swipes at her eyes, hugs Amanda quickly once more, and then retreats back around the house.

Amanda looks at me.

I look at the package in her hands.

"Oh my god," she whispers as she pulls out what looks very much like the red velvet pouch that Mrs. Briggs has carried with her in every Jingle Bell parade where she's played Mrs. Claus for as long as I can remember.

Inside, she finds a blue satin snowflake, an old tin cookie cutter in the shape of a Christmas tree, and a small new ornament that says *our first Christmas.*

To the best of my knowledge, Mrs. Briggs has never let anyone else carry her red velvet Mrs. Claus pouch.

It's clearly what's borrowed here.

But it's still huge.

We might be playing with fire.

All the way around.

And I'm not ready to stop.

Chapter 20

Amanda

I never thought I could be an overthinker until I opened my big fat mouth in a moment of panic and got myself a fake fiancé.

Now, I'm overthinking everything.

Did Dane mean it when he said he had a crush on me in high school? Does Lorelei know? What would've happened last night if Mrs. Briggs hadn't dropped off that gift? Was he kissing me because he knew she was coming and we needed to get caught looking like a couple madly in love?

Or was he kissing me for the same reason I was kissing him?

I like him.

I like him more with every minute we spend together. And we're breaking up in two days, and we haven't talked about how, and I want to kiss him again, but instead, I'm staring at the dresses I packed and thinking that neither one of them will work for the anniversary party that starts in an hour.

"Quit overthinking," I whisper to myself.

I close my eyes, mix up which dress is where in my mind, and I get ready to point when a voice behind me says, "The red one."

The other thing I'm overthinking about?

How after Mrs. Briggs left last night, Dane quietly said something about taking Chili out, and that was that.

No discussion about the kiss. Nothing else about what we're both hoping to get out of this. And today, he was on his computer when I got up.

"Work problem" was all he said.

Like it's normal for him to have work problems on Saturdays.

I fixed him an iced eggnog latte and let him be.

And now, forty-five minutes before we're supposed to be at his grandparents' party, he's weighing in on my dress.

Did he hear my telepathic invitation to come offer an opinion and put me out of my indecisive misery?

I peek over my shoulder at him. "What if your grandma's wearing red?"

See?

Overthinking.

"What if she's wearing gold?" he replies.

"Good point."

I'm in a towel, fresh out of the shower.

Semifresh out of the shower.

I've been standing here longer than I want to admit.

Dane doesn't seem to notice what I'm wearing. Or not wearing. He just nods to the dresses again, repeats, "The red one. If you'll let me know when you're done, I need five minutes in the bathroom."

He slips back down the hallway.

He's not rude. I don't feel dismissed. I believe he's been untangling a work mess all day, and I know he didn't get the hours in this week that he needed to for work.

But I only have a couple of days left with him.

How is it that a week ago, my life was completely fine, and today, I'm a wreck because I'll soon be headed back to New York solo?

And how is *that* the top problem on my mind when Grandma deserves to retire and Mom deserves to know she'll be able to one day, too, and I can't offer them a better option than me moving home, which is one thing I still can't see myself doing?

I've texted with my brother a lot this week.

He's madly in love with his new bride, and he adores Italy.

He's not coming home.

Ever.

And he doesn't have any magical solutions to the bakery either.

Even if we can solve this family feud, I don't see Grandma and Mom jumping at the chance to have anyone outside of the family take over. They've never said the phrase *we have to keep it in the family so the Silvers don't get it,* because it's always been assumed the bakery would stay in the family.

But the clear answer to this problem is *one day we'll have to sell the bakery.*

Which means I have to give up New York if we want *one day* to be many years' worth of days from now.

Maybe they can give me a few months so that I can see my play done back home.

Back home. New York is *back home* to me.

But it can't be. Because I have to move home to Tinsel to help Mom with the bakery.

I won't cry. I won't cry. I won't cry.

I take the red dress into the bathroom to change, then grab my hair and makeup supplies and move to the small powder room off the kitchen so Dane can have the shower.

When I emerge thirty minutes later, he's ready.

Despite the lingering heat, he's in suit pants, a white button-down, and a Christmas tie.

His hair is slightly damp and freshly combed. He's also freshly shaven, and he smells like a hayride on a Christmas tree farm.

I don't want to go to this anniversary party.

I want to stay here and turn on some Bing Crosby and Brenda Lee and have a private party, just the two of us, where he offers up some miraculous solution to my bakery problem that will work just as well as his plan to end our family feud.

He visibly swallows as his gaze rakes up and down my body, and his voice is husky when he says, "You look beautiful."

I blush, a mix of pride and desire making my chest swell. "Thank you. Here. Let me just . . ."

His tie isn't crooked.

Not in the least.

But I go through the motions like I'm straightening it for him anyway.

His breath catches. Mine speeds up.

"Thank you," he says, as if he doesn't know it was absolutely fine.

Maybe he likes it when I make excuses to touch him while we're alone.

"Do you have a large collection of Christmas ties, or do you stick to the snowflakes for general all-purpose winter wear?"

My voice is throaty. I might as well be purring.

And *all-purpose winter wear*?

Still overthinking.

"Just snowflakes."

My hands rest on his chest as I finish fiddling. Did I make it crooked? Or is it okay? Should we show up with his tie crooked to suggest that we were having our own private pre-party?

That would keep selling our story.

"I saw the most gorgeous snowflake dress once in a little boutique in SoHo. Your tie is like that dress in tie form."

Someone take my mouth away from me.

Please.

Dane's lips quirk up at the corners, though, and I suddenly don't care that I'm babbling about dresses in tie form.

"You must have to beat potential girlfriends off with a stick when you smile like that," I blurt.

He blushes.

Could he be any more charming and perfect?

"I make sure to wear my pocket protector when I leave my house," he says. "It helps."

He could walk out of his house in a hazmat suit, and women should fall all over him.

"We should—" I start, my hands still resting on his chest, feeling his heart beat while the engagement ring sits heavy on my finger, as he says, "I wish we didn't have to—"

"Same," I say at the same time he says, "You're right, we should."

We stare at each other for a beat.

And then we both smile.

Smiling leads to us cracking up.

It's ridiculous.

But it's also like being in a warm, cozy bubble of safety where no one's trying to attack anyone else, where no one's fighting, where no one *wants* to fight, where I'm not realizing I have to give up my home to move back to Tinsel, and likely where we both feel a little off-kilter.

Is he off-kilter?

I am.

I can't remember the last time I crushed this hard on a man.

I'm so distracted by myself and my overwhelming attraction to Dane that I almost trip over Chili on the way to the front door. Dane gives him extra pats and a treat while I stutter an apology.

And then we're headed out the door.

Except there's a big rock sitting in the middle of the front porch.

And I don't mean a rock like the one on my finger.

I mean a stone rock.

With an envelope underneath.

I freeze, then look up at Dane.

This is a change.

Whoever dropped it off wasn't afraid of being seen if it's all the way here on the porch. And it was *not* here two hours ago.

I took Chili out for a short walk. I would've seen it.

"Did you—" he starts, then shakes his head.

"Put it there?" I guess.

"See who put it there."

"Oh. No. I was—"

"Getting ready," he finishes for me.

He squats and retrieves the envelope, then tosses the rock off the side of the porch to join the rock bed scattered around the holly bushes.

I lean into him while he slides a finger under the flap and gently opens it.

And then we both devour the words on the paper, each of us holding one side of the letter, his free hand at the small of my back.

> *My dearest sister,*
> *We received your update that Maud's dowry was sent, but that rapscallion Anderson boy claims what he received was not what was promised, and he refuses to return it to our family.*

"Oh my god," I whisper as I scan the rest of the letter.

Dane makes a noise.

I look up at him, then back at the letter.

If George Anderson is my great-great-grandfather . . .

He's also a dowry thief.

He started this.

He stole something from the Silvers. He betrayed them.

"It's my family's fault," I whisper. "The feud is all my family's fault."

I know it's not *my* fault.

Logically.

But my family did this to Dane's family. We started it. We started it, and then we passed down the lie from generation to generation that *we* were the better family. That *they* were at fault.

And I didn't realize until exactly this minute how ingrained it is in me that *we*, the Andersons, were the victims.

Even when I was friends with Lorelei in grade school, there was a part of me feeling like I was the bigger person for being able to forgive her family for what they did to mine.

And how dumb is that?

How ridiculously stupid is it that even *as a child*, I'd been told so often just how bad Lorelei's family was that I occasionally had a sense of superiority over my friend?

I adore her.

I meant it when I said I'd donate a kidney to her. She's one of the kindest, most genuine people I know. And I know it's not my fault that I was taught to believe the Silvers were bad, but on some level, *I believed it.*

While it was all a lie.

It was *our* fault.

"This is one side of a story," Dane says. "We need the other half. We need to know what the dowry was. We need to know if he gave it back. Or what his reason was if he didn't."

He's trying to make me feel better, but I have this sick feeling in my stomach that the letters aren't wrong.

That whatever happened, it's on my ancestors.

Not his.

"The bigger point," he adds quietly, "is that whatever happened, it wasn't your fault."

I hear him, but the same part of me that used to think *look how special I am for being friends with a Silver* is now saying *you have asshole running through your blood.* "Yours either."

"Or Lorelei's or Esme's or your brother's." He tilts his head at me. "Is your brother a dick?"

I find a small laugh. "No. I've texted him since I got here and heard his news. He thinks the feud is dumb, too, and if he wasn't living his best life with his new bride in Italy now, he'd be sighing and going behind Grandma's back to be nice to Lorelei and Esme and you too. Of course, if he wasn't living his best life with his new bride in Italy, we wouldn't be doing this, because he'd be taking over for Grandma at the bakery and I wouldn't have told Grandma that we were engaged . . ."

Dane pulls me into a hug, putting his shirt in danger of my makeup. "It's not your fault that any of our ancestors did anything to any of our other ancestors," he repeats.

I set aside all my internal guilt at realizing I still have work to do to fully banish all thoughts, ever, forever, that the Silvers are evil on any level. "But I feel like it's my job to tell my grandma."

"Don't tell her it's her fault. Ask her what she knows about her own grandfather. Get her story. Get *his* story. We need the whole truth from all of our relatives so the whole damn town can move on."

He's right.

The town needs this.

But I can't quite make myself not feel guilty for the weight of what my family might've done.

Chapter 21

Dane

Amanda's fucking gorgeous, and I'm pissed.

I'm pissed because someone dropped off a letter telling her that the issues between our families are all her family's fault, and now she's gorgeous and sad when she should just be gorgeous.

We haven't been at my grandparents' party for ten minutes before someone quietly asks me if she's okay. Six more make subtle similar inquiries in the next hour as guests arrive and everyone mingles over appetizers and champagne before dinner.

"She's sad that our families haven't made up so that the rest of her family could be here" is my story, and the number of *I wish they'd all just get over it too* responses I get, in some form or another, once again resolidifies my belief that we're doing Tinsel a massive favor here.

The Andersons are the only family in town who aren't celebrating my grandparents' anniversary.

Their absence is even more noticeable in the face of Amanda being here. She's a glowing red beacon of *something is amiss but I'm trying my best.*

Uncle Rob pulls me aside to tell me that my fiancée needs to *smile more.*

That she's *bringing down the vibe.*

I tell him she just found out one of her favorite dogs died in New York. The one who humped my leg when we ran into each other and started dating.

I've never made up stories and lies so much in my life, but when I rejoin Amanda and quietly fill her in, I get a real smile for the first time all night. "Look at that. I'm rubbing off on you."

Huh.

She is.

We hug my grandparents and wish them happy anniversary.

Correction: I hug my grandparents.

Amanda tries, but my grandma makes a face, my grandpa makes a noise, and Amanda grabs my arm instead. "Oh, that's embarrassing. Predinner champagne doesn't usually affect me like this." She sways back and forth a little more, overdone to the point that I almost snap at my grandparents for making her uncomfortable.

She's trying.

She's hurting.

And this is their night, and I need to remember that.

So instead of making a scene about the way they're treating her, I squeeze her hand on my arm and vow to stop by their house tomorrow to inform them that I'm choosing her over them, and they can fucking deal.

"My fault," I say to my grandparents. "I didn't give her time to eat this afternoon."

Uncle Rob's right behind us, and he grunts out a mutter that my grandmother's echoing in her glare.

Awesome.

"Sorry," Amanda whispers as we head toward our seats for dinner.

"Don't be sorry that someone else has poor manners."

"You two going to Vicki Anderson's anniversary party tomorrow night?" someone asks.

"Unless we've both been cast out of our families and we decide to elope to Vegas instead," Amanda quips.

Then cringes.

I get the cringe. Feels like we might be cast out tonight. Or we might cast ourselves out.

Even if the Vegas plan is highly unlikely.

"Exactly that," I agree before she can correct herself.

It takes too long to find our seats, and when I do, irritation claws at my chest all over again.

We're at the far back table.

Our place cards say *Dane* and *Amnada*.

Spelled exactly like that.

Our tablemates are the local pest control guy and his wife, my high school nemesis and his new wife, and the mayor and her husband.

Being seated with the mayor is only offensive if you know that my grandparents have voted for her opponent at every election for the past twelve years, since Vicki Anderson always endorses her. And being seated with my high school nemesis is one more sign that we might fail.

That my grandparents are too stubborn to give up the feud, even for the sake of my happiness.

That hurts.

That fucking hurts.

Our very awkward dinner is wrapping up when Uncle Rob stands at the head table and clinks a spoon against his glass. "If I could have everyone's attention, please. I'd like to propose a toast to my parents."

Amanda and I have to scoot our chairs around to get a good view, as we've been placed with our backs to the head table.

I can't see my dad. Can't see Lorelei or Esme.

I can hardly see my grandparents, as the raised platform for their table is barely raised, and everyone in front of us is craning to see too.

The people who aren't looking back at Amanda and me, that is.

Have they been staring all through dinner?

I wouldn't have noticed.

My back was to the rest of the party.

"First, we want to thank you all for being here to celebrate Mom and Pops," Uncle Rob starts. "It means so much to them to see the appreciation the whole town has for the contributions they've made to Tinsel all of these years."

There's a smattering of applause.

Amanda claps with them. Not too loud, not too soft. Just fitting in.

Whereas I'm starting to sweat.

People are looking at us.

A lot of people. Not just a few. A lot.

We're at the back of the room. No one should be looking at us.

But they are.

Uncle Rob starts the story about how my grandparents met. And people are still turning to look at us.

Amanda scoots her chair closer to me and squeezes my hand. "Are you okay?" she whispers.

"Yeah."

She scoots even closer and squeezes my hand harder.

Quietly. There's no scraping of the chair legs on the floor. No grunting from the effort. It's all subtle motion bringing her closer to me and making my heart pound harder, which is making me sweat more.

I like her.

I've always liked her, but this week, I've seen how much more there is to like about her.

"If you'd asked my dad seventy years ago what he wanted to do with his life, the answer wouldn't have been *run the family fruitcake shop with a girl from the Bronx*, but that's exactly what their love story has been built on," Uncle Rob says. "Marrying a New Yorker still isn't something Pops would necessarily recommend for anyone else, but it sure worked out well for him."

My cheek twitches and my jaw tightens.

Grandma's from Kansas. She moved to the Bronx when she was eighteen, ran out of money at nineteen, and hopped the wrong bus back to Kansas, and Grandpa found her working a makeup counter in a mall in Grand Rapids not long after.

Amanda is more of a New Yorker than Grandma ever was.

That was a dig at us.

I'm positive that was a dig at us.

More people cast glances back at us.

"Pops won the in-law lottery, though," Uncle Rob says. "Doesn't happen with everyone."

Amanda makes a soft noise like that one landed.

Doesn't help that some people are getting restless, with more of them turning to peer at Amanda and me.

"But we all know wisdom comes with age, not hormones," Uncle Rob adds with a chuckle.

"Dad, stop," Esme hisses while a few people chuckle uncomfortably.

"What?" Uncle Rob says. "Pops is six years older than Mom is. And those were different times. He knew what he was getting into far better than a lot of you young people today. Especially *some* of you. Who should know better. And who should put family first."

That's it.

That's fucking *it*.

I jerk to my feet and tug hard on Amanda's hand. "We're leaving," I tell her.

"I'm okay," she whispers.

"I'm not."

She doesn't say another word. Instead, she squeezes my hand impossibly harder—*okay, I'm here for you*—and trots along a half step behind me as we head to the exit.

It's not far.

We're in the back, after all.

"Don't be rude to your grandparents, Dane," Uncle Rob says into the mic while more murmurs and whispers erupt around us. "This is their day."

I don't answer.

I *want* to.

I want to lift a stiff middle finger and let it do all my talking for me.

But instead, I keep walking, Amanda right on my heels, all the way out the door.

"I'm sorry—" she starts as we shove out into the thick, heavy, dark night air, but I cut her off with a look.

"You didn't put us in the back. You didn't treat me like an outcast. You didn't snub my grandparents when they tried to hug you. You didn't give a toast loaded with lies and insults. You didn't do a fucking thing wrong. So don't be sorry."

"Okay," she whispers.

She says *okay*.

I hear *but I'm the one who got you into this mess.*

"Continuing this was my idea," I say quietly as we reach the car. "Stop blaming yourself."

"They're your family."

"I don't want to be related to dicks. If they don't fucking knock it off, I'm never coming back. And that was true before tonight."

She peers up at me, briefly illuminated by a flash of lightning while a heavy gust of wind makes her free-hanging curls rustle.

Storm's coming.

Heat will break.

But this overwhelming desire to kiss Amanda, to assure her that this fake engagement might be the best thing to ever happen to me, that it might set me free, likely won't stop anytime soon.

Fuck my family.

I mean it. I don't want to be related to dicks.

Chapter 22

Amanda

I don't know what to say on the drive home.

Dane's jaw is tight, and he's focused straight ahead as we leave town and head back to the cabin.

He could be losing his family.

And it's my fault.

We've taken this too far. We're pushing too hard for something that will never happen.

And I don't know how to fix it.

I want to.

I want to fix this for him. I want him to be able to come home and visit Lorelei and see his dad and his family without feeling stressed.

But *how*?

Even if we figure out why the feud started in the first place, will that be enough to solve a problem that's been in this town for well over a century?

Can our grandparents actually get over it? And Dane's uncle?

Or at least keep it to themselves and not involve the rest of us?

I don't even care that we haven't found a solution for the bakery yet. I just want him to be at peace with however this week ends. To be happy.

The lightning in the distance is getting closer, the thunder growing from distant growls to pressing imminent threat. Wind buffets the car the entire way home, and big, fat raindrops splatter the windshield as Dane puts the car in park at the cabin.

"Can you run in those shoes?" he asks me.

It's the first thing he's said since we got in the car, and it's all about making sure I'm okay.

I need to do this for him. I need to make things okay for him.

"I can do my best," I say.

"I can't park closer."

"It's just water."

It's just water.

Oh, no, Amanda. It is *not* just water.

I haven't fully opened my door before the weather goes from a few fat, happy raindrops to a full-on deluge. One minute, you can race between the drops, and the next, you're swimming through air to get to the door.

It's cool.

It's heavy.

It's accompanied by a flash of lightning and an earth-shattering boom of thunder under a second later.

Dane grabs my hand while we race to the porch with more distant lightning flashing constantly around us, lighting the way.

It's not far, but we're both soaked by the time he unlocks the door and ushers me in.

My hair is dripping. My makeup is likely failing. My dress is dry-clean only and probably dead.

But more important—Dane's hair is soaked.

Raindrops splatter his angular face.

His white button-down is drenched, clinging to his strong, lean arms and broad shoulders and highlighting the outline of his undershirt. His nipples poke at the wet fabric. He swipes his face with one large hand, then brushes the water on his pants, which are also sopping wet and gripping his thighs.

"We shouldn't track water in," he says.

Our eyes meet.

My belly drops to my toes, my heart speeds up, and my vagina clenches.

He's about to offer to turn around so I can undress—I can see it in his eyes, I swear I can—and *no.*

I don't want him to turn around.

I want to stand here, peel my dress off, and watch him watch me. And then I want to unbutton his shirt, one button at a time, and relieve him of all his wet clothes too.

The engagement is fake.

My attraction to this man is not.

"I like you," I whisper.

He's watching me with guarded blue eyes.

Logic might not be my default, but I get it. I get why he's guarded.

Our families have fought for years.

We're "breaking up" sometime in the next two days.

All of this week has been an intense experience with my big mouth and his bigger idea throwing us together in intimate situations that we both know aren't real.

But I like him.

I do.

He's kind. He's patient. He looks at me like there's no problem in this world that we can't solve if we stay united, and it's so different, but so *right.*

"I like you too much," I add. "It makes me mad that the entire world can't see you for the wonderful man that you are."

He visibly swallows.

I close the half step between us and reach for his tie.

He doesn't stop me.

My fingers shake as I undo the waterlogged silk tie.

I can't fix his family. I can't fix mine.

But I can show him how much he matters.

How special he is.

"You're cold." His voice is thick and gruff.

"So are you." I get the tie off and move on to his top shirt button.

He still doesn't stop me.

I flick button after button until I reach where his shirt is tucked into his pants.

And *oh*.

He might be cold, but that's not stopping him from tenting the front of his trousers.

"Amanda—" he rasps.

I cut him off by leaning in and pressing a kiss to the bare skin of his collarbone while I pull his shirt out, feeling his chest rise as he sucks in a quick breath.

I want him.

I don't want to hurt him. I don't want to lead him on. I know that if I do this, if I kiss him again, if I keep undressing him, if we follow this path, everything changes.

We won't get married on Monday.

But maybe we'll be—something.

Something good.

He doesn't push me away. He doesn't tell me to stop.

Instead, he reaches behind me and tugs at the zipper on my dress while his lips brush my temple.

Yes.

Yes, *please*.

"You're shivering," he murmurs.

I push his shirt off his shoulders and let it drop to the ground, then tug on his undershirt. "You have goose bumps."

God, his body.

Sharp angles and hard planes and tan skin. Broad shoulders tapering down to tight hips. Dark hair across his chest that narrows to a line that disappears beneath his pants. I stared at his back when he came in from swimming the other day, and I know he has twin dimples at the base of his spine.

I wanted to lick them then.

Not just his dimples, though. I want to lick all of him.

Blinding lightning flashes through the front windows, and a thunderous boom shakes the cabin as Dane tugs my dress off my shoulders, down, exposing my bare breasts.

His breath catches. After the slightest hesitation, he brushes his thumbs over my hard nipples. "You're *very* cold."

"I'm very turned on."

His erection pulses under his pants, brushing my belly.

"And I'm not the only one," I add in a whisper as I reach for his belt.

"Amanda—" he says again, but he stops himself and shakes his head, and then he's kissing me.

Kissing me and tugging my dress down over my hips until it falls to the ground, leaving me in nothing but my stilettos and a red glitter thong.

He cups my bare ass cheeks and makes a noise in the back of his throat while his tongue thrusts into my mouth. I fumble with his belt with shaky, cold, overeager fingers, and it takes me longer than it should to get it unbuckled.

But it's finally free, and I make quick work of his button and zipper.

His pants easily slide off his hips.

He kicks out of them and pushes me deeper into the house, still kissing me, his fingernails scraping my ass cheeks and sending jolts of pleasure up the base of my spine that are more electric than the lightning storm outside.

Rain pounds on the roof.

The lights flicker and go out completely.

Chili yelps.

"Fuck," Dane mutters. "Sorry, pup."

"Sorry, Chili," I echo on a gasp.

The dog grunts.

Lightning illuminates the room in quick flashes. Dane's not looking at the dog.

He's looking at me. Not just looking at me.

Commanding me.

Owning me.

And simultaneously making me feel like the sexiest woman on the entire planet.

Like I have the power here despite all the ways I would do nearly anything he orders me to do in this moment.

He's holding me flush to his body, his hard-on rigid against my stomach. "I want you. Here. You. Me. Just us. No audience. No show. *I want you.*"

Yes. All of the *yes.* "I'm all yours."

Never—*ever*—have I said that to a man.

But I mean it.

I'm completely, hopelessly unable to resist Dane.

And he deserves all of me. No reservations. No second-guessing. No holding back.

All of me and nothing less.

And that's what I give him.

I give him all of me when I go up on my tiptoes in the unnaturally chilly room and kiss his lips while tugging his boxers down so that I can stroke his thick, long cock. I give him all of me when he presses me against the wall and I hook one leg around his hips. I give him all of me when he lifts me up, pinning me and kissing me until we're both panting for breath, his erection pressing between my thighs and rubbing my clit while I jerk my hips against him.

He snaps the waistband on my thong, tearing it completely, and rips it out from between us. "I want you," he repeats into the kiss.

"Take me," I gasp back.

"Condom—"

"I'm on birth control. *Take me.*"

He shifts, and then I feel his bare tip against my pussy, parting me, thrusting into me, and *oh my god.*

My eyes cross as he fills me, every inch of him new and hard and perfect and *right.* I'm so wet. My clit is throbbing. My breasts ache. And as he pumps into me, harder and faster, the walls shake again with another boom of thunder.

The light from the electrical storm illuminates his face as he fucks me against the wall, our gazes holding through every streak of lightning while I cling to his shoulders and ride his cock, the aching need for release growing deep inside me, tightening and building with every thrust.

"You—feel—better—ever—dreamed," he gasps.

"You are—a dream," I pant back. "The best—*oh god, right there.*"

My legs tighten around his hips as he hits the magic spot inside of me that has me right on the edge of an orgasm.

A true man-made orgasm.

"C'mon, my minx," he growls. "Come for me."

Oh god. I like bossy Dane.

I like bossy, naked, *fucking the ever-loving hell out of me against a wall* Dane.

And so does my body.

It obeys instantly, everything clenching in one hard burst while another massive round of thunder crackles through the stormy night. I fling my head back against the wall, my toes curling, while my orgasm rolls through me, everything spasming so hard and fast inside me that my eyes cross again, one ripple of sheer pleasure on top of another.

And then Dane moans my name and buries his head in my neck while he pushes deep inside me one last time.

I feel his cock pulsing inside me, and it makes me come harder.

I have never—*ever*—known sex could be like this.

I'm hot. I'm sticky. I have goose bumps myself from the chilly night air, but I don't feel cold.

I feel like I'm glowing.

Like I *am* the lightning.

My orgasm *is* the storm.

Dane blows out a shuddery breath and leans harder into me. He makes a noise like he wants to say something, but he doesn't.

Instead, he wraps his arms tight around me and just breathes.

My body has gone limp, but I make myself hug him back as hard as I can. "I think you're the best thing about home," I whisper.

I shouldn't say it.

I know I shouldn't say it.

But it's true.

I will never come back to Tinsel again in my lifetime without thinking about Dane and hoping he's every bit as happy as he deserves to be.

His grip around me tightens momentarily before he slowly pulls back. "Can you walk?"

A crash of thunder answers for me, though I don't know what it means.

We stare at each other for a beat as one more flash of lightning makes us both glow, and then the best-worst thing ever happens.

We both crack up.

He's fun. He's kind. He's strong. He's fabulous at railing me against a wall.

And he's only mine for two more days.

Fuck.

Chapter 23

Dane

It's a bad sign when I'm contemplating all the ways that we could go through with the wedding tomorrow so that this doesn't have to end.

But that's exactly what I'm doing as I lounge in bed with Amanda early Sunday morning.

I'm stretched out on my stomach while she sits beside me, trading stories about city life while she draws random designs on my back with light fingertips.

It's chilly this morning, so she's wearing one of my T-shirts. Her curly hair is wild around her head, and her face is fresh and clear.

No makeup.

We took care of that in the shower together after we banged against the wall.

I'm still completely bare assed. Ready for whatever she might want.

Wishing this was real.

It *feels* real. I believe her when she says she likes me. Lorelei's told me a few times this past week that dating isn't Amanda's priority. Amanda herself has told me the same.

But are we *dating* because we had sex all night?

Or is this the two of us blowing off steam after the stress of dealing with our families' reactions to us pretending we're together?

"*No*," she says as I finish telling her a story about accidentally crashing a black-tie formal in a seven-foot-tall bacon costume. "How did you not get the memo?"

"Just got back from a work trip to Hong Kong and I was looking at the wrong week on my calendar. Told Vanessa I'd meet her at the party, but when I got there, a week early for the venue, everyone else was in formal wear and I couldn't find my girlfriend."

Amanda cracks up. "What did you do?"

"Pretended I was a server, made a round with a tray of mini quiches, then ducked into the coat closet and called her."

"Where were you supposed to be?"

"A black-tie formal for her boss's wedding."

"Did you go in your bacon costume?"

"Yep."

"Were you mortified?"

"A bit."

"Aww. How long after that did you break up?"

"Well over a year. That was before we moved in together."

She dances her fingers over my shoulder blade, and I sigh and sink deeper into the mattress.

There are a few things in life better than getting a light back rub from a nearly naked woman who smells like sex, but only a few.

"It's not exactly the same, but that reminds me of the time Yazmin and I spent a day trying on clothes that we picked out for each other to see who could create the most epically wrong looks for our personalities," she says. "I walked out of a Bloomingdale's dressing room in pastel polyester pants pulled up to my boobs and a sweater that had *World's Best Grandma* knitted into it, and Yazmin laughed so hard we were asked to leave."

"You probably still looked perfect."

"I was ready to head to the accessories aisle and get some fake bifocals and a granny wig."

I smile as my eyes drift closed.

That's so easy to picture.

"When are tryouts for your show?" I ask her.

I don't tell her I know it's *her* show.

She doesn't volunteer it.

"Next week." She sighs. "Assuming I go back to New York."

"Why wouldn't you?"

"Because we still don't have someone else to help my mom at the bakery."

"Ever consider that that's a problem for your mom and grandma to solve?"

"Not without a lot of guilt."

I kiss her knee. "You should go home to New York and see what they come up with. Do your play. Have fun. Let them sweat for a while."

"Can I tell you a secret?"

"Mm-hmm."

"I miss being onstage, but it would kill part of my soul to do it as my job. That's why I love the community theater so much. It's bonus goodness in my life."

I slide a look at her.

Her cheeks are going pink. "And I wrote the play," she whispers.

"Send me dates. I'll come see it."

"It's probably—"

"Fucking amazing," I interrupt. "Something you should celebrate. Be proud of."

She wrinkles her nose. "Would you believe me if I said I was going to say that it's probably when you're on vacation?"

"Were you?"

The guilty look answers for her.

"Uh-huh," I say.

"It's just—I wasn't in New York more than six months before I figured out that acting as a career wasn't going to do it for me. But every time I leave my apartment, I see something new and fascinating and inspiring, so I wrote the play as an ode to my neighborhood. To celebrate what they'd done for me. And then I showed it to Yazmin, and she was like, *get out of my head*, and I realized we all love our community, we all love the city, and we all love different things about it, but it unites us. So it's . . . in a lot of ways, it's bigger than me. It's my thank-you to everyone who's become my family away from Tinsel."

"Think you'll write more plays?"

"Yes," she whispers.

"Good."

Her fingers drift up my neck. "You ever want to be on a stage?"

"I'd rather run naked through a town hall meeting with both of our families sitting together."

She laughs a little, then sighs.

She's about to say the thing I don't want her to say. *We need to talk about how we're breaking up tomorrow.*

Nope.

Don't want to.

I shift so I can kiss her knee again.

She runs her fingers through my hair.

I loop my hand around her calf and kiss her knee once more. Her breath hitches, and her fingers tighten in my hair.

And someone knocks on the door.

The sun's up. Clear blue skies are showing off outside the bedroom window, and before I shut it to keep more cold air from sneaking in, we could hear the birds chirping.

But it's still not even seven in the morning.

They knock again.

Both of us sigh in unison.

"Probably my grandmother." Amanda shifts like she's getting out of bed, but I move faster.

"Let me."

If her family heard that I dragged Amanda out of my grandparents' anniversary party last night and have come to gloat, they're going to have to gloat to me.

That'll be awkward for them.

If they're here to offer support, great.

They can do that for me, too, if they mean it.

Amanda lunges for her suitcase. I dash to the door.

My bag is still in the living room, and it takes me about three seconds to grab shorts and pull them on before I open the door after a second knock.

I take one look at who's standing there, though, and I shut it before he can say a word.

"Honey, it's for you," I call.

Front windows are still open. We forgot to close those.

He can hear me.

Amanda dashes into the living room, still in my T-shirt, but with pajama pants added beneath it. Her cheeks are stained pink and her eyes hold that half-wary, half-excited look of someone who's not sure they want the surprise on the other side of the door.

"It's my uncle," I say quietly as she joins me at the door.

"He wants to talk to me?" she whispers.

"I have no idea what he wants, but if he wants to talk to me, he'll have to apologize to you first."

She squeezes my hand. "You don't have to—"

"This one's for me."

I haven't checked my phone yet today. No idea how many members of my family have tried to get in touch. No idea if I'm facing screen after screen full of insults and yelling, or if there are excuses and apologies in the mix.

I just know that if my family insists on continuing to take joy in fighting with the Andersons, I'm done.

My dad's coming around. Lorelei's good. Esme's good.

If my grandparents and my uncle want to pick a feud over family, when they can't even tell me what the fucking feud is about, then I'm just done.

I *would* date Amanda.

I'd pick her over family.

She doesn't make me feel like a pawn in a game.

She makes me feel like her partner in doing something that no one else in our families ever had the courage or dignity to do.

"You don't have to talk to him if you don't want to," I tell her.

That earns me a devious smile. "You think I don't want to talk to someone who insulted my fiancé so thoroughly and publicly last night that he made you leave your grandparents' anniversary party?"

Oh, shit.

I might not have thought this all the way through.

But it's too late. She's flinging the door open and stepping out onto the porch. "Good morning, Uncle Rob. What can I do for you today?"

She pulls the door shut behind her before I can join her.

Fuck.

My stuff is still all over the living room.

Including my dog, who went out two hours ago, had breakfast, and is now giving me a one-eyed squint.

You sure that was a good idea, bud?

"Not at all," I tell him.

He snorts in amusement and goes back to snoozing.

I strip the quilt off the couch while I listen in on the conversation outside.

"I'd like to talk to Dane, please," Uncle Rob says stiffly.

"Why should I let you have access to him after the scene you made about us last night?"

Uncle Rob huffs. "I want to apologize to him."

"How well do you know your nephew?"

"I've known him his entire life."

"That doesn't mean you *know* him. What's important to him? Where does he see himself in ten years? Who are his friends? If he had to choose between peer pressure from dead people to keep up a family feud or leaving all of you behind to love who he wants to love and live how he wants to live, what would he pick?"

I peek out the window.

Amanda's on the front porch, looking down on Uncle Rob, who's retreated to the edge of the bottom step.

I spot Esme leaning against her car, parked next to my and Amanda's rentals.

So Uncle Rob isn't here completely willingly.

Good to know.

"You two don't belong together—" Uncle Rob starts, but he stops when Amanda snorts.

"Unless you're about to tell us that we're siblings or first cousins, I'm pretty sure neither one of us will care. *We didn't do this.* We didn't start this fight, none of you will tell us why it matters so much, and we have no interest in continuing to be the next generation of people who enjoy making conflict for no good reason. If you want to see Dane again, you'll let it go too. He deserves family who are happy for him and who honestly want the best for him. We all do."

Uncle Rob eyes her.

I can't see her face, but I can read her body language. Arms at her sides. Shoulders relaxed. Swaying left and right, just the slightest bit. Head up, but not so much that it's haughty.

Just enough to say *I'm not the enemy, but don't mistake me for a pushover either.*

I shouldn't have sent her out there alone.

I should be right next to her.

But she has this.

She's strong. She's capable. She believes in what we're doing.

And she believes in me.

My throat is thick. My heart pounding in a painful beat.

She's everything.

And she's not mine.

"Your family isn't innocent," Uncle Rob mutters.

"But Dane is," Amanda replies softly. "And so am I."

I sink to the couch as she lets herself back into the house, overwhelmed with gratitude, appreciation, lo—appreciation.

We're stopping at appreciation.

"Dammit," Uncle Rob says outside.

Amanda looks at me. *I'm sorry,* she mouths.

Her eyes get shiny.

Her chin wobbles.

Hell if that'll stand.

I'm on my feet pulling her into a hug in an instant. "You're fucking amazing," I murmur into her hair. "Thank you."

"I didn't—" she starts, but I shush her.

My heart is overflowing with more affection for this woman than I should let myself feel, but this pain?

The pain coming when it's over?

She'll have been worth it.

"I'm sorry," I whisper. "I shouldn't have sent you out there alone."

"Oh my god, *please*. I can handle this for me. I don't want to make things worse for *you*."

"This is on the way to better."

"Are you sure?"

Esme's voice drifts in through the window. "That didn't look like an apology."

Uncle Rob grunts something back.

"Amanda's right," Esme says. "She didn't do anything wrong. And neither has Dane. You're being a dick for the sake of being a dick, and I'm over it too. Good news for me, though, is that your dumb feud will die off with your generation. You can chew on that while you're rolling over in your grave."

Amanda stifles a noise that has my heart freezing in my chest.

I pull back and look down at her, prepared to wipe tears and reassure her that she's not the problem, when I realize she's holding back a snort of laughter.

"I should use that line on my grandma," she whispers.

And now I'm the one trying not to laugh as I pull her back in for another tight hug. "You're braver than I am."

"Eh. Not like I won't be breaking her heart anyway when I tell her I don't want to move home to take over the Gingerbread House."

If I squeeze her any tighter, she won't be able to breathe.

But there's a gravity in her voice that makes me want to carry this load for her.

"You need to tell her," I murmur into her hair. "You deserve to live a life that makes you happy. You glow when you talk about New York. It's good for you. And I think you're good for it too."

She squeezes me hard, then lets her arms relax as she changes the subject. "I should get ready and head into town. Grandma wants to talk to me before her anniversary party tonight."

"What can I do to help?"

"You're already doing it."

I might be.

But it's still not enough.

Chapter 24

Amanda

For how Dane and I spent last night, every cell in my body should be chill as an ice-cream cone.

But all my afterglow has disappeared before I've been at the Gingerbread House for a full thirty seconds.

It doesn't help that I'm alone. Lorelei called to request Dane's assistance with a playlist for the DJ for the wedding.

Which is tomorrow.

But not.

Which no one knows yet.

So my fake fiancé is off picking a playlist for the wedding that won't be happening while lying to his sister, who would probably understand, but who will find out with the rest of the town whenever we tell them.

Which needs to be soon.

Soon soon.

But I'm not announcing the breakup the same way I announced the engagement. I need a plan, and Dane needs to be in on it this time.

"I heard you and your fiancé stormed out of his grandparents' anniversary party" is how Grandma greets me.

Glee?

Glee has *nothing* on her attitude this morning.

This is so far past glee that there might not be a word in the English language to express how thrilled she is.

"Don't be a dick," I tell her. "Dane's hurting. Family shouldn't be assholes about love."

Her jaw hits the fake-gingerbread floor.

"Good morning, sweetheart." Mom flies into the kitchen and smothers me in a hug. "You okay?"

I don't have to look at her to know she's glaring at my grandmother. Probably mouthing a few things behind my back too.

Likely *this is the last one you have left to take over so I can retire one day, too, don't fuck it up*.

Everyone's getting more profane in my head right now.

Yay.

"I'm tired," I answer honestly.

Exhausted is more like it.

Not because I was up all night having sex with Dane, but because trying to convince our families to get along is draining.

So is the idea that I have to ask Grandma the hard questions today.

Winning over parts of our families has come with highs, but if we can't convince all our family members to get along, will that truly leave Tinsel better?

Or will it lead to infighting in our families along with more fighting with the other's family?

My head hurts.

I don't know if we can do this.

"I'm sorry you slept poorly," Grandma says. She doesn't add *if you were sleeping with someone better, you wouldn't be*, but I swear I hear it.

Mom makes a noise.

Grandma *pffts* at her.

I'm still being smothered in a hug.

"I have good news for you, Amanda," Grandma announces. "Today is the first day of the rest of your life."

"Technically, every day is," I counter as I shake my mom off.

"Bah. *Today*, you learn the family secret that keeps this gingerbread shop running. Today, you get inducted into the secret society of gingerbread magic."

"Did she fall and hit her head?" I whisper to Mom.

Mom pinches the bridge of her nose and inhales heavily.

"Mock all you want now, but in four hours, you'll be a brand-new woman," Grandma says.

"Vicki. It's a *gingerbread recipe*," Mom says.

"And it's magic. Amanda. Come. I considered not showing you, seeing as you seem to be turning your back *just a little* on your family, but your mother insists that I let you make your own mistakes. It'll likely correct itself within a few years."

"*Vicki*," Mom says again.

Grandma ignores her as she bustles around the kitchen, pulling the blinds on the windows that let people look in from the hallway to watch the gingerbread being made during normal business hours and locking the kitchen door.

That's not ominous.

"It's not magic," my mom whispers. "And I'm sorry she's stressing you out the day before your wedding."

My stomach follows where Grandma's jaw just was to rest on the fake-gingerbread floor.

We have one more day to convince our families to make peace, to get along, to maybe even find something to like about one another, before we have to either break up or go through with the wedding.

There's no chance we're going through with the wedding.

We might like each other, but *getting married tomorrow*?

No.

No way.

"It's time," Grandma announces.

"For . . . ?" I ask.

She hits the lights and plunges the kitchen into darkness. She flicks on her phone's flashlight, and then she produces and lights three Christmas candles that I've never seen before.

All three are shaped like gingerbread men, except they've been used enough that their heads are caving in.

And they're old.

You can smell it.

"Does the fire marshal know about those candles?" I whisper.

"Quiet. Don't disturb the ceremony."

I glance at Mom.

She's rubbing her temples and sighing.

Guilt hits me in the sternum. *Again.*

Mom's been trying. She's been working on Grandma all week. And she's going to find out it's all been fake very soon. Or at least for nothing when Dane and I "break up."

Will she feel betrayed?

Or will she understand?

Also, I'm supposed to be asking Grandma about her own grandfather. I did a little digging, and I'm sure George Anderson *is* my great-great-grandfather. But I don't know what Grandma might know about him and his romantic history.

"How far back does this ceremony go in our family?" I ask.

Look at me. Impulsive but *smart* this time.

"Shush. *Be present.*" Grandma hands me one of the gingerbread candles. The wax is thick and hard, with a texture that feels like years of grime has worked its way into the candle itself. Mom is handed a second, and then Grandma uses hers as a light to lead us in three circles around the main prep table in the center of the kitchen as she speaks.

"Ancestors, we come to you today with joyous news," she intones. "The next generation of gingerbread bakers is here to continue the work you've honored us with. May her spoons be accurate. May her mixer never lose power. May her frosting never melt. And may her molasses never crystallize."

Ben was supposed to do this. I wonder what my brother would say to Grandma's ceremony.

He'd probably be amused but hide it.

I'm just plain stressed. "Grandma, I have to tell you something," I say.

She ignores me. "From this day forward, one more generation of Andersons will benefit from the glorious gift passed from mother to son, father to daughter, grandparent to grandchild. But with this gift comes the duty to provide for the good of all of the town of Tinsel through baking, charity, and volunteer work. Amanda Elizabeth Anderson, are you ready to take your rightful place in our family and in our hometown?"

"Grandma, I don't think—" I start, but she cuts me off.

"Wonderful. We shall now proceed with the presentation of the recipe."

I start to speak again, but Mom grabs me by the arm and shakes her head at me.

Don't interrupt?

Or *we'll fix this later?*

Grandma leads us to the desk in the corner, still going on about how our family founded this town, about leading it into the Christmas years, about gingerbread being the root of everything.

It's overkill.

Mom keeps wincing.

I want to ask if she did this ceremony. If she was here with Dad. Or if this is something Grandma's making up the same way she fakes her heart attacks.

But I force myself to stay quiet while Grandma opens the top desk drawer, hits something inside, and exposes a secret compartment beneath the drawer organizer.

"Behold," she whispers reverently. "The original family recipe."

She removes a piece of paper that looks older than dirt, and I don't think that's just the flickering candlelight. The handwriting is old. The paper is nearly transparent. Smudges suggest it's had ingredients spilled on it over the years.

"Maybe enough with the candles now?" Mom blurts. "That's the only copy."

"As the family secret has been exposed, we now fall into darkness." Grandma blows out her candle.

Mom quickly extinguishes hers, then pinches mine out too.

"Amanda," Grandma says in the darkness, "this recipe has been a family secret for generations. *Generations.* It is now your duty to continue in the tradition, to share this recipe with *no one*, not even your ridiculous—"

Mom clears her throat.

"To include anyone to whom you've been married for fewer than fifteen years," Grandma amends, "and to use it to make the world's best gingerbread, from now until retirement."

"But—"

"There is no one else, Amanda. It must be you, or this town will fall apart. This is not just gingerbread. This is the glue that holds Tinsel together. The core of everything that makes our community run. It is our origin, and it is our future. Come. Come take the recipe, and continue the work of our family."

For the love of New York pizza. The only thing about our family uniting this town is that they all wish we'd stop fighting with the Silvers. "Grandma, *I can't bake.*"

"The recipe will fix you."

"*Vicki,*" Mom says, sounding just as frustrated and sad as I feel.

"It fixed me. It will fix my granddaughter."

Grandma couldn't bake?

"When I married your grandfather, I couldn't operate a stove. I once served him spaghetti with raw hamburger and burnt noodles. *Burnt noodles.* But this recipe—once I was given this recipe, everything changed."

"Grandma—"

"The first batch of gingerbread I made with this recipe was perfect. So was the next batch. And the next. With this recipe stored in my heart and in my brain, I have never—*never*—ruined a batch of gingerbread. And I once set fire to a chicken casserole inside my oven. This recipe works. It's magic. It worked for me, and it will work for you."

"Even if it does—" I try, but she interrupts me again.

"Then I get to retire in peace and you find that this *is* what you're meant to do. Just like I did."

Stab stab stab. Guilt guilt guilt.

"Okay," I blurt. "Okay. I'll make the gingerbread."

Dammit.

Not okay.

Not okay.

What happens if the recipe *is* magic?

What if I *do* bake good gingerbread with it?

How is this different from the coded recipe on the wall by the mixer?

A recipe can't make me fall in love with running a bakery in my hometown.

But I'm starting to realize there's no way out of it.

No matter what Dane says about letting my family figure this out themselves.

They need me.

"I knew you could do it," Grandma says.

The lights flicker on.

Mom's watching me like she knows I'm on the verge of tears, but Grandma shoves the delicate yellowed paper at me. "Let's get started. We open in an hour."

My pulse is hammering. My mouth is dry. My throat feels thick.

I didn't have any problem standing up to Dane's uncle earlier this morning, but I can't tell my own grandmother that I don't want—that I *can't* run her bakery.

I keep messing this up.

And I don't know if there's any way for me to fix it.

Chapter 25

Dane

"You're very stressed for a man who's marrying the love of his life tomorrow," Lorelei says as we stroll down Kringle Lane toward the Gingerbread House.

I slide a look at her.

We're both in light jackets and sunglasses. Everything's still wet from the storm last night, though the sky is blue and cloudless and the sun is working on clearing up the puddles. The crews are out placing the life-size snow globes where they'll fit downtown, with the rest planned for a display in Reindeer Square.

Yes, it's early to set out holiday decorations.

But that's how we do it in Tinsel.

"Just saying, weddings should be happy," Lorelei adds.

"Uncle Rob gave us a shitty apology this morning."

"Esme stopped to get gas after they left Amanda's place. She kicked him out of the car and told him to walk the rest of the way home and think about what he'd done. You could uninvite him if you don't want him there."

"That'll be great for the rest of our lives."

She doesn't answer, and I cringe to myself. "Sorry for the sarcasm," I say quietly. "Not your fault some of our families are still being dicks."

She loops her arm through mine and squeezes. "No apology necessary. It's frustrating for me, too, and I'm not the one trying to marry an Anderson."

"You've been friends with Amanda longer than I've known her name. This matters for you too."

"It's a lot easier to sneak around being someone's friend when they're only in town a couple weeks a year than it is to sneak around being married to someone."

I glance at her again.

She grins. "It *is*."

"This sucks."

"It does, but look what you two have already done. You've won over our parents to the point that I think they might even become friends. That's something. And I like Kimberly. A lot, actually. Which makes sense, considering how much I like Amanda."

She's right. We've made progress.

But it's not enough. And I don't know if we can finish what we started before we have to break up or get married.

We reach the Gingerbread House. I start to turn in, but she tugs my arm and stops me. "I've never been in here," she whispers.

"If you don't want—"

"Are you serious? Of course I want to go in. But give me a minute. I need to make sure I'm prepared."

I smile my first real smile since leaving the cabin this morning as she closes her eyes and sucks in a large breath beneath the fake arch of the gingerbread doorway. Smells like cinnamon and ginger and nutmeg here in the doorway.

Honestly, it smells a little like Lorelei herself.

Dad used to say she's loved baking since before she was born. She brings all the baked goods except the fruitcake anytime there's a family gathering.

Never gingerbread, though.

Unless it's just the two of us, and even then, only when she's visiting me in San Francisco.

I stop and stare at her.

Fuck me.

Fuck. Me.

That's the answer. *Lorelei* is the answer.

At least, she should be.

But I don't think either of our families are ready for that.

I don't know if *Lorelei* is ready for that.

"Okay," she says. "I'm ready."

I hold the door for her, brain puzzling again if this could work, and the two of us step inside the bakery.

"Oh, wow," my sister whispers as she pauses to take in everything from the gingerbread floor to the gumdrops and candy canes to the menu and the candy light fixtures, which I hadn't noticed the other day. Peppermints light the bakery.

That's awesome.

If you're into this kind of thing. Which I would like to be without remembering how many times my family has insisted that the people running this bakery are terrible.

I stifle a sigh.

It's killing me at the moment that there are solutions that would likely make everyone happy if it weren't for a family feud that we've only begun healing.

Lorelei and I are the only people here except for a lone woman I don't know behind the counter. She's arranging gingerbread men on a plate, and her entire expression lights up when she sees us.

"Amanda's in the kitchen," she says. "You can go on back."

"It's like a magic candy land," Lorelei says.

"Without Hansel and Gretel," I mutter.

She bumps her shoulder into mine with a laugh. "You *are* in a mood. We're gonna have to fix that before tomorrow."

Tomorrow.

When somehow, Amanda and I will be breaking up.

That's what has me in a mood.

It's not Uncle Rob. It's not wedding stress. It's not last night. It's not any of our grandparents.

It's breaking up with Amanda.

She's been in my life for less than a week, but I already miss spending hours of every day with her. I miss how easy it is to smile at her. I miss how funny she is and how thoughtful she is.

I tell myself both of us are on our best behavior this week, putting more effort into being the perfect partners than either of us would if this were real, if we lived in the same city, but I don't believe myself.

I'd race her to the kitchen to make coffee in the mornings.

I'd order her fruitcake as often as she wanted it.

I'd go explore with her anytime she wanted company.

I'd take her with me to Thailand just to watch her face light up every time she discovered something new.

But that's not my future. This isn't *real.*

No matter how real it felt last night.

Lorelei and I head down the hallway toward the kitchen. Unlike the last time I was here, it sounds like the mixer is running just fine. The hallway smells even stronger of fresh gingerbread.

We crack the door and peek inside.

Amanda's bent over a sheet of dough, pressing cookie cutters into it while her grandmother supervises, pointing to the dough and making Amanda move her cookie cutter.

"She's really not built for this," Lorelei murmurs.

Agreed.

She looks like she belongs in the kitchen about as much as a zebra belongs at a spa.

Or possibly less so.

A zebra might enjoy a spa day. Who am I to judge?

But Amanda's jaw is tight. Her lips are turned down, and her shoulders are bunched. I've had only a few days to get to know her, but I have a pretty good idea that she's up in her head, unhappy with how the morning has gone but uncertain how to say so.

The exact opposite of how my sister would look if she were in this kitchen.

But that's not happening.

We've worked a few miracles this week, but getting Lorelei hired in the Gingerbread House?

That's a pipe dream.

I push into the kitchen. Lorelei follows.

Vicki glances at us, and her cheek twitches.

But when Amanda's gaze meets mine, all I feel is gratitude.

Gratitude from her that we're here. Gratitude of my own that I can bring a hint of a smile back to her face, even if her eyes are shiny and her chin is doing that wobbling thing again. "Hey," she says. "I have successfully not murdered any gingerbread this morning."

"Kitchen's closed," Vicki says.

Kimberly rolls her eyes. "Good morning, Dane. Hello, Lorelei. Lovely to see you both. Did you need the bride?"

"We do," Lorelei answers for me. "My dad's experimenting with fruitcake flavors for a special side cake that he's making just for Amanda, and he wants to know which kind she prefers."

"Today's *my* day with her," Vicki says. "Your family had their chance yesterday."

"I like all of the flavors," Amanda says to Lorelei.

"If you can't leave, we'll bring them by. You can sample on your lunch break."

Vicki sucks in a breath.

Kimberly visibly suppresses a smile.

Amanda looks at me again. The utter misery in her face is so opposite how she looked in bed this morning, and it's pissing me off.

Family shouldn't make you miserable.

"We just have three more batches to make," she says. "I might get the thickness right by the last batch. Maybe."

She hasn't told them.

She hasn't told her grandmother that she can't take over the bakery.

That's why she's stuck here. She's still playing along.

Or maybe this isn't playing. Maybe she's completely given in.

That's why she's so unhappy.

Because she's giving up a life she loves to fulfill an obligation her family's putting on her shoulders so that they don't have to change anything about their lives.

Fuck unhappy. Fuck obligations.

Fuck the continued stubbornness from family members who are standing in the way of everyone else's peace.

"You can watch from the windows," Vicki says, shooing Lorelei and me away.

Fuck watching from the windows too.

I slip around the prep table until I'm standing behind Amanda, settling my hands on her waist and pressing a kiss to her hairnet-covered hair. "You okay?" I ask softly.

"Fantastic."

If that's fantastic, I don't want to know what she'd sound like if she ever confessed to being miserable.

"I could use your opinion on a tux today," I say, louder.

"She's busy," Vicki says.

"I can make the gingerbread," Kimberly says.

"Amanda needs to."

"She's getting married tomorrow and we all have your party tonight and the world won't stop if we run out of gingerbread one or two days in late summer."

"She's marrying the enemy and trying to get out of her family duties."

"She doesn't owe us this, Vicki."

"And what happens to the Gingerbread House next?"

"Stop," Amanda says. "Please. Please stop. Grandma, weddings are hard enough when the families *do* get along. And you can't just tell someone that she has to give up her entire life to move home and expect her to just go along with it when I've never been able to bake, I've never loved baking, and I've always been told Ben would do it, and now I'm supposed to walk away from a job I love and a community I love and volunteer work that I love to move home because you don't want to consider that maybe it's time for the Gingerbread House to have new owners." She yanks off her prep gloves and sets them on the table. "I can't do this today. I need a break. I need to breathe. I need to think. Okay?"

She spins to me and grabs my hand. "Let's go pick a tux. Lorelei, tell your dad we'll be by to try fruitcake soon, okay?"

"Amanda, if you walk out that door . . . ," Vicki says.

Amanda's shoulders bunch even higher.

And that's when Lorelei breaks through the tension with a single question. "Where's your engagement ring?"

Chapter 26

Amanda

The ring.

The ring is gone.

I had it when I left the house this morning, and it's no longer on my finger, and I don't know where it is.

I don't know where it is.

Was it on my hand when Grandma chastised me to put on gloves?

Oh my god.

It wasn't.

It wasn't.

Was I wearing it when I got here? Was it on my hand during the gingerbread candle ceremony? Did I have it on when I left the cabin?

Yes.

Yes, I had it on when I left the cabin. I smiled at it glinting in the light when I was driving into town.

But I stopped to thank Mrs. Briggs for her gift the other day. And then I got distracted when I saw Pia walking down the street, and I popped into her bakery to get cookies for Dane.

I decided today and tomorrow require my soon-to-be-former-fake-fiancé to have a stash of his favorite cookies.

And I don't remember if my ring was on my finger when I was talking to Mrs. Briggs and Pia.

I'm already off-kilter from telling Grandma that I don't want the bakery, but now, I'm gaping at Dane. I need to say something. Anything. Apologize. Make this better.

For him.

He paid thousands of dollars for that ring and *I lost it.*

I'm completely and totally frozen.

This is it.

This is when he's going to break up with me—for real and for pretend—and it's all over.

We're done.

He's going to yell at me and dump me and our grandparents still hate each other and his uncle is still not convinced and all of this is over and I just told my grandma that I don't want the bakery and we didn't get done what we wanted to get done.

We'll leave the town worse off now than it was before we agreed to our plan.

I still can't speak, but suddenly I'm being crushed against his chest, both of his arms around me. "It's okay. We'll find it. And if we don't, it's just a ring."

It's just a ring.

But it's not.

Not to me.

It's every kind thing he's done for me this past week. It's how he's gone so far above what I expected. It's his patience and understanding and quiet acceptance of me no matter what I do, big or small, from blurting out that I was engaged to him to now, losing the engagement ring.

And I'm supposed to let him go.

"I didn't take it off," I whisper.

"So it's probably here in the kitchen somewhere."

If the situation were reversed, if he'd lost the engagement ring I'd given him, my family would take the first opportunity to say he'd never deserved it.

"I stopped a few places on my way here. I don't—I don't remember when I last knew I had it on my hand."

"I don't remember either," Mom says quietly next to us. "I don't remember looking at your ring today. Vicki, did you look at Amanda's hand? Was she wearing her ring when she got here?"

"I . . . did not," my grandmother replies.

She's not gloating.

She doesn't sound happy.

But why would she be happy after what I just told her?

"Why don't we start looking here—" Lorelei starts, but that's apparently too much for my grandmother, who snorts loudly.

"You can go look in Amanda's car," she says. "I won't have strangers snooping around my bakery."

"*Vicki*," Mom says again.

"I'd say that about anyone who doesn't work here coming into my kitchen," Grandma says. "And it's still my kitchen until I actually retire. With a *family member* taking over."

Mom sighs.

Dane sighs too. He still hasn't let me go, and he's stroking my back like a comforting pat can somehow make this all better.

I appreciate that he's patient.

But I lost my engagement ring. My *fake* engagement ring.

The one that he deserves to have back.

Every time I think I'm doing something good, I mess it up.

"Can you check my car?" I say to Lorelei. "And I saw Pia. And Mrs. Briggs. It could—it could've fallen off anywhere between their shops."

I can do this much.

I can ask my hometown best friend and my fake fiancé to check the other places I've been today while Mom and Grandma and I search the kitchen.

"I'm on it," Lorelei says. "And I'll text and give them a heads-up to look for it too."

I look up at Dane. "I'm so sorry."

He quirks a brow at me, and then the best-worst thing ever happens.

He smiles.

He freaking *smiles*.

"We'll find it," he says. "And if we don't, it can be the next great Tinsel mystery for all of the tourists to look for it. People love a good treasure hunt. And as you so wisely pointed out earlier this week, you don't need a ring to get married."

It's the best and the worst thing he could possibly say.

He spent thousands—*thousands*—of dollars on a fake engagement ring, and I lost it, and he's already on the bright side.

"I don't deserve you," I blurt.

It's the absolute truth.

But he doesn't take advantage of my statement to break up with me.

Instead, he pulls me closer again and squeezes tightly, like he never wants to let me go.

"You deserve so much more than you know," he murmurs quietly.

It's been years since I actively wanted a man in my life.

And I don't know how I'll ever let Dane go.

Chapter 27

Dane

Vicki Anderson is breaking.

In the good way.

We've been searching the bakery for hours. Every time Amanda tears up, Vicki flinches.

I'll never claim to be an expert at reading people I don't know, but I don't think those are flinches of a woman who's horrified that her granddaughter has made a terrible choice in fiancés and doesn't want to inherit a bakery.

I think that's the flinch of a woman who's starting to feel bad for standing in the way of her granddaughter's happiness.

She might never like me.

My family.

She might never like *my family.*

But I think she's starting to see the harm that the feud has done.

"Did you get on the floor and look under the prep table?" she says to me at one point. "My old bones don't like me bending that way anymore."

I look under the prep table. I shine a light under the fridge and under the ovens. I help pull everything out of the fridge and ovens. I help put it back. I search the dining room. Behind the counters, even though Amanda says she wasn't behind the display cases and checkout counters.

I don't get kicked out.

And honestly, they'd have to call the sheriff if they wanted me to leave. So long as Amanda wants me here, I'm here.

By early afternoon, it's pretty clear the ring isn't in the bakery.

Lorelei's activated the entire town.

Everyone's looking for the ring outside the bakery too.

Including Uncle Rob, apparently.

"Are you *sure* you were wearing it when you left the cabin?" Kimberly asks Amanda as we all sit together at one of the tables in the dining room.

Amanda won't make eye contact with me. Her eyes are dull and her lips angled down, and even her hair seems to have lost some of its curl. "I'm absolutely positive I was wearing it in the car."

I've thoroughly searched the car.

It's not there.

We've retraced basically every step she made since getting here, though there were some glances between the women that tell me I'm missing something.

I loop my arm around Amanda, feeling absolutely helpless. "It'll turn up."

She meets my gaze for the first time in what feels like an eternity. "I'm so sorry."

"It will turn up," I repeat.

It was a hefty chunk of change.

But I wasn't going to return it. I knew what I was investing in when I bought it, and it wasn't a fiancée, no matter how much I like Amanda.

Damn thing's working to soften up Uncle Rob because it's lost.

And I know she didn't lose it on purpose. The Amanda I know—the Amanda I believe in—would not have lost it.

But maybe she's devastated that this was supposed to be my excuse to break up with her because she doesn't want to do it herself, and I'm not playing along.

That thought, more than anything else today, is what has my heart twisting itself into a knot.

"You don't need a ring to get married," Kimberly says. "Dane's right about that."

My phone buzzes with an incoming text message.

I check to see if it's Lorelei with good news, but it's a number I don't recognize.

> Is this Dane? My name is Winona. I'm the Tinsel town historian. I got a message you wanted to talk about some letters.

Amanda makes a noise next to me. She's reading it too.

"Did someone find it?" Kimberly asks.

"Cake emergency," Amanda blurts at the same time as I say, "Tux shop needs me ASAP."

Kimberly and Vicki stare at us.

I shove my seat back.

Amanda leaps out of hers too.

"What's going on?" Vicki asks.

"I forgot I stopped at the bridge to make a wish that our entire families would be happy for us on my drive in, and someone just texted that they thought they saw something shiny in the water but they can't dive in, and I didn't want to tell you how much it hurts that you're being an asshole about me marrying Dane, but we're going to go see if we can find my ring in the creek," Amanda says. "I'll be back for your party tonight. Probably."

She's operating at half-strength perkiness, but the *asshole* comment still lands.

Vicki and Kimberly are both slack jawed as Amanda and I push back from the table and head out the front door.

I'm calling Winona the minute we're a shop away from the Gingerbread House.

And fifteen minutes later, she's showing us into the archives room at city hall again.

"You're not the first people to ask about this in the past month," she tells us as she lays out a spread of original letters on a wooden table in the musty-smelling room. "I got curious, so I dug these out myself and took them home to look them over during my off hours."

"You've been sending us copies," Amanda says.

Winona shakes her head. "I have not."

"But these are the letters we got," I say.

There's the letter about George breaking Maud's heart.

The one about George stealing the dowry.

And more that we haven't seen yet.

At least a half dozen more.

Including letters back from Lucy, my great-great-great-great-aunt.

I've read all of them three times, but I'm not learning anything new.

George and Maud were engaged. Lucy sent the dowry. George got the dowry, broke up with Maud, and married Minnie instead.

Okay, we learn Minnie didn't give birth for another thirteen months and that my great-great-great-grandmother was convinced that it was either the world's longest pregnancy or that Minnie had lost a baby and not told anyone.

And we learn that my family has a deep and abiding dislike of Amanda's family.

"So my family couldn't let go that a romantic relationship didn't work out, and they claim a dowry is missing, but we have no record of what the dowry was," I say quietly.

"That's my read," Winona agrees.

"Do you have any letters or records about the Andersons?" I ask.

"Nothing until they built the original Gingerbread House right after the war."

"The Gingerbread House," Amanda whispers. "Oh my god. *Oh my god.*"

I arch my brows at her. "The Gingerbread House?"

"This one." She points to a letter from Lucy. "May I please have a copy of this letter?"

I skim the letter again. "What are you seeing that I'm not?"

"The handwriting."

I lift my gaze to her.

Her eyes are shiny, but not sad.

Not completely.

There's a level of triumph in there too. "I think I solved the rest of the mystery. But I need a copy of this. And then I need to do something. Alone."

She pinches her lips together, and her eyes go shinier. "Oh my god," she whispers again. "This could change everything."

Chapter 28

Amanda

"You haven't broken up with me yet," I say quietly to Dane as we head back to the Gingerbread House. I have to concentrate on something other than my suspicions if I'm going to keep my cool.

"I don't like to ruin fun" is his only answer.

He doesn't parrot it back at me—*you haven't broken up with me yet either*—and he doesn't say *I was thinking we should do blah blah blah to break up* either.

I slip my hand into his and squeeze.

He squeezes back.

And we walk the rest of the way back down Kringle Lane looking exactly like what we're pretending to be—a happily engaged couple who apparently forgive each other nearly everything.

No one would look at us and think we were faking this. That we're breaking up sometime in the next twenty-four hours. That in three days, hopefully I'll be back in New York running auditions for my play and Dane will be back in San Francisco.

They wouldn't even know I lost Dane's engagement ring.

"I'll pay you back for the ring," I say.

"No need."

"But I—"

"It'll turn up."

"Dane!" someone calls from across the street.

We both look over at his uncle, standing in the doorway of the Fruitcake Emporium.

Rob winces. "And Amanda," he adds. "Have you found the ring?"

We both shake our heads.

"Your grandpa said to tell you that your grandma lost her engagement ring once too," he says. "She found it later inside a fruitcake."

"If you're offering to let me eat your whole stock to see if my ring's in there, I'm game," I call.

Dane looks down at me and smiles a soft smile. "You are truly one of a kind."

"I'm pretty sure every person who's ever bought an expensive engagement ring for another person is very grateful for that."

"*Stop.* It'll turn up."

He doesn't add *and if it doesn't, it's probably because it was stolen.*

But that's another thought that's started lingering in the back of my mind.

Did my grandmother steal my ring during the ceremony this morning?

Did we hold hands at any point?

I can't remember.

But I know she doesn't want me to marry Dane. I know she's known all week that I'm hesitant about taking over the bakery. And it wouldn't be the first time someone in our family did something shitty in the name of winning.

Or so I'm reasonably certain I'm about to prove.

"I'm happy to get you as much fruitcake as you want, Amanda," Rob calls. "I'll even ship to—to wherever you are."

Dane and I both look at him.

Have we done it?

Have we convinced him to give up the feuding too?

"I won't make the same offer to your grandmother until she apologizes for telling me that the raisins Dad painted on our shop a few years ago looked like turds, but you're not your grandmother. You make my nephew happy. So I—I'm sorry. I'll try to do better."

"And this is why I don't give two shits if that ring never shows up again," Dane murmurs to me while he squeezes my hand tighter.

"Does this mean I can call you Uncle Rob?" I call back across the street.

Rob flinches.

Then squeezes his eyes shut.

I can almost hear him sigh too.

"You know what? Sure. And not because it would piss off your grandmother. Just because if it would make you happy, and you're marrying my nephew, why not?"

"Aww, thank you! I promise I'll send good Christmas presents. My relatives get only the best."

Shut. Up. Amanda.

That could make it worse.

Dane snorts quietly beside me, and when I glance up at him, he's repressing a smile.

But he can't hide the amusement in his eyes. "Very nicely done," he murmurs.

"See you soon, Uncle Rob," I call across the street with a wave. "I'm glad we don't have to uninvite you from the wedding."

Yep, that's me, still not listening to my orders to myself to shut up.

"Don't make that face," Dane calls to him. "She's funny. The sooner you appreciate that, the happier you'll be."

Quieter, to me, he says, "Wave goodbye and let's leave well enough alone now."

I blow Uncle Rob a kiss. "Toodles!"

"I fucking adore you," Dane says.

Oh, my heart.

For all that it's prancing happily in a field of sunflowers while swooning over this man today, it will hurt like hell tomorrow.

But that's why I have today.

Right now.

This moment where Dane's smiling while he opens the door of the Gingerbread House for me, the familiar *Ho ho ho!* announcing our arrival.

Mom's behind the counter, checking out some customers. "Did you find it?" she asks.

"Not the ring, no," Dane says.

"I need to look in the kitchen again," I tell her.

Mom looks at Dane, then back to me. "Okay."

"Is Grandma back there?"

"She went home to get ready for the party."

So the kitchen is empty.

Good.

I pull Dane down the hallway and into the kitchen, where I lock the door and shut the blinds.

And then I head to the desk.

I didn't clearly see Grandma pop the secret compartment, but when I can't figure it out on my own, I tell Dane what I'm trying to do, and within moments, he has it open.

But the recipe isn't there.

"What the hell?" I mutter.

I lean into the drawer, peering into the corners, looking under the cover to the compartment, feeling around. "Is there another lower compartment?"

"What are you looking for?"

"A recipe."

"Stored in a secret compartment."

"It's old. And . . ." I pull out the folded photocopy of Lucy's letter. "I think the handwriting matches."

He sucks in a breath. "You think the recipe was the dowry."

"I do. But the recipe isn't here, and I don't want to jump to conclusions. I want to see if the handwriting matches."

"If the dowry was a recipe, and Lucy wrote it for Maud, why wouldn't she have just written it again?"

I bite my lip and stare at him. "That's a very good question."

An excellent question, in fact.

My shoulders droop.

My entire *body* droops.

"There could be a logical explanation," Dane says. "You could be right. And it would explain continued hostilities."

"I don't *like* this as an option," I whisper. "It means my family did really shitty things to yours and then benefited from it for years. *Decades.* Generations. But—"

"It makes sense," he says quietly.

I sigh and drop my forehead to his chest like I've leaned on him for years, and he loops his arms around me like he's comforted me just as long.

How does this feel so right when it's so new?

And when it's ending tomorrow? If not sooner?

"I am so grateful for you," I tell him.

His grip around me tightens. I wrap my arms around his waist and hug him back, our bodies lining up. A hard ridge presses into my belly, growing harder and thicker with each passing second.

My nipples tighten, and my panties are instantly wet.

"Sorry," he mutters.

I shake my head, then go up on tiptoe to kiss him, holding his face in my hands. "I like it," I whisper.

"Fuck, Amanda, I can't resist you."

"Same."

I barely register that I'm pushing his jacket off his shoulders until it hits the floor. My hands slide up under his T-shirt without conscious thought. He cradles my ass in his large hands and holds me tighter against his fabulous hard-on until I can't help myself as I hook one leg around his hip and let him pull me up so I can wrap both legs around him.

He kisses me hard, deep, his tongue hot and demanding, while he turns us to settle me on the desk.

We're in the kitchen.

We should *not* do this in my grandmother's kitchen.

But when he palms my breasts and presses his thumbs to my aching nipples, there's zero chance we're *not* doing this in my grandmother's kitchen.

He makes me feel so good.

Not just my body.

My heart. My mind. My soul.

He makes my entire being float. Makes me believe there's nothing I can't do. That everything I am is perfect, just as I am.

"I shouldn't—" he starts, pulling out of the kiss, his thumbs still working magic on my nipples.

"You absolutely should," I gasp in response.

"Just—so—perfect." He nibbles my neck.

I pant and try to tug him closer, but he's bent over the desk, over me, and I can't get him as close as I want him.

"I want you," I whimper. "I can't get enough of you."

The door rattles across the kitchen. "Amanda?" my mom calls.

"*Dammit*," I gasp.

"Fuck," he agrees.

He lifts his head and drops his forehead to mine. "We're going to have to stop."

I don't know if he means stop *now*, or stop altogether.

Either way, I don't like it.

"Amanda?" Mom calls again.

"Come in," I yell, aware that she can't.

Can she?

Does she have a key?

Dane yanks upright and adjusts his cock, giving me a *please don't invite your mother in while I can't control my dick* look that shouldn't make me smile, but does.

He wants me.

I like that. And I want him. I want him *so* badly.

I adjust my nipples, which isn't really a thing, but it's the closest I can think of to make him feel not so alone in being visibly turned on.

He squeezes his eyes shut for a brief second, but a smile is playing on his lips.

"Am I ridiculous?" I ask.

"In all of the best ways."

"Amanda, I'm unlocking this door," Mom calls.

I slide off the desk and hastily put the secret compartment back together.

The lock clicks open behind me.

Dane turns to studiously examine the worker schedule, or possibly the requisite workplace signs, on the bulletin board next to the desk.

And Mom totally catches me in the drawer.

"What are you doing?" She's looking at me like she was afraid of what she'd find when she walked in here.

"Trying to solve a mystery," I answer honestly.

"What mystery?"

"Why our families don't get along."

She sighs. "Your father always told me the only people who knew the full story were dead and buried, and I've never gotten anything more from your grandmother. I can't fix this for you two, but I promise I'll be better myself. It . . . wasn't right of me to decide to hate people just because my husband asked me to."

"Could be worse reasons," Dane says.

"Dad wouldn't have asked you to hate the Silvers if he didn't have a good reason." Loyalty is my default when it comes to my dad.

I miss him. He wasn't perfect, but he was my dad, and I will always miss him.

But Mom shakes her head. "He never gave me a reason. Your father was a good man, but that's a red flag. You two are correct. There's no reason why our family shouldn't get along with the Silvers. No reason why we can't start fresh with a clean slate."

"Grandma doesn't agree," I say.

"My grandparents aren't there yet either," Dane says.

He's being as polite as a person can be while angling his body away so she can't see the way his pants are still bulging in the crotch.

This man.

I need five minutes alone with him in a broom closet, stat.

"That might have to be their problem," Mom says. "I'm on your side. But I can't work miracles this fast."

Dane nods to her. "Thank you. Your support all on its own is more than enough."

I would very much like to go a full hour without my eyes welling up and my sinuses getting hot and my throat feeling froggy.

But today will apparently not be the day that that happens.

"It only extends as far as you don't hurt my daughter," Mom says.

"Mom."

She crosses her arms and goes full-on Mom on me. "I'd say that to any man. Even a serial killer. Are you still going to your grandmother's party tonight?"

I sigh. Then wince at myself for sighing. Then sigh again. "Yes."

"Then you'd better head back to the cabin and get ready. It's getting late."

I look up at Dane.

He nods.

He's in.

"Mom?" I say quietly. "I'm not the best person to join you here. I'm honestly not."

She blinks quickly as her eyes start to shine too. "I know, sweetheart. But I don't know what else to do."

"I need the recipe."

"Why?"

"Just . . . trust me. Please. I need the recipe. I think—I think it might be able to tell me what to do."

"It's not in the drawer?"

I shake my head.

"Then your grandmother must have it." Her brow furrows. "Or it's with your engagement ring."

"Or both."

"Oh, honey . . ." She crosses the kitchen and pulls me into a hug.

She doesn't tell me Grandma didn't take the ring.

She doesn't tell me I won't find answers in a recipe.

She just hugs me.

And then the best-worst thing ever happens, and Dane loops his arms around both of us and hugs us too.

Chapter 29

Dane

Wanting to punch something isn't my default, but I want to punch something now.

For the second night in a row, Amanda's on edge as we head into town for a family event where everyone in town except the other's family is invited.

She's in the gold dress tonight, and all I can think of is how much I want to peel her out of it.

"I know we need to talk about how we're going to not go through with the wedding," she says as I drive us into town for her grandmother's announcement, "but can we maybe wait until after the party tonight?"

A million knives slash my heart, but I give her the only answer that anyone could possibly give. "Of course."

"I just—it's dumb to think a recipe could've been Maud's dowry."

"It's not dumb." Especially since she can't find the recipe. It's not in the desk where it was this morning. It's not in any other hidey-holes that Amanda knows of at the bakery.

Kimberly either.

She knew a few more safe spots to look.

But the recipe is gone. It's as missing as the engagement ring.

"Maybe your grandma wants it with her for something tied to her retirement announcement," I say. "We should still compare the handwriting. You said it was old?"

"*Old* old. Definitely as old as the letters Winona showed us." She has her hands twisted in her lap, and I notice she reaches for the missing ring to fiddle with more than once.

"It does make sense that something like a recipe would've been a dowry," I say slowly, ignoring the voice whispering *and that means the recipe should belong to Lorelei*. One step at a time here, and we are *not* at that step yet. "My ancestors' letters said that George said he was tricked about the dowry. Getting something like a recipe when you're expecting cash or jewels or even a dozen chickens or something would be . . . surprising."

"It would suck," she says, not dancing around it. "Recipes can't lay eggs to feed you."

Despite the heavy atmosphere in the car, I smile. "Exactly. Recipes cost as much money as a bride."

Thankfully, she laughs a little at that.

But then she sighs one of those heavy sighs that says there's entirely too much weighing her down when tonight should've been so different. For so many reasons. "It would be amazing if someone tonight just *knows* something and flat-out tells us . . . wouldn't it?"

"It would," I agree.

We pull into the parking lot of the community center fifteen minutes before the party is scheduled to begin, but we're not the first guests.

Not by a long shot.

Half the town seems to already be here.

"We were all looking for the ring all day, so we just came early," Mrs. Briggs tells us when we run into her inside.

High-top tables are situated around the room, all of them adorned with baskets of individually wrapped gingerbread men. Brown and pink streamers and balloons line the edges of the room, and there's a giant stuffed gingerbread man sitting on a chair on the small stage at one end of the room.

"I warned you about this tragedy thing," Mr. Briggs says to me.

"Mr. Briggs. We are *not* breaking up over a silly ring," Amanda says.

Is it weird that I can feel her cringing on the inside? That I can practically hear her thinking *We're breaking up because this was fake all along but we need one more piece of evidence to fully put this feud between our families to bed before we can*?

Possibly I'm projecting.

Because that's how I'm feeling and what I'm thinking.

Amanda leans into me and gives the older man a cheeky grin. "He's just learning early how much I'm going to cost him."

I force an amused smile of my own. "Worth every penny."

Everyone in town wants to know details of the wedding. No one's talking about Vicki's anniversary and the rumor that she's announcing her retirement, unlike last night, when everyone wanted to talk about how long my grandparents had been married.

Except Uncle Rob.

Who's walking into Vicki Anderson's party in suit pants and a button-down shirt, Aunt Teeny and Esme and Jojo beside him.

My jaw unhinges.

And then it snaps shut while irritation chokes me right about the same place my tie is sitting.

"I invited your entire family," Kimberly says to me as she joins us. "I called your father and told him I was ready to present a united front of support for you two and that he could bring anyone he wanted who was willing to do the same."

The irritation choking me morphs into something different as Uncle Rob's gaze meets mine, and he gives me an awkward smile.

Esme beams.

Amanda sucks in a breath that comes with a hitch that I feel in the pit of my stomach.

She's touched too.

I subconsciously reach for her hand. She meets mine halfway.

Three to go.

Just our grandparents now.

The hardest of the bunch.

Silence descends among the early party guests as everyone watches my family approach us. Dad's not here. Lorelei's not here.

But if Uncle Rob is here, they're likely not far behind.

Uncle Rob extends a hand to me as he reaches us. "Never too late to admit you've been wrong and start over, is it?"

"It is not." I'd like to be more eloquent, but I wasn't prepared for this and I'm not always quick on my feet.

Uncle Rob turns to my fake fiancée. "Amanda, I apologize. You've done nothing to me or my family that would justify the way I've treated you."

"Thank you," Amanda says. "I know this isn't easy for anyone, and I can't begin to express what it means to Dane and me that you're all here and willing to try to get along for our sake."

"It's a summer Christmas miracle," Esme murmurs.

"I just married into this baloney," Aunt Teeny says.

Kimberly smiles at her. "Same. Did I hear you quilt? I've always wanted to learn."

Esme hugs me. "I'm so proud of you," she whispers. "It's about time someone ended this so that no one else ever has to suffer in love."

There's something in her voice that has me lifting a brow at her.

What's in it for her if our families make up? She was in Amanda's brother's grade in school, but to the best of my knowledge, they weren't secret friends.

But they could've been.

She blushes, then gently shoves my arm. "That was a long time ago," she mutters.

I look at Amanda. Then back at Esme. "Did you—" I start, but she cuts me off.

"I'm a happily married woman with the best daughter a woman could ask for. Don't go telling yourself stories."

Amanda's eyes are dinner plates. "Wait, wait. Did you and my—"

"*Happily married woman,*" Esme repeats.

"You gave us the letters," Amanda breathes. "Winona said she didn't. But *you* did."

"What letters?" Kimberly asks.

"Mama, can I have a gingerbread man?" Jojo asks.

"Absolutely," Esme says. "Let's go find the prettiest one. Thank you for the invitation, Kimberly. It's fascinating to see how Andersons party after all of these years."

Amanda whips out her phone, mutters something about time zones, and fires off a text. I'm not trying to spy, but I can't help but notice it's a message to her brother in all caps and demanding an answer to the same question I have. DID YOU HAVE A THING FOR ESME SILVER IN HIGH SCHOOL??

She doesn't get an answer before Vicki arrives.

Vicki's wearing a gold dress with frilly sparkles that hangs down midcalf. I realize her short hair is brighter with the red and green stripes, like she had it touched up, and I wonder if I just didn't notice earlier today. She's also wearing makeup, including something glittery that makes little spots all over her face glint in the light.

Amanda sucks in a big breath and squeezes my hand tighter.

On her mom's recommendation, she's going along with whatever Vicki says tonight.

We'll fix everything else later, Kimberly said. *I don't want you to spend your life miserable. I want you to be happy.*

I want her to be happy too.

I want to be what makes her happy.

And instead, our breakup is looming over us.

Our engagement has always been fake, but it never felt more so than it does tonight.

Chapter 30

Amanda

I used to love parties, but this week, they're the absolute bane of my existence.

Last night's anniversary party was awkward.

Tonight's party is even worse. On top of the questions about the wedding, I'm getting questions about where Dane and I will live with Grandma passing her share of the bakery to me.

Grandma hasn't even made the announcement yet, but everyone knows it's coming.

Fiftieth anniversary of taking over the bakery party.

No one believes that.

Everyone knows I'm the only one of her grandchildren here because she plans to name me as her successor.

Secrets in this town are apparently only well kept when they're about why two families are feuding.

Grandma makes her rounds visiting with all her guests and making sure they're enjoying their gingerbread and insisting that they enjoy the light appetizers and the wine bar too. Mom's pulled in, too, doing much of the same.

But the deeper we get into the first hour of mingling, the more questions pop up about where Dane and I will live.

It gets overwhelming enough that I escape to the bathroom, feeling like a complete asshole for leaving Dane to handle the questions solo.

Lorelei follows me. She and her dad arrived not long after Grandma. "Are you okay?" she demands after checking all the stalls to make sure we're alone.

"I don't want to run the bakery," I blurt.

"Duh. You belong in the city." She visibly clamps her mouth shut like she's keeping herself from asking *which city, by the way?*

"And I really wanted my grandma and your grandparents to get over this stupid fight before my wedding." God, I hate lying to Lorelei.

She trusts us.

What will she think tomorrow? Will she figure out that we've been faking when we break up? Will she be brokenhearted that we've called it off?

Why can't she see that we're lying *right now* and give me some sign that she's been going along with it for the good of Tinsel?

She wraps me in a tight hug. "There's a reason you two have always been my two favorite people in the world, and everything you've done this week has cemented it. This will work out. I promise you, this will all work out, and you'll be happy. I can *feel* it."

Not. Helping. "I want to feel it, too, and tonight, I just *can't*."

"You'll feel it tomorrow. Tomorrow is what matters."

I suck in a heavy breath at the thought that tomorrow, Dane and I have to break up in just the right way to make sure our families don't start arguing again, while knowing we'll be breaking Lorelei's heart probably almost as much as I'll be breaking my own.

Which is not what I need to think about tonight.

I inhale again and get a hint of nutmeg and ginger on my bestie. "You smell nice."

"I perfumed for the occasion."

Lorelei doesn't wear perfume. She's allergic.

But she bakes.

She's always baked.

The only reason she's not involved in the fruitcake side of her family's business is that she doesn't like it.

"I wish you could take my place in the bakery," I whisper, not even realizing how true it is until the words escape my lips.

But I do.

I wish she could take my place.

Especially if the recipe was originally her family's.

She sucks in a heavy breath of her own. "I think that's a stretch too far."

"For you?"

"For our families."

"Fuck our families," I grumble.

She laughs. "Next week. For now, let's pretend we're all very happy for our families."

We take a few minutes where I ask Lorelei if she knows anything about Esme possibly having a crush on my brother back in high school—she swears she knows nothing—before we emerge from the bathroom to return to the party.

I instantly wish we'd stayed inside.

The party is breaking out in pandemonium.

Why?

Because Dane and Lorelei's grandparents have arrived.

And my grandmother is not happy about it.

"I said, *you are welcome to leave*," Grandma says loudly.

Not that she has to speak loudly.

No one else is saying a word while they have a stare-down in the middle of the room.

"We're here to make amends at the request of our grandson," Dane's grandpa says.

"You're here to *look* like you're making amends," Grandma replies. "I know this game. Look like the bigger person while someone else is out putting salt in my gas tank."

Dane slips to my side.

He looks as weary as I feel.

"Could you quit being a suspicious ass for one minute for the sake of someone else?" Dane's grandmother snaps.

"Could you quit acting like I'm the problem here?" Grandma snaps back.

"You *are* the problem."

"This is *my party*. I didn't interrupt yours, did I? No. No, I didn't."

"Maybe it's good to let them get it out before the wedding?" Lorelei murmurs.

"And don't even think about passing gas in here," Grandma adds to Mr. Silver.

"*He does not have gas, you hussy*," Mrs. Silver screeches. "That was *your* husband! *He* always tooted in the market!"

Dane and Lorelei's father and uncle both hustle over to the Silver grandparents while Mom leaps between them. "Vicki. Let's go get a drink and take a deep breath. This isn't worth making a scene."

"*They're* making a scene."

"No offense, Amanda, but I don't think it's my grandparents making a scene," Lorelei murmurs.

"No offense taken. I don't think you're wrong."

"We should sign them up for a reality TV show," Esme says from Dane's other side. "*Old People Fighting over Stupid Shit.* It would be a train wreck and it would make millions."

"Mom, Dad, maybe we should go," Dane's dad says.

"*We were invited*," Dane's grandma snarls.

And suddenly, I can't take it anymore. "*Enough*," I snap.

Every eyeball in the room turns to stare at me.

"That's. Enough," I repeat.

Dane squeezes my hand.

"We're not actually engaged," my mouth says before my brain can stop it.

Exclamations of surprise go up around the room.

Dane jerks a look at me.

I squeeze his hand tighter. I don't want to let go.

But I've started this and now I can't stop it.

"I made it up," I tell the entire community gathered here. "I made up the whole lie about being engaged to a Silver because I don't want to move home and make the Gingerbread House my whole life. I have a life and a community and a job I love in New York. And a play. I wrote a freaking *play* and we revitalized our community theater to put it on."

I need to shut up.

I need to stop talking.

But Dane squeezes my hand, a quiet *I've got your back*, and more comes tumbling out of my mouth. "When I told Dane, he agreed to go along with it because he hates how much our families fight, and because he knows Lorelei is one of my favorite people in the entire world and he just wanted us to be able to go to dinner without having to sneak around for fear of making any of our elders upset. And *that's so fucking stupid.*"

"Amanda," my grandmother whispers.

It's so quiet in here.

So quiet.

"Your grandfather stole our family's secret gingerbread recipe from the Silvers," I say. "He was engaged to Dane's great-great-grandmother, but he dumped her because he said he was tricked, and he refused to give the dowry back. The dowry was the gingerbread recipe. Everything we've built our family fortune on started with a recipe that was a stolen dowry."

"*Amanda*," Grandma says stronger.

"Ooohhhhh, that makes so much sense," someone in the crowd says. Winona. The town historian. "All of those letters . . ."

"Great-great-great-however-many-times Lucy saying that she couldn't send it again because her mom had been struck with the fever and wasn't lucid," Esme whispers. "She couldn't recite the recipe again."

"I can't find the recipe to prove it, but the handwriting matches," I say. *"I know the handwriting matches."*

It does.

I'm not making that up.

Why would I make up something that would hurt my family?

Grandma Vicki gapes at me.

I can't give up my grip on Dane's hand.

This is it. I've ruined it all. It's over.

And I can't let go of his hand.

I don't want to let go of his hand.

At the same time, I can't bring myself to look at him.

I got us into this with my big mouth.

And now I've ended it with my big mouth.

"I'm sorry," I add in a whisper.

I don't know if I'm apologizing to Dane or to Grandma or to my mom or to the entire Silver family on behalf of what my family did to them.

I just know I'm sorry.

So, so sorry.

"You faked being engaged so that we'd get along with the Andersons?" Rob says.

"Without a single regret," Dane answers. "I'm done being a pawn in your feud. Find something else to brag about or shut the hell up."

He's not trying to shake me off. Not trying to get away from me.

"You promised no tragedies," Mr. Briggs says.

"That's in our family's hands now," Dane replies. "But as for my generation, the Silvers are completely good with the Andersons. This feud ends with us."

My eyes water. My throat threatens to close in on itself.

He's a good man.

Doing the right thing for all the right reasons.

The community center door bangs open, and one of the daytime Gingerbread House staff comes dashing in, wearing an apron and a hairnet.

"I found it!" she shrieks. *"I found the engagement ring in a ball of dough!* And look at it—the mixer didn't mess it up a single bit."

She lifts the ring, making it sparkle in the light.

My breath catches in my throat.

The mixer didn't mess it up.

I look at Grandma.

She stares back at me with the guiltiest of guilty expressions on her face as her entire complexion goes paler than real winter snow.

"Amanda," she starts, and then she clutches her chest.

"Oh, no, you don't," I say. "You are *not* pulling that again."

"Sincerely, Vicki, don't do this," Mom says, quieter, but everyone can hear her.

"I didn't want—" Grandma starts, but she doesn't finish.

And that's when I start to realize she might not be faking it this time.

What's whiter than snow? That's Grandma's face. Her breathing is rapidly growing labored, and she's reaching for one of the tables for support.

Mr. Briggs leaps to her side and holds her while she slumps against him, gasping. "Someone call 911," he says. "I think this one's real."

Chapter 31

Dane

Does anyone like hospitals?

I don't. They smell like badly covered sickness and death.

Amanda looks as comfortable as a fish in a desert. Her mom can't sit still and keeps pacing the waiting area. Lorelei's picking at her fingernails.

She doesn't merely dislike hospitals. She actively hates them.

But she's here.

"I'm sorry," Amanda says one more time.

"This is *not* your fault," her mom says.

I squeeze her knee while a new kind of guilt beats me over the heart. "It's not your fault," I agree.

It's mine.

I'm the one who insisted we stay fake engaged. I egged her on. I pushed to get the engagement ring. I kissed her in public to sell this.

And then I fell for her for real.

How could I not?

But I fell for her for real, and I just wanted to be with her more and more, and I lost sight of the fact that we could be doing real damage to our families in our pursuit of ending the feud.

I know we did this for the right reasons.

I know I deserve better than to feel like my accomplishments have more worth than being used to make our family feel better than theirs.

But I should've seen how much stress it could put on our grandparents.

That they're too set in their ways.

Victims of what they were fed their entire lives who didn't have the resources to get over it the way my generation does.

"It *is* my fault," Amanda whispers.

"Not yours alone," I reply quietly.

"Stop. You didn't do anything wrong."

I rub my eyes.

We've officially—and very suddenly—broken up in the eyes of the town, our secret out there for everyone to know, and I don't know where that leaves us personally.

I still like her. I still want to be here for her.

Especially now, when she keeps grabbing her ring finger like she wants to twist the engagement ring that's no longer sitting on it.

The engagement ring she wore for show, and only for a few days.

But there's no reason for me to do anything other than head back to the cabin to gather my dog and my luggage and fly home.

Clear my head.

Decide who I need to apologize to for the lies this week.

If I even deserve to think about how much I enjoyed this week with Amanda.

How much I still don't want it to end.

"I think what you did was wonderful," Lorelei says.

As one of Amanda's oldest friends, she has more of a right to be here than I do. But we both followed along behind the ambulance and Kimberly's car to come wait for news about Vicki.

"I don't even care that I thought you were faking the whole thing and didn't trust me enough to tell me why," Lorelei adds. "I wanted it to be real. I thought if I treated you like it was real, I could manifest this being real."

So did I, sis.

So did I.

And it could be . . . but how?

Do we do what we claimed we did and date long distance?

Would she even want to?

And how inappropriate is it for me to sit here thinking about wanting her when we almost killed her grandmother?

I need fresh air. I need time and space to think. I need to recenter myself.

"You seemed so happy," Kimberly says quietly. "I've never seen you so happy with a boy—a man—before."

"I couldn't have pulled this off with anyone else," Amanda replies.

I want to look at her, but I can't.

What if I look at her and she's just being nice?

What if I look at her and I think she wants more, but I misread her expression?

What if she does want more?

Would she move to San Francisco? Would I move to New York?

How guilty will I feel for the rest of my life if her grandmother doesn't make it?

Why do I feel like the spot where my heart was two hours ago is now occupied by a black hole?

And don't ask what the ring in my pocket feels like.

"I'm sorry you had to do it at all to get the rest of us to pull our heads out of our collective asses," Kimberly says.

She's pacing.

Pacing in ivory flats over a blue rug patterned with concentric rings while the rest of us sit on stiff gray waiting room chairs.

They're cushioned.

That's nice.

Possibly the only *nice* thing in this situation.

"Grandma still hates the Silvers," Amanda whispers.

"She's retiring. She can go live in her own misery and completely step out of the Tinsel community if she insists on continuing to hate them over what our family did to them."

"Maybe after we're sure she's gonna pull through?" Amanda says.

I steal a glance at her.

She looks tired. Utterly beaten down by this entire situation. Like she needs an eggnog latte and to be thoroughly satisfied in bed.

Fuck me.

Was it just a few hours ago that I was ready to tear her clothes off inside the bakery kitchen?

And what now?

I can't fix her grandmother for her. Not her health. Not her opinions. Not her behavior.

And who was I to think that I could change the minds of people who've been set in their ways for seventy or more years?

"She'll pull through," I tell her. "Can I get you something? Eggnog latte? Fruitcake? A dog to pet?"

Her eyes go shiny while she blinks at me. "I'm sorry."

"*Stop.* You don't have to be sorry."

"We were supposed to plan the breakup story together."

"Your version worked very well." I wince. *Good job handling the breakup that I didn't want to have but don't have the courage to tell you.* "The moment was right. You did exactly what you—what we needed you to do."

"Pia says she's donating the cake to your reception even if you don't get married," Lorelei says. "And Mrs. Briggs wants to see you in your wedding dress having the time of your life, enjoying what you did for the community with bringing our families together."

"See?" I nudge her knee with mine. "All's well that ends well. And your grandmother will pull through. She was talking. She was breathing better. Whatever happened, she's in good hands."

Nothing is well.

I'm sick to my stomach, ignoring the constant humming inside my own head.

Vicki Anderson wouldn't be in the hospital right now if you hadn't faked your engagement. You tortured old people with weak hearts.

And when I drown that out, I go back to thinking about wanting to kiss Amanda.

I shouldn't be here.

I'm not helping.

"What if I was wrong about the recipe?" Amanda whispers.

Kimberly stops pacing to take the seat on Amanda's other side. "Even if you were, there's *something* that set the families at war, and it's something that doesn't matter anymore if none of us can remember it."

"Agreed," Lorelei says.

An older man in scrubs enters the waiting room. "Mrs. Anderson? Ms. Anderson? Vicki is asking for you."

Amanda and her mom both bolt to their feet.

"Is she okay?" Kimberly asks.

"How bad is it?" Amanda adds.

"We're still monitoring her, but indications are she'll be just fine."

I don't know whose exhalation of relief is loudest. Could be any one of the four of us.

"Indigestion again?" Amanda asks.

"I don't believe so. We can talk more in her room."

Fuck.

Fuck.

We *did* do this to her.

The man in scrubs nods toward the hallway. "This way, please."

They both start to follow the doctor, but Amanda pauses to turn and look at me. "Thank you. Again. For everything. I—I meant it when I said I hope we can stay friends."

Stay friends.

She has a lot on her plate right now. Her grandmother. Figuring out the bakery. Probably a lot of truth to share with her mom, much like I need to fully clear the air with my dad about how our families' feud has impacted me.

Dating is the last thing on her mind.

As it should be.

This was a week of purposeful fun with an expiration date.

And how utterly boring is *purposeful fun*?

I know I'm not boring. I got over Vanessa's reasons for breaking up with me a long time ago, especially as I started working through how all the negativity I've been surrounded with my entire life has impacted me.

But I'm not the vibrant ray of *life* that Amanda is either.

I nod to her even though my heart is screaming for me to kiss her in direct opposition to my brain screaming at me to apologize until I'm hoarse for trying to kill her grandmother. "Let me know if there's anything I can do to help."

Her smile is pained. "You've done so much already. I couldn't ask for more."

And she doesn't.

She walks away, scurrying to catch up to her mom and the doctor, their footsteps fading down the hallway.

"You like her," Lorelei whispers.

I don't deny it.

I can't.

"This week has been . . ."

Special.

Unexpected.

Fun.

Mine.

I can't accurately put into words what my time with Amanda has meant to me, much like I can't put into words how I feel knowing that it's over.

That she'll head back to New York. That I'll head back to San Francisco. That Tinsel will be better for what we did while we were here.

I shake my head. I don't want to talk about Amanda. "You should talk to Kimberly about working at the bakery once Vicki's fully retired."

"Because the recipe was ours to begin with?"

"Because you'd be happier there. You love to bake. You love this community. You love Christmas. You could fit there if you and Kimberly can work through all of the feud shit. And I have faith in you. In both of you."

She blinks at me, and then her eyes get shiny. "You did this for me."

"I did it for all of us. Definitely for you. So you could see Amanda in the open. Probably subconsciously to give you a shot at working at the Gingerbread House too. But I didn't mean—I didn't mean it to end with us in a hospital waiting room."

She throws her arms around me, and I take advantage of the opportunity to lean right back on my little sister.

"She likes you, too, you know," Lorelei says.

She might.

But does she like me in an *I would date him* kind of way, or in a *he was fun to hang out with for a week* kind of way?

And can I handle it if the truth is the latter?

She's free spirited. Impulsive. Fun.

It's half of what I adore about her, but I'm not.

Not regularly. I'm . . . quieter.

She'd get bored with me if there wasn't something like a fake engagement and a series of mysterious letters keeping us together.

"We nearly killed her grandmother."

"*Stop*," Lorelei orders. "You're the first person to catch a fly and let it loose outside instead of swatting it. I know you, Dane. You did *not* do this with the intention of harming anyone. You did it to make things better. Amanda knows it too."

"She has bigger things to deal with." I take a shuddery breath. "This week—it's felt very unreal. Good, but unreal. I need—I think I need a little normal to see where my head's at."

"You're going home. San Francisco home."

I don't answer out loud.

But it's exactly what I think I need to process everything and decide what I want to do next.

Chapter 32

Amanda

The rest of the town might be in quite the festive mood, but my heart is hollow tonight.

Not because of Grandma.

She'll be okay.

She's retiring immediately, no questions. She had stupidly high blood pressure when she got to the hospital last night, and she'll be monitored by her doctor regularly while they figure out what happened.

But the bigger point is, she'll be okay.

I apologized for lying to her. She said apologies were unnecessary between family, and that was that.

It feels . . . incomplete.

But that's not my biggest heartache tonight.

My biggest heartache is wrapped around all the little reminders that Dane left.

He and Chili went back to San Francisco.

Work emergency is what Lorelei told me when I left Grandma's room and found her in the hospital waiting room solo. He texted himself and said something had come up and he had to get back ASAP.

He also promised we'd stay in touch, but there's this lingering question of *how much of what I felt was real, and how much was all an act*, and it has me forcing every smile at what was to be my wedding reception on a beautiful evening in Reindeer Square.

Not that Tinsel needs a reason to celebrate, but everyone insisted on keeping the party in honor of us mending the feud between our families.

It's not fully mended—my grandmother has some apologizing to do to people outside of our family, and I suspect Dane's grandparents could own up to a few things with a sincere *sorry* as well.

But my mom is chatting with Dane and Lorelei's dad and uncle over a plateful of food from the potluck tables. My uncle and one of my cousins flew in, and they're talking to Esme's husband while watching Jojo on the play set at the edge of the park.

Grandma is here too. I can't look at her without picturing her being loaded up onto the stretcher and into an ambulance last night.

It sucks that you can be trying to do the right thing and still feel so guilty about it.

"You two were so cute together," Pia says to me over an amaretto sour while we linger on the grass between the gazebo and the food tables. The owners of Holly & Mistletoe insisted on setting up a bar for the party, and they insisted on amaretto sours as the drink of the evening.

In honor of the sweet-and-sour nature of my relationship with Dane.

Hi, my name is Amanda, and I'm irrationally angry at the implication that Dane was the sour one in our relationship.

I know it's supposed to be an opposites-attract homage, not a true sweet-and-sour thing, but I'm still put out.

"Dane is a very good man," I tell Pia. "The absolute best. He's even better than your cake, and you know how much I love your cake."

The cake that's displayed inside the gazebo, waiting for someone to cut it.

Probably me.

But I don't want to cut it. It's not truly my cake.

It's the town's cake now.

Maybe the mayor can cut it. Or Lorelei. Or Pia herself.

"I wish you'd been for real," Esme says. "The way he smiled at you—*swoon*. How could anyone not want you to be happy together?"

"Lorelei has always been one of my favorite people. It makes sense that her brother would be, too, once I got to know him." The words sound hollow to me.

He's so much more than one of my favorite people.

He's someone who made me believe that there could be someone out in this world who could love me in all my flighty, unpredictable glory. When I told him about my play—all I felt was support. Belief. Pride.

"What I want to know is whose idea it was," Mrs. Briggs says as she joins us, also carrying a plate overflowing with food from the potluck tables.

I spot the sausage balls that the mayor brings to everything—the sausage balls that have been my second favorite after fruitcake my entire life—and the sight of them does nothing but turn my stomach.

The sight of the fruitcake did the same.

I think I hurt Dane.

I don't know exactly how, but I think I did, and I want to fix it and I have no idea if he'd let me try.

"It was my fault," I tell Mrs. Briggs. "I didn't know how to tell my grandma that I didn't want to work at the Gingerbread House, so instead of telling her the truth, I made up a fake fiancé. Dumb, right?"

"I'd say it was brilliant," Esme says with a sweep of her arm, indicating the party where Grandma and the eldest Silver generation keep eyeing each other across the square.

I shake my head. "That wasn't me. The brilliant part was when I told Dane and he insisted we keep up the act. For exactly this reason."

Which he's not here to see.

Because he's hiding from me?

I shake my head, pull out my phone, and snap a few pictures, then text them to him. It's what a friend would do, right?

Good job, partner. The whole town turned out to celebrate the end of The Great Silver-Anderson War.

It doesn't show as immediately read, so I pocket my phone again.

Maybe he really did have a work emergency.

Maybe he's tied up.

He doesn't owe me anything. We didn't have a real relationship.

But it certainly felt real to me.

"You were behind the letters," I say to Esme. "How long did you have them?"

She blushes. "I first saw them in high school, but when I heard that you two were engaged, I decided it was time to share what I knew. But I couldn't do it openly without pissing off my dad at first."

"You knew the whole story?"

She shakes her head. "The letters never said what the dowry was. I assumed it was something like a lock of an ancestor's hair or the confession of our serial killer great-great-however-many-times-grandfather or uncle or whatever he was."

"You have a serial killer in your family tree?" Mrs. Briggs says reverently.

"Family secret. But since we're airing family secrets . . ."

"Dane told my mom and grandma," I tell them. "Mom had just listened to a podcast about him. And speaking of secrets . . . I got a fascinating text message from Ben this morning."

Esme smiles. "We were young and idealistic, more in love with the idea of doing what you just did than we were into each other for real. I'm glad he found someone who makes him happy."

"I'm glad you both did. And that you did all the heavy lifting to help solve the mystery of why our families fought in the first place."

Winona slides into our group. "Amanda. Have a minute?"

I nod and excuse myself from Pia and Esme and Mrs. Briggs. "What's up?" I ask Winona as she leads me into the gazebo.

"I have a confession."

Two weeks ago, I would've been frothing at the mouth with excitement over the idea of one more confession in a string of tumbling truths.

Right now, though, I'm bracing myself. "Yes?"

"I might have latent talents related to guilt and manipulation."

What would Dane say to that? I open my mouth, then slowly close it again.

Winona grins. "That's code for *I convinced your grandmother to give me her gingerbread recipe in the name of the town records.*"

My mouth opens again, and this time, I hear myself making an inhuman choking sound.

There's no way Grandma gave up the original recipe.

Zero.

Chance.

None.

Winona smirks. "She gave me the recipe *and* the gingerbread candles that she says have been used in family rituals for generations."

I squeak.

"I think what you did this past week made a huge impact on her." Winona squeezes my arm. "What you did this past week made a huge impact on all of us. Mrs. Briggs is donating the dress you were going to wear to the historical society, and Dane gave me the ring before he left too. We're putting together a display at city hall to commemorate the end of the feud. With the letters and the recipe too. The handwriting matches, by the way. You were correct. The gingerbread recipe was to be Dane's great-great-grandmother's dowry. It was *her* grandmother's recipe, only written down one time before the poor thing succumbed to a fever and passed away."

My eyes water.

I'm so tired of being a Weepy McWeepy-Face.

But I'm also so glad that it worked.

That Dane and I accomplished the impossible. And in a week, no less.

"Do you think they'll stay at peace?" I ask Winona.

"They'll have to," Lorelei says as she joins us inside the gazebo. "Your mom just asked me if I'd be interested in joining the bakery staff."

I look at my hometown BFF, take in the implications of what she's just said, and burst into full sobs.

"Oh my god, don't cry." Lorelei smothers me in a hug. "I'll tell her no if you changed your mind and you want it instead! Don't cry. Please don't cry."

"Just—so—happy," I sob.

She pats my back and keeps hugging me. "I've . . . never seen you . . . happy . . . like this."

"So happy," I insist.

I am.

Lorelei *should* join the bakery. She loves to bake. It was her family's recipe. She's always been a sister of my heart.

She belongs there.

I'm thrilled that my mom is willing to recognize it.

Provided Mom's also willing to make everything *fully* right, considering the stolen recipe.

"Are you sure this is happy?" Lorelei says.

"Amanda, honey, what's wrong?" Mom rushes into the gazebo and pets my hair. "Sweetie, what happened?"

"I love Lorelei," I wail. "So—happy—for all—of us."

"This is . . . happy?" Mom asks dubiously.

"Furiously . . . *hic!* . . . happy!"

Dammit.

Dammit.

I'm crying so hard I have the hiccups.

My thighs shake. My belly grumbles. My heart—

My heart is being pulled in so many different directions.

Happiness for Lorelei and Mom and the Gingerbread House. Relief that I haven't been disowned. Lingering irritation with my grandmother for all the times she faked heart attacks, making me doubt a true medical emergency, and gratitude that she seems to be turning a corner, willing to face that this long-standing feud might have been our family's fault. Utter misery for being alone at what was supposed to be my wedding.

But it wasn't real.

None of it was real.

I know this, and yet—"But I—miss—Dane," I gasp out.

"Oh, sweetie," Mom whispers.

"He's such—a good—man."

"He's the absolute best," Lorelei agrees.

"I think—I—love him."

Lorelei squeals a short squeal, like she's reining it in, while she hugs me tighter.

"And he's—gone," I finish on a desperate, sad sob.

"He's not *gone*," Mom says firmly. "He's just in another place. Physically."

"He had such a crush on you in high school," Lorelei says.

"I know." I hiccup. "Kind of. He—*hic!*—told me."

"And the way he looked at you this past week . . . ," Mom says.

"But he *left*."

Lorelei heaves a sigh and releases the hug, but grips me by the arms and holds me so she can stare me square in the eye. "Amanda. You're *Amanda Fucking Anderson*. Do you have any idea how intimidating it is to like you?"

"I don't mean to be intimidating."

I don't. But I know when I'm home, I feel like that girl who was always the best actress on the stage, universally loved by all the shop-keepers and former teachers and postal workers.

And while Dane never said he still feels like the band geek, and while he clearly has more confidence, he's also quieter and more reserved than I am.

We are vastly different people.

And I absolutely adore every bit of him exactly as he is.

"This past week was a lot for both of you," Lorelei says. "But it's not too late to see what things would be like for you in normal times."

"I wouldn't have truly supported you marrying a serial killer," Mom says. "But it was so obvious how much you liked him."

"Was it?" I swipe at my eyes.

"*Yes*," they reply in unison.

"And don't get me started on how obvious it was that he still thinks you painted the stars in the sky," Lorelei says. "He was always on edge when he was dating Vanessa. Like he was waiting for the next bad thing to happen. But this past week—he was so happy. Like he found where he belonged. He has a quiet kind of happy—it's not a *big* happy, you know?—but he was happy. I could tell."

And now I'm crying again.

"*Amanda*," Mrs. Briggs hisses from just outside the gazebo. "Honey, I don't know what's wrong, but you need to see this. *Look.* All of you. Just look."

She points to three people standing near the start of the potluck line.

My grandma.

Dane's grandparents.

All going for food at the same time.

"She better be getting a fucking salad," Mom mutters.

Lorelei stifles a whimper of amusement and hooks her arm through mine as we watch my grandmother extend a hand to her grandfather.

There's definitely wariness in the way Grandma's holding herself. I can see it in Mrs. Silver too. Hesitancy. Caution.

But a willingness to still shake my grandma's hand too.

"You did it," Lorelei whispers.

"*We* did it," I correct, my voice thick as I try to suppress even more tears. "Because Dane thought it would work. And he was right."

My phone dings in my pocket.

I absently pull it out as I keep watching the stiff conversation happening between our grandparents.

But when my gaze snags on Dane's name with a text message alert, I instantly swipe my phone open and hungrily read his message.

Success all around. Great job. Wish I was there to see it.

He's attached a picture of our grandparents from another angle.

I look around, searching for him, but I can't find him.

He's not here. He's not waiting behind a bush to surprise me and ask me to be his girlfriend and give this a shot for real.

I see Esme's husband tucking his phone back into his pocket, though.

Oh.

Oh.

If it wasn't Esme's husband sending him the photo, someone here likely did.

Gossip spreads like wildfire, and geographical separation is no match for cell phones.

"I can't do this," I whisper.

"Can't do what, sweetie?" Mom asks.

"I can't *not* go talk to him. I have to. I have to go see him. I want to know—I want to know if we can work."

Lorelei squeals and hugs me again.

Applause breaks out among the townspeople gathered in the square.

I know they're not clapping for me. I know they're clapping for my grandma and the Silvers' grandparents attempting to make up.

But it gives me more determination anyway.

I want to date Dane Silver.

And I'll do whatever it takes to prove to him that I mean it.

Chapter 33

Dane

Leaving Tinsel was the stupidest thing I've done in my life.

I don't want to be in San Francisco. I don't want to go to work. I don't want to walk my dog in my neighborhood. I don't want to swim laps in the pool on the roof.

I *want* to be where Amanda is.

I *want* to ask her to give me a chance—a real chance.

The pictures of her from the town party last night that everyone kept sending me—her halfhearted smile, the way she was crying while she hugged Lorelei, one of her staring at her bare left hand when I'm sure she had no idea anyone was watching, much less photographing her—I was an absolute asshole to leave her.

Especially in the midst of feeling so guilty.

How was she feeling? How much support could I have offered her instead?

I'm fixing it.

Today.

Instead of heading into the office, I'm packing and getting ready to leave for the airport.

Chili's giving me heavy side-eye from his spot in his doggy bed beside my bed.

"It's a nonstop flight," I tell him. "And we should land the same time Amanda does."

He lifts his head and woofs once.

I think that's approval.

Not entirely certain.

He's been cranky with me since we hopped on the last flight out of Michigan and back home to San Francisco two nights ago.

Or maybe I've been cranky with myself.

My phone dings, and I drop everything to dive for it on my nightstand.

Not a friendly text from Amanda like the few I got last night.

It's a sign when my heart sinks this low at the sight of my sister's name in my messages.

I'm never disappointed to see Lorelei's name light up my phone.

But she's not Amanda.

How much of a sign is that as to how much I need to take this leap?

Winona needs to know how big you want the statue of you to be.

I stare at the message from my sister.

Stare harder.

And then I call her.

"What the hell?" are the first words out of my mouth when she answers.

"You're basically a superhero at home now," she replies. "They're asking Amanda the same. I think I heard your snow globe will be the centerpiece for the statue they're putting up of the two of you in Reindeer Square."

"I don't need a fucking statue."

"Too bad. They're making one of you anyway. It's not every day people fake *Romeo and Juliet* to end a generations-long family feud.

This is the best thing to happen to Tinsel since they renamed the town in the sixties."

I squeeze my eyes shut. "I don't want a statue."

"Take it up with the mayor. Who, by the way, is Grandma's new favorite person. Oh! Did I tell you I got a new job? Vicki Anderson herself stopped me at the party last night to ask me if I'd be interested in working at the Gingerbread House. She's retiring, basically effective immediately, which we all knew, and Kimberly Anderson had already asked me, but having the Big Grandma's approval is cool."

"You did not just say *the Big Grandma*."

"I did. It's my new nickname for her. How's work? You get that emergency all sorted?"

She knows there wasn't an emergency. "Yep," I lie.

"Good. You were missed at the party last night."

I missed the party too.

I've never been sad to miss social events. They're things I do, but they're not things I look forward to or miss when I can't make it.

But last night, I wanted to be at that party.

I wanted to be there with Amanda, watching her sparkle and shine and listening to her tell the story of our fake engagement.

Listening to her tell everyone that she fell hard for me the same way I fell for her.

No idea if she would've. But it's what I want.

It's what I want to believe in.

We had something. I know we did.

"I do have to get to work," I tell Lorelei, which is yet another lie.

I'm not going to work.

I'm flying to New York.

"You don't want to hear details about the party last night?"

"We'll catch up this weekend."

"I might forget a lot by then."

I blow out a breath.

My sister rarely frustrates me, but I have a plane to catch. "I'll make a list of questions and send them to you so you remember."

"Dane, before you go . . ."

My heart stutters. Does she have something to tell me about Amanda? "Yeah?"

"Thank you. I don't think I'll ever be able to say thank you enough, but *thank you*. I really like Kimberly so far, and I can't even tell you how excited I am to get to bake all day, and this wouldn't have happened without everything you did last week. And I know how big of a risk it was. And I know it had to be hard in a lot of ways too. I'm joking about the statue. I am. But I will forever be so, so grateful for what you and Amanda did for Tinsel and our families and for me. Expect the best Christmas presents ever from now through eternity from me, okay?"

Fuck. My vision is going cloudy and my throat is getting thick. "You don't have to do that."

"You pulled off a miracle and changed everything for the better. I won't be the only one getting you the best Christmas presents."

"Gotta go, Lorelei."

"I know. You hate the mushy stuff. Love you. And thank you."

We hang up. I finish tossing the last few items into my suitcase, zip it up, and then grab Chili's leash. "About time to call a ride. You ready?" I say to him.

He grunts and lumbers to his feet.

"If all goes well, this time tomorrow, you could be getting walked around Manhattan by Amanda. With new friends. Wouldn't that be awesome?"

He gives me the look of *if you didn't fuck it all up already, dumbass.*

Yep.

I'm projecting.

Because that look doesn't usually come with a little tail wag and a happy pant, which is actually what he does when I say Amanda's name again.

We head through my condo to the front door, Chili moping along while I pull my suitcase.

And when I open the door to step out into the hallway, I find myself facing a mirage.

Has to be.

There's no way Amanda's standing at my doorway, arm raised like she was about to knock.

Her mouth forms an O, then morphs into a smile.

A very hesitant smile.

"Hi," the mirage says.

I blink once. Then again. Then a third time.

She's still there.

So I do the only logical thing I can think to do.

I poke her in the shoulder.

The woman of my dreams is standing at my doorstep and I just *poked her in the shoulder.*

And now I'm blurting, "You're real."

Her smile shifts from hesitant to full-on blinding. "I am."

"You're here."

"I missed you. I didn't get to say goodbye. I didn't want to say goodbye. And I thought, *what would Amanda do*, and since I *am* Amanda, I decided the best thing to do was hop on a plane and come see you."

Chili's circling her, rubbing his body against her legs. No luggage. Just a backpack.

She really did spontaneously fly out here to see me.

"I don't want to be friends," I say.

Her brows lift in surprise.

Fuck. That came out wrong. "I was on my way to the airport. To come see you. To be more than friends. If you want. Because I want. I want you. And I—"

I thrust a hand through my hair.

I was supposed to have five hours on a plane to figure out what to say to her, and instead, I'm a stuttering, stammering mess.

"I want," she whispers. "I'm here because I want."

It's not real until she steps into my space bubble and goes up on her tiptoes, wrapping her arms around me and pressing a kiss to my lips.

The feel of her against me jolts me back to reality.

And this *is* reality.

She's here.

She's solid and warm and she smells like cinnamon sugar and tastes like dreams come true and she doesn't have to be here for any reason beyond *wanting* to be here.

"I wanted you to be at the party so bad last night," she whispers between soft kisses to my lips and my chin and my jaw. "It felt like I was missing half of myself. The better half."

A shudder ripples through me.

Relief? Overwhelming joy? Love?

All of it?

I boost her up into my arms, and she wraps her legs around my hips, kissing my face while I push my suitcase back into my apartment, pull my dog inside, and shut the door.

And then I take charge of the kissing.

All my awkwardness melts away, leaving me with nothing more than a feeling of utter adoration and desperate need for this woman who came to get *me* before I could leave to go get her.

She wants me.

She's here. She wants me.

And I'll leave zero question in her mind that I want her too.

I almost trip on my dog as I turn to carry her to my couch, but he grumbles and scoots out of the way, barely avoiding the backpack Amanda drops on the floor, which lands with a *clunk*.

"Your cookies," she gasps.

"I'll give you cookies."

We don't make it past my couch before Amanda's tugging at my shirt and I'm kneading her ass.

Clothes have to go.

They're unnecessary.

So is the tie in her hair.

I'm not smooth, but there's nothing clumsy about my motions, either, as I help strip her out of everything from her shirt to her shoes, leaving her bare for me to just stare at as she tugs me toward the couch by my open pants, which are the only clothes I have left on now too.

"Last week was the best week of my life," I tell her as I shuck the pants and climb onto her on the couch.

"Mine too," she breathes as she runs her hands over my chest. "I didn't want it to end. I was so mad at myself when I told everyone we were fake. You weren't fake to me. Not how I felt about you. How I *feel* about you."

"You're not just a girl I had a crush on in high school." I press a kiss to her jaw beneath her ear, loving the way her breath hitches. "You're a kind, fun, beautiful, smart woman who has absolutely captured my heart."

"You're the only man who could convince me my life is better with a relationship. Only a relationship with you. Only you."

"I'm sorry I left you without saying goodbye. I don't ever want to leave you again."

"I get it." She squeezes my ass. "I do. It was overwhelming. You needed space. It's okay. It'll always be okay if you need space."

I stare down at this remarkable woman telling me everything I've always wanted the people in my life to say but have never heard.

It's okay to need space.

She doesn't need space, but she gets it.

She understands.

"I love you," I whisper.

"Oh, my heart, I love you too," she whispers back.

Everything inside me glows warm and happy as I touch my lips to hers again.

This.

This wasn't my plan. It wasn't my goal. But being with Amanda—this is everything.

It's so easy to fall into kissing her until I don't know if she's breathing for me or if I'm breathing on my own. To stroke her soft skin, knowing that this isn't temporary this time.

It's not a situation we've thrown ourselves into.

It's not a thunderstorm making us lose our minds. It's not stress. It's not pressure.

It's simply right.

Perfect.

Easy in that way that says this is meant to be.

With every stroke of her hands, every nip of her lips and teeth against my mouth and my skin, every sweet little noise and every arch closer into my body, she sets me on fire. It's the most natural thing in the world to thrust inside of her, feeling her slick heat envelop me as she matches the rhythm of my hips, pulling me deeper and deeper into all of her.

Her body.

Her soul.

Her heart.

And I'm giving her mine with every stroke while my body tightens in anticipation.

"I love you," Amanda gasps as she wraps her legs tighter around me, her pussy clenching around my cock, and I'm done for.

"I love you," I groan into her neck as I come fast and hard, holding her as tight as I can while she squeezes me to the point that I can barely breathe.

And it's perfect.

So damn perfect.

My throat clogs and my eyes get hot as my body shudders with every pulse of my release until I'm spent. Amanda's body goes limp beneath me as I flop against her side, both of us panting.

She touches my cheek and watches me with heavy lids. "I love you."

"I can move to New York. We have an office there."

Her eyes go shiny. "There are dogs in San Francisco."

"We can try both places. See what we like best. *After* your first play is a resounding success. I want tickets for every night."

"And this is one more reason why I love you," she whispers, softly kissing my cheek.

"I can't count the reasons I love you. There are too many."

Chili nudges my bare hip with his wet nose, then snorts on me.

Amanda's peal of laughter brightens the gray and blue tones all over my apartment, and I smile again.

She makes my world brighter.

We still have things to figure out, but she's here.

We're doing this together.

"Promise me something," I murmur to her as I pet Chili, silently promising to take him out soon.

"Anything."

"No more faking anything, ever again."

She beams at me. "I think you've just proved there'll never be a need."

Epilogue

Amanda

Three months later . . .

Tinsel is sparkling as only Tinsel can in early December when Dane and I pull into town the night before the Holiday Parade. The normal year-round number of twinkling lights has multiplied by at least seven thousand. Instead of one hot cocoa stand, there are six on Kringle Lane. Thick scents of pine and cinnamon waft into the car through the heater, and real snow is overflowing the sidewalks.

"Look!" I exclaim, putting a hand to Dane's thigh and pointing with the other. "They put our snow globe in the old tree lot!"

There are no other snow globes on the street.

Lorelei called laughing so hard she was crying not long after Dane and I arrived back in New York for our first trial month there, reporting that traffic had completely shut down in downtown Tinsel while the Jingle Bell Fest Committee gathered to try to figure out how to fit twenty snow globes that were wider than the sidewalks onto the sidewalks when someone objected to putting them in Reindeer Square instead.

Wait.

Not the *entire* Jingle Bell Fest Committee.

My grandmother was absent from discussions.

She's been asked to step down and put her health first.

Which was a kind way of the town saying *your generation is done here.*

Dane and Lorelei's grandparents have been relieved of their roles in some of the smaller holiday committees too.

And speaking of Lorelei—"Park! *Park!*" I squeal at Dane.

He smiles that patient smile of his while he takes his time finding a safe spot to pull over on the side of the road.

"I'm going to go hug your sister so that she's all yours by the time you get there, deal?" I say.

"It'll cost you a kiss."

I peck his cheek, knowing that's not what he wants, and laugh when he hooks his hand behind my neck to pull me in for something deeper.

I love this man.

I don't care if we're in San Francisco or New York or Tinsel or anywhere else in the world.

I love him.

His quiet smiles. His warm eyes. His gentle patience.

The way he asks, "Do you want company, or do you want to go alone?" when I tell him I feel a desperate need to go to a museum or show or that I'm craving Greek but want to try a place I've never been.

The way he gets along with Yazmin.

The way he not only came to every night of my play last week, but also insisted on making half of his office in New York come, too, so that we sold out nearly every night.

The way he calls my mom.

He calls *my mom.*

It started by accident, but he does. He calls and checks on her roughly every other week.

Some days I still wonder what he sees in me.

Other days, I make sure to spend as much time naked as possible so that he remembers what he sees in me.

"Take Chili?" he says as he releases me.

"Of course."

Maybe that's what he sees in me.

That his dog and I are besties. Mr. Lazybones accompanies me to work nearly every day when I'm working close to our neighborhood, and he even keeps up.

I hop out of the car and get Chili out of the back seat, and then the two of us dash up the street to tackle Lorelei in a hug. She's outside the Gingerbread House with samples.

"You're here!" she squeals.

"I missed you!" I squeal back.

Chili woofs.

It's a halfhearted woof, but he does it like he's saying hi too.

"Amanda!" Mom says in the doorway. "Welcome home, sweetie."

I shift from Lorelei so I can hug Mom as Dane reaches us.

It's a hug-a-palooza on Kringle Lane, and I'm here for it.

Once we've all hugged our fill—including Dane hugging Mom—we slip into the shop to get out of the cold.

The changes are small, but they're there.

Instead of Dolly Parton, Mariah Carey is singing to us.

The nutcrackers by the bakery counter are wearing ugly Christmas sweaters instead of elf outfits.

There's a new note on the menu.

Ask us about gingerbread-baking classes!

But the biggest change—Grandma is sitting at one of the tables with Dane and Lorelei's grandmother.

I freeze in my tracks. Dane makes a startled noise.

They're playing dominoes.

Our grandmothers are eating gingerbread and playing dominoes.

"Oh, close your mouths," Grandma Vicki says. "Doctor's orders. He says we'll live longer if we make up."

"I think he's full of crap," Dane's grandma says.

"We fully agree, which is why we're here," Grandma Vicki says. "We're proving him wrong. Oh, Opal, look, you have crumbs on your sweater."

"I'm saving them for later."

"You're saving them to torture Warren when he does your laundry and sees gingerbread."

Dane's grandma giggles.

Giggles.

"Surprise," Lorelei whispers.

"I'm still highly uncomfortable every time they come in and do this," Mom murmurs. "I'm waiting for the gingerbread to start flying. But I'm going with it."

I hug my grandma. Dane hugs his.

They both tell us to shoo before we break their concentration. They'll see us later.

Santa Claus *Ho ho ho*s, and a blast of cool air sweeps through the shop as Mrs. Briggs enters. "Oh, look! Our parade king and queen have arrived!"

Dane's ears go pink.

Absolutely. Adorable.

I squeeze his hand. "Don't worry. We'll be so bundled up, they won't recognize us."

"Have you seen Reindeer Square yet?" Mrs. Briggs asks.

"People over places," I reply.

"Tell me there's not a statue," Dane says.

Mrs. Briggs grins.

So does Mom.

And Lorelei.

Our grandmothers?

They *cackle.*

Dane winces.

I squeeze his hand harder. "It's okay. We don't have to come back here ever again if you don't want to see a statue of us."

"There's not a statue," Mom says. "You don't have to threaten to never show your faces again."

"What *is* there?"

"Something . . . else."

That's ominous.

I look at Dane.

His smile is more on the resigned side, but I love all his smiles, and I love how frequently I catch him wearing one. "Let's get it over with and see what they did."

"Wait for us," Lorelei says. "We'll close up early."

The grandmas insist we let them finish their game so that they, too, can come along.

Almost an hour later, with Dane, Chili, and me all getting hungry, we finally make it to Reindeer Square.

It's lit up almost as bright at Times Square, but instead of a skating rink and a giant tree, the square is full of the snow globes.

There's a path cut through the snow to lead us through the display of snow globes, but the best part—the very best part, the surprise—are the guides for the path.

They're all the statues that either of our families have decorated over the years.

The elves and snowmen and reindeer and other creatures that were in storage, except for the ones Dane and I used in our own snow globe.

Which is in the very center of the square, under the gazebo.

It's modified, though.

Instead of just the Silvers' snowman holding my family's elf with snow swirling around inside, my family's elf is holding the engagement ring, and Dane's family's snowman has my wedding dress draped over one stick arm.

And there's a plaque affixed to the base of the snow globe, illuminated for easy reading.

TINSEL'S JINGLE BELL FESTIVAL IS DEDICATED TO DANE AND AMANDA, WHO RISKED IT ALL TO FIND PEACE BUT FOUND LOVE ALONG THE WAY INSTEAD.

"Instead?" Dane says as he tucks an arm around me and presses a kiss to my hair.

"Our grandparents all still insist the peace is temporary," Lorelei says with an eye roll at her own grandmother.

"Like Esme says, they can fight it out in the afterlife," he replies.

Grandma Vicki squeaks.

Grandma Opal glares at him.

He tucks in a smile, but his eyes can't hide how amused he is. "Feud's over, ladies. If another family wants to start one, that's their business. But we're only coming back if you agree to get along."

He doesn't mean it. We'd both miss Lorelei and Esme and my mom and his dad too much.

But our grandmothers don't know that.

They eye each other.

"Same time on Tuesday?" Opal says to Grandma Vicki.

"Unless my goiter's acting up."

"Clearly, I meant if *my* goiter isn't acting up too."

They sniff at each other.

But they also smile.

Almost.

Close enough, anyway.

"Any more surprises here?" Dane asks Lorelei.

She grins. "Of course not."

No sooner have the words left her mouth than a rousing chorus of "We Wish You a Merry Christmas" erupts behind us.

Someone hands me a hot cocoa. I pass it to Dane, and he trades me for a fruitcake log.

"You get me," I whisper. "I love you so much."

He just smiles.

And that's all I need.

Bonus Epilogue

Chili, a.k.a. the world's laziest dog

We're back here *again.*

You'd think after three trips already since last Jingle Bell Fest, my pets would be tired of coming to Tinsel, but no.

We're here *again.*

It's cold. *Again.*

And no one's feeding me fruitcake.

Again.

At least we're staying at the cabin. It has a fireplace and both of my pets know how to light it so that I can sleep in front of it most of the time.

But tonight, our third night in this town with all the bright lights, we're not in front of the fire.

We're freezing our paws off in the square again.

There aren't any snow globes this year.

This year, there are Christmas trees.

Too many to mark all of them. At least in one night.

Unless I can make the right puppy dog eyes at my girl pet to get her to share some of that spiced cider with me to really fill up my bladder.

They're always shocked that I like it.

But I do.

It tastes like when my pets are happy.

I'm making a slow meander toward a tree I know I haven't marked yet when people start clapping and cheering and then singing.

Ah.

The big pet in the red suit must be making his way through the square.

I whine at my girl pet.

I don't like the big pet in the red suit.

He's scary.

He smells like he hides dog bones in his big bag so that he can lure dogs like me away from our favorite pets who don't care if we play a game where we try to be even lazier today than we were yesterday.

I don't trust him.

I think he'll be the reason this town has another family feud, and I don't even know what he looks like in real life.

No one else in town smells like him.

I whine at my girl pet again.

She squats next to me and gives me a big fluff-rub. "Are you cold? Do you need to go find a place to warm your paws? Hold on. Dane? Do you have those paw warmers?"

"Of course." My boy pet hands over a package, which makes my girl pet smile at him even brighter than she smiles at me.

I like the paw warmers.

They do the work of keeping my paws warm for me.

But I don't like the big red pet, so I whine and lean on my leash, away from the noise.

"Need to go potty, sweet thing?" my girl pet asks.

"Yes," I woof back.

I don't.

I just don't want to be close to the big red scary pet.

"Okay. Potty and then paw warmers. I don't want you pottying *on* your paw warmers."

Good.

Good.

We're getting away from the big red pet.

I make myself trudge along while my girl pet leads me to a tree I haven't tinkled near yet—she won't let me tinkle on the decorated trees—and I concentrate extra hard to make the tinkle come.

I really have used it all up.

But having to work hard means it takes extra long.

The big red pet guy should be gone before we get back to our boy pet.

But as we meander back, with my girl pet pausing to put my paw warmers on—*oooh, so nice*—and then getting herself more cider and our boy pet more hot chocolate, I realize something's off.

The smell of the big red pet is getting stronger the closer we get to where we left our boy pet.

I don't like this.

I whine again and slow down.

"What's wrong, Chili-boy?" my girl pet says. I'm so glad she lives with me and my boy pet now. She's nice. And fun. And she always gets down close to me when she talks to me, especially when I whine. "Are you still cold?"

I whine again.

Let her think I'm cold so she'll take me home.

"Aww, poor thing. Let's see if your daddy can cuddle you. That'll help. And then we'll go home. Not much longer, I promise. I just want to see them light all of the trees and see Aunt Lorelei wish everyone Merry Christmas in the dress that her grandma used to wear. It's her first time. I'm so excited for her."

This isn't the answer I wanted.

But she said home *soon*.

And I like my aunt Lorelei pet.

She makes me homemade dog treats and sends them in the mail with fruitcake for my girl pet and cookies for my boy pet.

I slow down even more as the smell of the big red pet gets stronger.

And stronger.

And stronger.

But I can't slow down enough, and then we're there.

Back with our boy pet, who's talking to the big red pet like he's not a scary old crazy dog-napper.

I whimper and sink to the ground, getting snow all over my ugly Christmas sweater, and I cover my nose.

"I think Chili needs to go home," my girl pet says to my boy pet.

"Huh. You okay, pup?" my boy pet says as he bends over me too.

I give him my best *noooo, I want to go hooooome* look.

He gives me back a look that I don't see very often on my boy human.

It's a look of *please give me five more minutes.*

Weird.

My boy human never asks me for five more minutes.

He's the chillest boy pet ever.

Maybe I'm reading this wrong.

Maybe this is a cry for help.

It's my time to shine. It's my time to save my boy pet.

I eye the big red pet.

He shakes his belly. "Amanda Anderson! I hear you've been a *very* good girl this year, *ho ho ho*! And look at this . . . I have a special present *just for you.*"

I growl low in my throat.

No one gives my girl pet *special presents.*

"Down, Chili," my boy pet murmurs. "It's okay."

It's *not* okay.

The big red pet who smells like he eats the blood of chickens by the light of the full moon is holding out a package to my girl pet and it could be poison.

It could be a dead rat.

It could be one of those things that springs out confetti when you open it, which is the scariest fucking thing in the entire world.

Even scarier than having to exercise.

Shudder.

"Aw, Santa, you shouldn't have," my girl pet says.

I growl again.

"Whoa, boy, it's okay," my aunt Lorelei pet says as she joins us and squats beside me.

No.

No.

The big red pet will take down the whole family.

I have to stop him.

My girl pet is opening the present.

It's now or never.

Has to be now.

I'm doing it.

I'm leaping.

I'm leaping and I'm grabbing the present and I'm running.

I'm runnnnnniiiinnnnnng.

Fuck, I hate running.

I hate that I'm probably sacrificing myself, too, with whatever this scary present is, but I'd do anything to protect my pets.

They love me just the way I am.

I will protect them at all costs.

"Chili!" my boy pet calls as he races after me. "Chili, drop it!"

Not a fucking chance.

I don't know what this is, but I know it's bad news.

Nothing good ever comes from the big red pet with all his *Ho ho hos*.

"Chili!" my pet girl calls. She's falling farther behind. "Chili, come back! It's not a squirrel!"

Squirrels.

My downfall.

They trick me into running every time too.

"Chili, *halt*," my boy pet commands.

My feet stop on their own.

Stupid obedience training.

Oh.

Oh.

My paw warmers feel nice.

They're working really—*focus, Chili. Focus.*

The good news—I've gotten my pets away from the big red pet.

My boy pet has caught up to me. "Drop it."

My jaw obeys.

Stupid jaw.

I whimper.

My boy pet snags the wrapped box.

It smells familiar, but I can't place it.

Why can't I place it?

"Chili!" My girl pet slides to a stop and drops to her knees, hugging me around the neck. "Silly dog. What's gotten into you?"

"*Ho ho*—no?" the big red pet finishes as I bare my teeth at him.

My pets look at me.

Then back to him.

Then back at me.

My girl pet cracks up.

My boy pet sighs. "Santa, can you give us a minute?"

Santa.

They call him *Santa.*

I call him *the megalomaniac who should be put in doggy prison.*

Who trusts a pet with a beard and a suit that smell like that?

The big red pet shuffles away.

Of course he does.

He's already planted the bad things in the present.

I start to leap for it again, but my boy pet catches me by the collar and holds the present to our girl pet. "For you, my love."

She beams at him.

I growl.

He shushes me.

I growl again just on principle.

"Can't blame him," Aunt Lorelei pet says. "Santa's creepy."

"Oh, he is not," my girl pet says as she opens the small box.

Her mouth forms an O. "Dane," she whispers.

He's still holding me, but he gets even closer, right down on my level.

He's not facing me. He's facing her, holding me behind him. "Amanda," he says just as softly.

"Is this . . . ?"

"The ring that I hope you'll wear for the rest of our lives?" he finishes.

"Dane."

"Marry me."

It's a good thing I have excellent hearing, or I wouldn't know what they're saying. More pets are gathering around us, and I can hear them asking each other if they can hear anything.

"*Yes*," my girl pet shrieks as she throws herself at us.

My boy pet catches her while she kisses him all over his face, saying, "Yes, yes, yes, always and every day, forever," over and over again.

"And you too, Chili," she says to me as she topples our boy pet into the snow, making his stocking cap fall off. "You're a package deal with this guy. I'll take you too. Even if you tried to steal my ring, you goofball."

Her ring.

I know that ring.

She hasn't worn it in forever.

That's why I couldn't place the smell.

I look around, wondering where the big red pet went.

He did good this time.

This time.

But I still know who he is. I still know what he is.

And I'll still be on guard every time my pets bring me here to this town.

ACKNOWLEDGMENTS

This book would not have happened without the love and support of my readers. Thank you for being on this journey with me.

Massive thanks to Maria and Lindsey and the team at Montlake for believing in the potential of this book.

To my agent, Jessica Alvarez, thank you for your unending support.

And last but never least, thank you to my behind-the-scenes support systems. To my family, thank you for rolling with all the quirks of life that go with living with a writer. And to Jodi, Beth, Jess, and Emily, thank you for being the best group of people I could ever work with day in and day out.

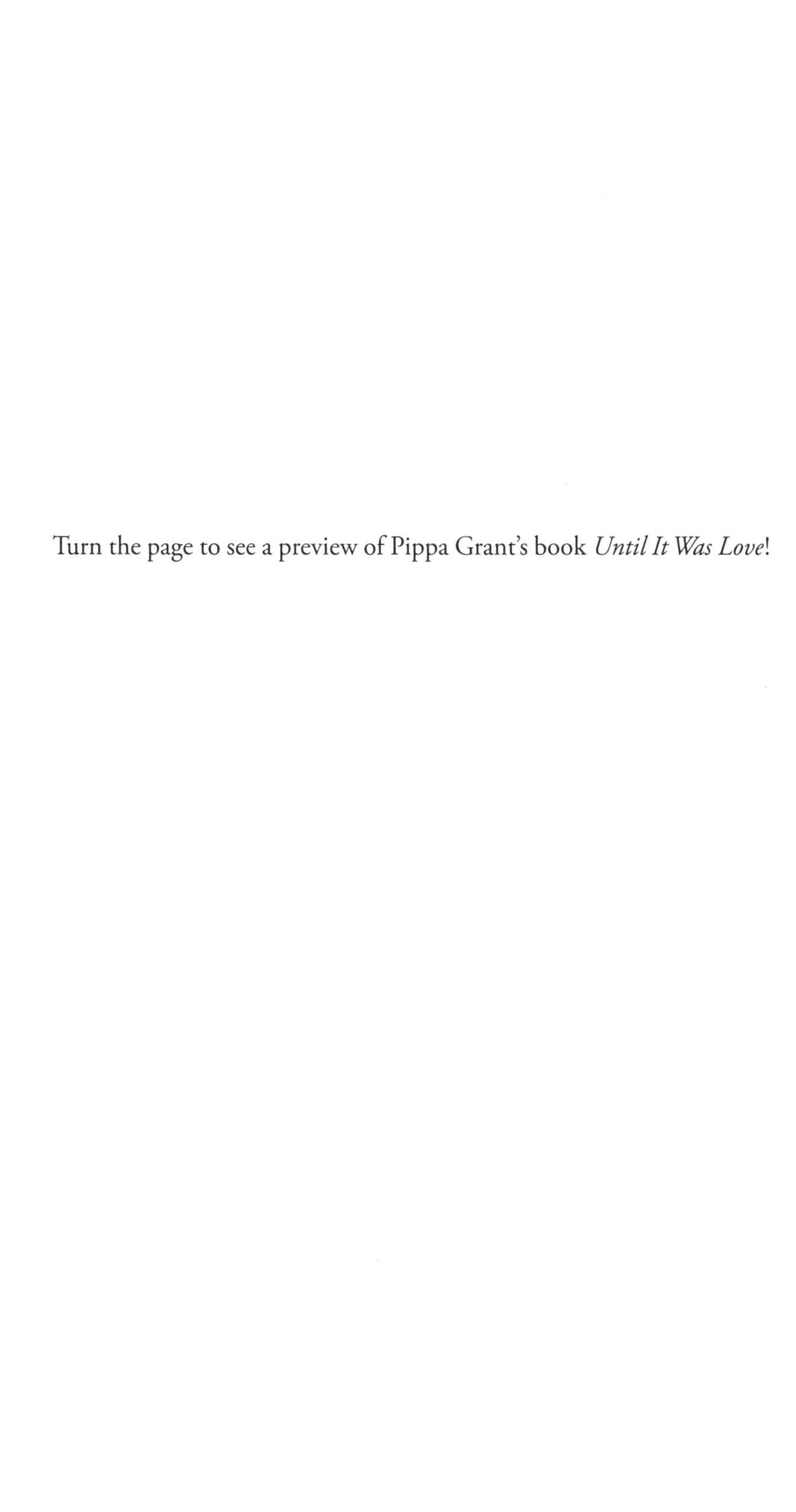

Turn the page to see a preview of Pippa Grant's book *Until It Was Love*!

Chapter 1

Goldie Collins, a.k.a. a life coach not currently regretting any of her decisions . . . which is about to change drastically

Is there anything more satisfying than watching someone you don't like make a **SERIOUS** mistake with their facial hair?

Yes, yes, I know. In the grand scheme of life, there are probably worse decisions than neglecting to take a razor to your upper lip for ten years.

But Fletcher Huxley's absolutely horrific mustache is giving me the kind of glee that probably can't be balanced with a simple donation to a food bank or volunteer stint at a blood drive.

And considering he showed up to this blood drive with a camerаperson in tow, and that he's recording himself looking like that, apparently with the thought that it'll help advance his social media side hustle—yep.

My petty glee meter overfloweth.

"Oooh, Evelyn, look at that," Odette, my seventy-two-year-old neighbor and one of my pro bono clients, says. "Goldie's making eyes at one of the rugby players."

"Ew." I wrinkle my nose at the Black woman in the bright-pink *Outlive Our Ex-Boyfriends Club* T-shirt. "No. *Never.*"

"Mm-hmm." Her smug grin and dancing brown eyes say she doesn't believe me.

"Which one?" Evelyn replies. She's a sixty-nine-year-old white woman in a matching T-shirt, though both her jeans and her dyed brown hair are the height of stylish. She's also three inches taller than Odette and the VP to Odette's president in their seasoned ladies' club.

"The one that looks like MacGyver," Odette tells her.

Now all three of us are staring at the large tattooed white man sitting in the blood-draw chair. We're at a senior center near the hockey arena, and my companions are tracking how many donors we get today. They want to beat the number that their rival club, Old Man Bikers, got last week.

"If I were forty years younger, I'd make a pass at him, but not before I told him to shave," Evelyn says.

I grab a warehouse-size box of single-serving Goldfish cracker packets from beneath the refreshments table along the wall. "The 'stache isn't all that's wrong with him," I mutter to myself.

"I couldn't date him," she continues thoughtfully. "I'd kick the bucket before him, and what fun would that be?"

"None at all," I assure her, louder so that she can hear me. "Even if he kicked the bucket before you, I'm sure it would be awful to date him."

"We could murder the mustache, though," Odette says.

Evelyn cackles. "And we could write its obituary."

"The facial hair of the scowly tattooed giant died an untimely death when runaway kitchen shears—"

"No, when there was an accident with a Weed Eater," Evelyn interrupts.

"*When a runaway Weed Eater older than color television picked the wrong time to malfunction*," Odette intones.

The visual makes me smile.

For the record, there are very few people in this world that I genuinely dislike. Three, to be specific.

My ex-boyfriend.

My former best friend.

And Fletcher Huxley.

Trust me when I say they all earned my dislike.

I rarely spend time dwelling on any of them, but there's Fletcher, *right there*, impossible to ignore with that mustache. The sight of him is making my chest suck in on itself a little at the memory of what he did the last time I saw him.

Which was supposed to be the *last* time in my entire life.

And unfortunately wasn't.

ABOUT THE AUTHOR

Pippa Grant wanted to write books, so she did.

Before she became a *USA Today* and #1 Amazon bestselling romantic comedy author, Pippa was a young military spouse who got into writing as self-therapy. That happened around the time she discovered reading romance novels, and the two eventually merged into a career. Today she has more than thirty knee-slapping Pippa Grant titles and nine published under the name Jamie Farrell.

When she's not writing romantic comedies, Grant is fumbling through being a mom, wife, and mountain woman and sometimes tries to find hobbies. Her crowning achievement? Having impeccable timing for telling stories that will make people snort beverages out of their noses. Consider yourself warned.